STORIES OF SEX IN COLLEGE FRATERNITIES

EDITED BY
GREG HERREN

alyson books
los angeles

MANUFACTURED IN THE UNITED STATES OF AMERICA.

THIS TRADE PAPERBACK ORIGINAL IS PUBLISHED BY ALYSON PUBLICATIONS, P.O. BOX 4371, LOS ANGELES, CALIFORNIA 90078-4371.
DISTRIBUTION IN THE UNITED KINGDOM BY
TURNAROUND PUBLISHER SERVICES LTD.,
UNIT 3, OLYMPIA TRADING ESTATE, COBURG ROAD, WOOD GREEN,
LONDON N22 6TZ ENGLAND.

FIRST EDITION: MAY 2004

05 06 07 08 09 **a** 10 9 8 7 6 5 4 3

ISBN 1-55583-789-1
ISBN-13 978-1-55583-789-1

LIBRARY OF CONGRESS CATALOGING-IN-PUBLICATION DATA
    FRAT SEX : STORIES OF SEX IN COLLEGE FRATERNITIES / EDITED BY GREG HERREN.—1ST ED.
        ISBN 1-55583-789-1; ISBN-13 978-1-55583-789-1
            1. GAY YOUTH—FICTION. 2. GAY COLLEGE STUDENTS—FICTION.
    3. GREEK LETTER SOCIETIES—FICTION. 4. EROTIC STORIES, AMERICAN.
    I. HERREN, GREG.
    PS648.H57F73 2004
    813'.01083538'08664—DC22   2003069634

CREDITS
COVER PHOTOGRAPHY BY JONATHON BLACK.
COVER DESIGN BY LOUIS MANDRAPILIAS.

This is dedicated to
every gay man
who lived through the fraternity closet.

Contents

Acknowledgments

It would be incredibly remiss of me to take full credit for this anthology. In addition to the wonderful contributors, to whom I owe an enormous debt of gratitude, there were a number of other people who in some way or another were of assistance to me in a variety of ways—be they emotional, physical, intellectual, or spiritual. I will attempt to name them—please bear in mind that the excesses of my own fraternity days destroyed innumerable brain cells, so some might be forgotten.

From my days as a brother of Theta Chi fraternity, I'd like to thank Mike Smid, Craig Freeman, Bill and Kara Warnke, Rees and Diane Warne, Larry Ford, Dawn Lobaugh, Karen Bengtsen, Darren Brewer, Gail Nagata, Coni Hintergardt, Rob Heatherly, Matt Kennedy, Barbara Jacques, Jodi McCreery, Wendy Westfall, and a few others whose names are lost in the mists of time. I hope none of you mind being mentioned in a gay erotic anthology—you were all wonderful friends and we had a lot of good times I remember with a smile, although at times I wonder how we survived.

Nick Street, my wonderful editor at Alyson Books, is a dream to work with, understands my mood swings and is always supportive. I never once get the impression he is rolling his eyes when he talks to me on the phone—I know, in his place, that *I* would be.

Some other people deserve mention, for being wonderful friends: J. M. Redmann, Mark Richards, William J. Mann, Paul Marquis, Michael Huxley, Lawrence Schimel, Victoria A. Brownworth, Patricia Nell Warren, Felice Picano, Julie Smith and

Lee Pryor, Kelly Smith, Jay Quinn, Bill Cohen, Kevin Allman, Clark Broel, Michelle Tea, Dorothy Allison, the tennis girls, and far too many others to mention.

I need to thank the board, staff, and volunteers of the Lesbian and Gay Community Center of New Orleans for all of their support and understanding—it's not easy having a program coordinator who is constantly needing time off to finish a book.

And my partner, Paul J. Willis, who inspires me every day to face the day with a smile, no matter what it may bring, because every night I come home to his love.

Introduction

The Greek Life

Since leaving college and coming out of the closet, I've always wanted somehow to explore the college fraternity system. I've started any number of novels, all of which petered out in some way. After the completion of my first erotica anthology, *Full Body Contact: Sexy Sweaty Men of Sport,* I was casting around in my head for yet another theme to build a second anthology around. One night I was in a bar, nursing a beer, when I noticed two exquisitely beautiful young men wearing tank tops with the Greek letters Sigma Alpha Epsilon emblazoned across the front. The proverbial lightbulb went on over my head: fraternities. I had been in one, and so had my partner. I had met over the years any number of gay men who had been college Greeks. My then-editor at Alyson Books, Scott Brassart, was a Greek alum as well. Scott green-lighted the project, and then it became a matter of deciding whether I wanted the content to be fiction or true stories.

I eventually decided to go the fictional route. The concept of true stories, while on some levels appealing, at the same time made me more than a little wary. I didn't want to get into the personal experiences of others—some of them, I was certain, would be painful and might bring back painful memories of my own. Besides, Shane Windmeyer and Pamela Freeman already did an excellent job of covering gay Greeks from a nonfiction perspective with their brilliant *Out on Fraternity Row.* I thought it would be more interesting to see what other writers of fiction would come up with—after all, isn't most fiction based in truth of some sort? Would I get stories of *Animal House*–like conduct, or would I get erotic stories of desire, love, and passion? I was also afraid I would be overwhelmed by stories about homosexual conduct between a closeted gay brother and the straight object of his desire loosened up by the influence of drugs and/or alcohol. After all, as the old joke goes, what's the difference between gay and straight? A six-pack, of course.

When I myself was in the fraternity, I was terrified the other brothers would find out. I was pretty sure what it would mean—expulsion from the house and ostracization by my friends. Because of my attraction to other men I had never felt like I belonged anywhere, but within the hallowed halls of Theta Chi I felt accepted, even though this acceptance was underscored by my absolute terror of being found out and losing it all.

At first, to hide my "condition," I treated women like the other brothers did: as targets for our sexual desires and needs. This was not something I could keep up, however. I empathized with the women too much; they weren't objects but people with feelings, and so I stopped playing along. I repressed my sexuality completely, becoming completely asexual, my only release coming at 3:30 in the morning in the shower, when the rest of the house was safe, quiet, and still. I never dared, despite the enormous temptations, to trust anyone enough to make a drunken pass…and over the three years I was a brother, anything that might have been a drunken pass made at me was neatly deflected and defused.

After all, I never could be completely sure that the "drunken pass" wasn't a test.

And despite the physical beauty of some of my brothers, I kept a strict hands-off policy. I completely sublimated my urges, desires, and needs; if someone was a pledge or a brother of Theta Chi, he was not a sexual being to me. This, despite the frequent exposure to nudity, young men in their underwear, and the highly charged sexual energy that seemed to course through the fraternity house like a pulse.

This isn't to say I was completely a eunuch. I was having gay sex, but entirely with young men outside the fraternity system. I wouldn't bring anyone back to the house, even when I'd lived there long enough to rate my own private room. The door locks, after all, were easily enough popped with a credit card—and everyone knew I always had a bag of pot in my room I gladly shared, at any time, with anyone who wanted to light up.

The stories I've heard from other gay fraternity alums since I left Theta Chi certainly opened my eyes. Apparently, most gay brothers had an amazingly active sex life with their brothers. Yet to this day, thinking back on my fellow active brothers, I cannot pick out a single one who might have experimented with homosexuality after a sixer and a few joints. The law of averages is certainly against its never happening, but there you are. I can't even think of one that I would indulge with if I could go back in time and he were available. Even after almost 20 years I still have the mental block that prevents me from thinking of my brothers as sexual entities.

It's funny how the mind works. After two decades I can still recite the Greek alphabet, sing all the words to "It Is to Thee," and recite the "Badge of Theta Chi" without thinking twice or stumbling. I still can't refer to Greek houses as "frats." (After all, you wouldn't call your country a "cunt," would you?)

I still have one of my old Theta Chi shirts. It's a mesh football jersey with the letters proudly printed on front. Every once in a while I trot it out and wear it in public, despite the obvious incongruity of a balding man in his early 40s wearing a college shirt.

It never fails: Someone, somewhere, will come up to me and

ask me in the secret fraternity way whether I'm a brother. It's happened at circuit parties, in bars, and on the street. It always makes me laugh, and I automatically reply in Theta Chi code that yes, indeed, I am a brother.

Some of my friends from back then know I'm gay—the ones I've stayed in touch with and who still remain close to my heart. None of them cared when I came out to them; in fact, most of them were absolutely delighted I finally admitted it to myself. As for the others, to whom I wasn't as close and with whom I lost touch when I walked out of the house for the last time—I neither know nor care if they have a problem with it. Some bonds simply weren't as strong as others.

Do I regret my time at Theta Chi? No. Despite the excesses, the mistakes, the unhappiness of being in the closet, I learned a lot about people and how to deal with them. I learned the importance of friends who love you no matter what, and the importance of giving that back.

And knowing the Greek alphabet really comes in handy when doing *The New York Times* crossword.

Enough of this! If you haven't already moved on to the erotic tales inside this volume, shame on you! Get the lube and a towel—you're going to need it.

Desire Under the Blankets

Todd Gregory

Blair lights a cigarette. The match flares for a moment, casting shadows in the darkened room. He shakes it out, tossing it into an overflowing ashtray as he sucks in the smoke. The menthol fills his lungs for a moment, and he tries to hold the cough fighting its way up his windpipe, wanting to expel the poisons. He gives in to the cough at last, eyes watering, closing his mouth to muffle its sound. The clock on his desk reads 4:15. The rest of the fraternity house is silent. The majority of his brothers, undoubtedly passed out from too much alcohol, would hate themselves in the morning. Some of them, he was sure, were behind locked doors, smoking pot out of bongs or snorting cocaine off the glass in picture frames. His own supply of cocaine sits in a small pile on a framed photograph of his mother on the desktop, next to a bong made of glass and plastic in the shape of a dragon.

He opens his small refrigerator and gets a can of Pepsi, still a little drunk from the evening's festivities. Big Brother Night, a tradition every semester in which the pledges received their protectors and advisers amongst the group of the already initiated, ended around 2 in the morning when the keg ran dry and the last pledge had vomited. His own little brother, Mike Van Zale, sleeps off his drunkenness in Blair's bed, snoring a little softly. Mike puked around midnight, thanks to the Jose Cuervo shots Blair kept pouring down his throat. After Mike staggered down the hallway to the bathroom and lost the contents of his stomach, Blair took pity on him, leading him up to his room.

Some of the other brothers would force their new charges to drink again after throwing up, but Blair was a little more compassionate. Besides, the previous semester, one of the Alpha Chi Omega pledges almost died from alcohol abuse. Blair's brothers at Beta Kappa, for the most part, only paid lip service to the new university regulations regarding alcohol hazing of pledges. *They are idiots,* Blair reflects, stubbing out his cigarette and making another line from the cocaine. It wasn't the first time he'd thought that, nor was it likely to be the last.

His nostrils are already numb from previous snorts. This one wouldn't restore the high the first one had given him hours earlier. The first exploded in his head, making his fingertips and scalp tingle, bringing an indescribable rush—almost like an electric shock to his brain. This latest one would merely make him grind his teeth and his hands shake. *I shouldn't waste it,* he thinks, but he is firmly in the grip of the *I want*s. *Must have more cocaine,* he thinks, almost giggling at himself. He takes a hit off the bong, to lessen the edge of the coke when it hits. He holds the smoke in as long as he can before it explodes out of him in a massive coughing fit. He grabs a tissue and spits out a wad of phlegm. *Nice.* He almost starts giggling again.

On the bed Mike shifts, moaning a little.

Blair sips his Pepsi to cool his burning throat, walking over to the bed. Mike is sprawled on his back on top of the covers. In the moonlight coming through the slightly parted curtains, his smooth skin looks like alabaster, his hard chest gleaming in the ghostly light. Thick wiry hair sprouts from under his arms. A thin line of drool hangs from the corner of his mouth. His face is serene in his sleep. A thin trail of wiry black hairs runs from his navel to the waistband of his white briefs.

Beautiful, Blair thinks, *just beautiful.*

Mike is his third little brother and the first he has felt attracted to. Usually a pledge he found the slightest bit attractive he refused to accept as his little brother, instead taking a scrawny pimple-faced 18-year-old one semester, then an overweight drunken mess the next. Blair carefully keeps his sexuality a secret from the brotherhood. Some of the brothers who don't like him speculate. Every once in a while one of them, when drunk or stoned or both, makes some snide comment to him at a party. His sexual activity is kept away from school. At home in Los Angeles he might hit a couple of the bars in West Hollywood for sexual release, but that life stays away from the University of California at Woodbridge. He avoids the small gay bar in one of the seedier parts of the small mountain city, just as he avoids the students who belong to the campus gay group.

Some of the other brothers are attractive—beautiful young men with hard muscles and smooth skin; round, hard asses; and thick cocks hanging limply between their legs as they parade naked through the group shower. He never dares do more than cast surreptitious glances at them, replaying the pictures in his mind when alone in his room late at night beating off, imagining those limp cocks aroused and needing release. In his mind's eye he sees their firm, hard asses arching up at him as he rubs his cock until he comes all over himself. No matter how drunk or stoned he is, no matter how horny he gets, no matter how he reads signals from other guys in the house, he sticks to his hands-off policy.

But Mike is different somehow, and even though he told himself it was a mistake, when Mike picked him he said yes.

He looks at Mike's relaxed form. *I'm playing with dynamite,* he thinks, looking at the smooth throat with just the barest hint of razor stubble, aching to press his lips against it. *How does it taste?* he wonders. *Is his skin as soft as it looks?*

Rush was alcohol-free by university mandate these days. Strict regulations against smoking pot, usually ignored most of the semester, were vigorously enforced during rush. There were rumors of undercover cops, pretending to be prospective pledges, infiltrating the rush system to look for drugs. The Executive Council of Beta Kappa took these tales as holy scripture. Still, it didn't stop Blair from going over to friends' apartments and getting stoned before the activities began. The only way he could cope at those events was to be stoned. He was cursed with an inexplicable shyness that years of drama courses and performances in plays had never cured. So on the first night, Casino Night, with brothers and the little sisters acting as card dealers and roulette croupiers, he'd wandered in about 10 minutes after prospectives started arriving, standing in the doorway to the big activity room. He made a name tag for himself and stuck it to his shirt, longing for a beer. *Rush sucks,* he thought.

"Hi," a voice said from behind him. "Are you one of the brothers?"

He'd turned and came face to face with Apollo, God of Light and Beauty, in human form. Cropped dark hair, pale-blue eyes, a smattering of freckles sprinkled across a snub nose, thick lips, and muscles bulging out of a tight Polo shirt and tight-fitting blue jeans. He went into what he called Joe Fraternity mode: big phony smile, stick out hand for firm handshake, pretend the guy is your best friend. "Yes, Blair Blanchard, Fall '85 brother. And you are?"

"Mike Van Zale, sophomore from Visalia. Majoring in anatomy and physiology." He smiled, showing white teeth, some of them slightly crooked.

Of course you are, Blair thought. Mike was only about 5 foot 7, the top of his head reaching to about Blair's mouth. "Let me show you around and introduce you to some of the brothers."

Mike attached himself to Blair. Blair guided him through the house, feeling like a museum docent. He introduced him to various brothers whose friendliness seemed a little forced. Mike's effect on the little sisters was almost painfully obvious. Mike seemed unaware of the looks he was getting from the girls, remaining focused almost entirely on Blair and everything he said. He'd accepted a pledge bid that night with the glee of a child on Christmas morning. On his daily visits to the house he always stopped by Blair's room first. As the weeks passed leading up to the selection of Big Brothers, Blair knew Mike was going to pick him. He also knew Mike had slept with some of the little sisters after parties. The girls, who for whatever reason always seemed to confide in him, told him Mike had "a big one."

Like he needed to know that.

Mike crept into his fantasies every night as he lay in bed stoned, trying to go to sleep. Mike in nylon jogging shorts and a tight white ribbed tank top, practicing on the flag football team. Pulling off his shirt after practice and mopping the sweat off his face with it. The hard round ass, white as marble, showing every once in a while when the shorts rode up as he ran with the ball or bent over to stretch his leg muscles.

He was aware of his growing attachment to Mike: dreaming about him, fantasizing when he masturbated, picturing them lying in bed together naked, kissing, nibbling on Mike's big nipples, trailing his tongue down the flat stomach. He could feel Mike's strong arms around him, pulling him in closer and more tightly as their lips met, Mike's full sensual lips parting and his tongue sliding into Mike's mouth, feeling his slightly crooked teeth with his tongue. Mike's beautiful slate-blue eyes slightly closed in pleasure as he slowly began to grind his crotch against Blair's, their erections straining against each other.

Blair would lie in the darkness, his cock hard, aching for release, as he tried to imagine how big Mike's dick was.

And now there it is, covered only by a thin layer of white cotton, just inches from him, semi-hard as he sleeps. The girls weren't wrong.

I want you, Blair whispers.

Blair reaches his trembling hand out toward Mike, pausing just above his half-dollar-size right nipple. Mike's even breathing raises his chest almost to where it would touch Blair's hand before dropping back down. *How does your skin feel?* Blair wonders. *Is it cool and smooth and velvety? Is it hot and fevered?* Would the connection of Blair's hand touching his skin give off an electric shock as he imagined it would?

Did Mike want him as much as Blair wanted Mike?

As though in answer, Mike moans a little in his sleep and shifts again, his right arm going up over his head, revealing the deep armpit formed by the thick shoulder, chest, and back muscles, the damp black hairs lining the center.

Blair's hand shoots back. He reaches for the bong again. He lights the bowl, inhaling gently until the water begins to bubble. The cool smoke snakes its way up the long glass neck of the dragon and enters his mouth and lungs. He puts the bong back on the desk and holds his breath as long as he can before expelling it toward the ceiling, a fog of curls.

Mike shifts again in his sleep, muttering incomprehensible sounds, the gibberish of the sleeping. His left hand slides up from the bedspread and rests on his lower abdomen, just above the elastic waistband of his underwear.

Blair looks at the hand as the smoke begins to do its magic on his mind. Mike's hand is beautifully shaped, big and strong with black hairs curling along the side of it just below his pinkie. His fingers are strong rather than stubby and meaty—graceful, the hand of an artist.

Yeah, right, an artist's hand, Blair's voice mocks inside his head. *He has the IQ of a doorknob. He doesn't get the jokes on* Alf, *for God's sake. His favorite movie is* Rambo. *He has never read a book he didn't have to for a class. He has the body of a god and the soul of a…well, face it, the soul of a peasant.*

But not mean-spirited, no. Never mean-spirited. He is sweet and gentle and kind, with never a bad word for anyone or about anything, almost like a child in his simplicity.

Blair reaches out again toward the nipple, the mound of muscle lying on the rib cage. He wants to touch the nipple, tweak it softly, pull on it a little bit, just to see what would happen, to see if he would wake.

What if Mike did wake to find Blair hovering over his nearly naked body? To having his nipple toyed with?

His eyes might open with a slow moan. "That feels good, Blair, I like that." Giving him that lazy smile, the one exposing the slightly crooked teeth.

He'd take Blair by the hand and pull him onto the bed with him, using his free hand to release his huge cock from its white cotton restraints. They would kiss, Blair fumbling out of his clothes until both were naked on the coverlet. They would roll over, their tongues entwined, arms and legs entwining until Blair was on his back, his legs going up in the air as Mike spit on his hands and wet his cock, sliding it into Blair. Blair would open for its invasion, its pleasure-bringing hardness sliding deep inside of him until he has to clench his teeth to keep from screaming. It would feel so damned good, better than any other man he'd been with. Mike would gently rock his hips back and forth, teasing, taunting him, slowly sliding back and out before plunging back in deeply, clenching his butt, pushing in as far as Blair could take it. Blair's breaths, practically groans of pleasure, coming in gasps until he could hold himself back no longer and would start shooting long ropy strings of come, raindrops of white falling on his chest and stomach as Mike smiled down at him before pulling out and finishing himself off as well.

And they would kiss again, more tender than urgent, as the first kisses were, and wrap their arms around each other, falling asleep that way.

Mike would move in with him, in this very room. They'd put another bed in, for appearance's sake, but every night they would slowly undress each other before climbing into bed, kissing and caressing and loving each other, before making love and going to sleep, to wake in the morning in each other's arms, loving each other, happy, content. When they both graduated they would move down to L.A., getting a great place up in the Hollywood hills, with a pool and a hot tub, and invitations to parties at the Blanchard-Van Zale's would be the most sought-after, the most prestigious in the West Hollywood social scene.

Other men—models, actors, directors, producers, agents— would try to steal Mike away from him by offering to make him a star, offering him cars and clothes and jewels and money, and Mike would always just smile and say, "Thank you, but no. I'm in love with Blair and can't imagine not having him in my life." And they would grow old together, a permanent fixture on the scene, Blair writing his books and Mike doing—well, whatever it was he wanted to do. And every night they would share a glass of red wine before making love and going to sleep, celebrating their life together.

Desire Under the Blankets

Their love.

Blair smiles. *It could happen that way,* he thinks as he lights a cigarette.

Or Mike could open his eyes. "What the hell are you doing?" he would say, shaking his head, trying to clear it from the raging hangover and the overwhelming sense that something was wrong, something was terribly wrong.

"I, uh, I…" Blair would panic, the cocaine and the pot and the alcohol rushing together in his clouded mind as he tried to think of a plausible reason for tugging on Mike's nipple. *Let go, you idiot, let go!*

Mike would sit up, awareness dawning on his face. "You're a fag," he would say, his beautiful eyes narrowing in disgust, revulsion, and hatred, lips curling back over the crooked teeth into a sneer. "A fucking faggot. Were you going to suck my dick next?" And then, aware he was only in his underwear, he would shove Blair back and away. Blair would fall backward and hit the wall with a thump loud enough to wake up everyone in the house as Mike grabbed his pants and pulled them on, his voice rising as he continues his rant. "A fucking fag! Beta Kappa, some fucking fraternity! Are you all butt brothers? Is that what this place is? A faggot recruiting center?"

Voices in the hall, pounding on the door, Mike pulling his sweater over his head.

"Mike, please—" Blair would beg from the floor, unable to move, unable to do anything as Mike opens the door and other fraternity members pour into the room. Then Mike is telling them, telling them what Blair had been doing. And Blair's carefully protected life, the one of acceptance and fraternity and friendship he has worked so long and so hard to build, would collapse as Mike screams at them all that Blair is a fag, Blair is a fag, Blair is a fag…

"He's lying," Blair would try to say. The words, clogging in his throat, wouldn't come out, and then his brothers turn to look at him, disgust on their faces. The face of his pledge brother and best friend, Chris Moore, twists with loathing and contempt and hatred as he spits out the word: "Fag."

Blair stubs out the cigarette and stands up. He looks down at Mike and then peers through the curtains. The sun is coming up.

He reaches out and touches Mike's shoulder. "Mike."

Mike's eyes open, his mouth working slowly. "Blair? What the—"

"I let you sleep in my room, but it's time for you to get back home." Blair smiles as he speaks the words slowly, softly, gently. "The worst thing in the world is for a pledge to be in the house the morning after Big Brother Night." He bends down and picks up Mike's clothes from the floor and hands them to him.

Mike stands up, rubbing his eyes. "I feel like shit."

"Go on home and get some sleep."

Mike yawns, stretching, muscles flexing and contracting all over his nearly nude body. Blair turns his head.

He can't watch.

Mike pulls on his clothes in an agony of movement, tying his shoes, giving Blair a hug. "Thanks for watching out for me."

"What are big brothers for? Come on by tonight and I'll take you out for a nice dinner."

"Thanks, Blair." Mike smiles.

The door closes behind him. Blair lights another cigarette and walks over to the window. He stands there until Mike walks out the door, watches as he walks up and away down the sidewalk. His right hand makes a fist and gently pounds on the window twice as Mike disappears into the distance.

Then he puts out the cigarette and undresses. He slides

beneath the sheets. He can still smell Mike's presence there, and the sheets are still warm from his body.

"I love you," he whispers to the ceiling, then closes his eyes and goes to sleep.

Tucker the Spy

Davem Verne

I'm not in the habit of spying on my friends, but late in my second year at college I began to acquire a delicious desire to catch off guard the naked male butt. Not *any* buttocks, prone to pimples and bruises and stretch lines around the hips—I mean a firm, virgin, collegiate ass, ripe in the jockstrap, bold and full of power.

At college there is a lot of young butt on parade. I didn't expect the onslaught, the attack, the abundance. At the gym, in the pool, beside the lockers, fresh butts seemed to breed, expand like balloons and explode out of shorts. Idling in the Yard or lined up in the dining hall, they tagged their owners, butt upon butt rivaling one another for trophies. Some were hairy, others spanking, smooth.

Studious guys sit on it during class, and fraternity boys lounge on it recklessly at night. A healthy butt is second nature to its owner, neglected like a puppy. But to me, a burgeoning spy in my sophomore year, the vision of penetrating a welcome fraternity ass seemed the predominant purpose of my college years.

I spied on my fraternity mates in the gym, where perspiring hips melted through damp sweats and I could discern the contours of their fleshy posteriors. I spied on them in the showers, a wet sleuth without scuba gear. Schoolboy inhibition warranted that the guys face the blank tiles instead of scrubbing in a convenient open circle. However, this gave me a full view of their well-developed buns, with a variety to choose from like a butt buffet.

Tucker the Spy

Always the provocateur, I often removed their towels and waited in the locker room with a photographic memory as each dripping stud barreled out of the showers and voiced his dissatisfaction. They slipped and cursed and exposed their gleaming cocks, pink thighs, and bubbling buttocks for my favor. There were too many to count, and I succumbed to posterior paralysis as they engulfed me with their raw behinds.

My best routine was late at night. Under the disguise of fraternity father, I prowled the corridors of Henry House and sniffed my way to the uncompromising moments when a star jock let his strap slip and crossed the common room in the buff, ass preening. There were quite a few moments like this, and I always retired to my room exhausted, with a handful of come.

In my fraternity there was no shortage of succulent specimens to follow. I engaged them in conversation when I sensed their hormones were out of control and attempted to initiate fratsex. My successes were few, but I made encrypted notes during my second year, where I philosophized and founded the golden rule of Peeping Tucker–hood: make friends, memorize their intimate schedules, then feel them up real fast.

As time went on I selected a few favorites, those with perfect pumped packages. But this is a no-no in my profession, since a spy must be prepared at every corner to spot an even healthier subject than those previously studied. I don't think any of them suspected me, lurking stealthily, that I was spying on their hind ends or that my reasons for chatting with them in the partial nude in their dorm rooms was part of an undercover operation. I managed to fly under their numb-nut radar and lull their butch egos without a raised eyebrow questioning my ways.

My evolution as spy was ordinary. In my freshmen year I was green about guys. The pervasive display of gladiator backs and hardened torsos frightened me and made our fraternity house seem cagey, with two-legged animals pacing back and forth for release. Inevitably a fight broke out, two jocks bickering about a score or an upcoming meet, and the reign of bare fists on clenched jaws exposed the reality of masculine cohabitation.

I grew to welcome these events. Like a dutiful housefather, I separated the combatants at the moment when the first pair of shorts was torn off, and escorted the broken bit of elastic into the labyrinth of my dorm. This is when my indecent behavior first surfaced. My childhood inclination toward butt love and butt play rekindled in my dorm room where my brother stood, his shorts in ruins.

In the fraternity house, this primal need to eliminate privacy aroused me because it was a rebellion against my family and home. My fraternity brothers were comfortable sharing their bodies in public. They enjoyed grabbing and patting their fannies aggressively, though mostly kept what they found to themselves. Occasionally there was rumor of a midnight spooning, but everyone suppressed that talk. A general thick-hided reaction was given to the unexpected appearance of a guy's stark derriere or ample college meat. After a few giggles the vision was quickly forgotten.

"Get your bottle back in the brewery," they said, a favorite expression.

My spirited pursuit of freed buttocks all began when I was a kid. Tucker Sr. used to call me Skin Boy because I ran around the house naked. I jumped on the sofa like I was flying through the air, a superhero startled out of my trunks with my rear end as my only weapon. I won't tell you what superhuman powers I managed to employ at that young age, but my older brother often covered his face with a towel whenever Skin Boy revealed his true identity. Tucker Sr. encouraged me—that I remember—until I outgrew my exhibitionism. He eventually packed my bags for college, paid my tuition, and told me how proud he was that I had grown up and learned the importance of male privacy.

"A man needs privacy, Tucker," he said. "Respect a man's privacy and you'll always make a friend for life."

But Dad, why is it that the guys in my fraternity like to stay up at night reporting their family secrets like they were writing for a campus paper? How come they fart in public and grab their crotches and pick their asses for anyone to see? Where were they born, if not in a stable, that allowed them to think nothing of urinating in a favorite cup, prop a beer bottle up their butt during parties or pull another guy's shorts off when a flock of sorority girls walked through the door? And remember my most humiliating moment ever, when I woke up with pubic hair in my teeth and a picture e-mailed to all my friends with some guy's nuts bouncing on my face? Remember? Remember?

Obviously, Tucker Sr. could not have anticipated that the dorms at Henry House were anything but private.

Our fraternity house motto was "Climb the Spire of Desire," referring, of course, to intercourse with the male reproductive organ. Proving to your fraternity brothers that you had the biggest spire on campus, worthy to be climbed at any hour, was the preoccupation of our days and nights. There were various ways to prove this: You could strut around the common room with your dick hanging out of your jock. You could leave the bathroom door ajar while masturbating. You could roll out from underneath your covers with a conspicuous boner in your unconscious grip at about the time your roommate was getting ready for class. You could piss in a senior's cup because you were too lazy to get up and go to the john. Or (the oldest trick in the fraternity book) you could get your girlfriend to talk about your woody in front of your buddies.

I remember one conceited junior named Walter, who opted for the last choice on two infuriating occasions. Once, during our house formal, he made his girlfriend add up the latest count of comeloads he shot off during the day—12, I if recall. And another time at the Harriet House formal, where his girlfriend lived, Walter made her talk about his thick cock, like they were discussing a child whom they had recently adopted.

"It's big and red with bushy hair and sits stubbornly on two huge balls like Buddha," she said.

Obediently, she tugged him under the cummerbund, performing his hypermasculine act for him. She finished by asking if he thought he was thicker inside or outside her pussy, to which he responded that he was thicker when inside and invited anyone to measure him next time he climbed on to make love.

Walter, you show-off! You oversexed pig, humiliating our luckless company of fraternity dogs with your high-and-mighty spire of desire. Grow up, you pumped-up bulldog. Then again, you had a great ass.

I remember Walter like this:

The hallway was dark. Henry House lay still. The scent of unjerked cock hung like a vulgar idea in the air, pendulous. The laws of attraction were in full operation that night and made themselves evident as flesh unfolded before me.

I had been studying the atheist's love of modernism, burrowed at my desk, with my swollen dick sore at me for delaying its dinner, when Walter, a.k.a. Self-appointed Spire of Desire, lumbered through the doorway and interrupted my studies. Walter appeared from the shadows like an Nordic god descending from a steel-gray chariot. His crown of blond hair cast about his face and his blue eyes illuminated the room. Thunderbolts of testosterone danced off his skin as he approached me.

He was 6 foot 2 and 210 pounds, every inch of him polished and *naked*. His powerful legs extended and his hips protruded as he walked towards me, a steady hand covering his crotch with a campus newspaper.

"Tucker, the lonely man's fucker," he droned.

Walter flexed his pectorals and angled his backside in profile to me, sensing that I didn't want to miss any inch of him. His was an awesome ass, deliberately oversize and generously cuffed with yellow fur. It rose when he walked; it spread when he fucked. Like the rest of him, it presented itself in grand scale, recalling memories of a well-stocked supermarket, a gilded staircase, a poet's dream.

He wasn't hungry for gay action; I could tell. His hand didn't grope the paper at his waist, repressing an erect dick. So I immediately knew he hadn't stumbled into my room by accident, hung over with that groggy need to get blown. I had seen such stares in the blurry eyes of my fraternity buddies on Saturday nights but never answered the call of the wild. Tonight Walter was on duty, rounding up his crew like the Pied Piper.

"What are you doing with your clothes on, Tucker?" he asked, astounded.

"Clothes suit me," I responded, confused.

"Not tonight, Tucker. Time to get skinny, boy!"

The name's Skin Boy. Or at least it was.

"Is it initiation?" I asked. I knew we were near the end of our fourth term, but I became excited anyway by the chance to spank a freshmen behind.

"You wish, pervert. Take those layers off and get running. Last one in the Yard has to suck my dick!" He flashed me with his newspaper but covered himself quickly, and all I saw was an overly groomed navel.

Walter turned. His full buttocks exploded into view, white, reflecting the lamplight into my eyes before vanishing down the hall. I chased after him, following his bouncing cheeks. He sprinted out of Henry House and joined the tide of naked fraternity boys on campus taking part in the annual ritual, Primal Run.

College hunks abounded, stripped and hung. I nearly tripped on the steps.

Primal Run occurs several nights before finals, when the Yard suddenly fills with buff, bare students chasing in delirious circles. The ritual dates to the founding of our college, when disaffected intellectuals and deviant professors ran unclad through the Yard on election night, ridiculing the academic nominees. By the next year everyone got in on the act. The student body adopted the rite and soon made it a tradition. The campus has grown 10 times since then, with more fun and flesh than in years past. It is the perfect rite to expel the year's academic demons. And for the intrepid voyeur, it's heaven.

I stood behind an unoccupied tree and spied on my fraternity. They ran in a steady pack behind Willard House. Ahead of the pack was Walter, who led his teammates Martin, Dunster and Finkle. Their varsity cocks swung wildly, bouncing off their balls and thighs with little else than a mound of uncombed pubes protecting them. I ducked around the trunk and followed their progress around the Yard. Walter's ass bubbled comically in the night air. From the distance it appeared as if Martin and Dunster were chasing after two soccer balls, ready to tackle and pounce on the hole in between.

I laughed, clinging to bark.

Then Finkle tumbled out from behind, a defensive lineman cutting off his friends and giving Walter a run for the money. There was unspoken hostility in his attempt. Finkle wanted everyone to know that he was the real Spire of Desire.

I voted on Walter finishing first only because he loved me, but I was wrong.

By the time the whistle blew, Finkle was ahead and escorted Henry House indoors, a rowdy bunch of naked fraternity males cavorting up the stony steps. Each one of them covered their spire of desire, but I could see their ripe rumps clamping shut in the cold. I returned a half hour later, leaving come marks on the tree roots.

From that day forward I swore never to close my door, since there was always the opportunity of an unexpected slice of male ass appearing out of nowhere. A naked fraternity butt, like a bowl of fruit, is a welcome sight at any hour of the day, so I must be prepared. In the morning it is like an offering from the academic gods to feast and gain sustenance for the day. At noon it is the gentle inspiration for all schoolboys to find a healthy hole and plant a seed. And in the evening it is the warm reward for labors spent in the stadium or classroom.

I believe that a solid fraternity bottom rising out of bed or slipping down from the bunk overhead offers the sleepy, roaming eye a magnificent object to focus on. It speaks to the scholarly hunter to follow it, greet its coach and make a wish in the well. And the seat of an athletic boy just out of the shower and drip-drying in your bed is an incomparable treat.

After Primal Run, Finkle became the object of my finest spying. He had a powerful male figure, chiseled from small-town clay, with blond curls blanketing his thick arms and thighs. His father was a traveling preacher, unable to attract a dime; thus, Finkle attended college the only way a jock knew how: on a football scholarship. I spied on him in the lockers; I studied him in class. I could tell Finkle was torn inside between the ankle-deep mud of Christianity he grew up in and the prospect of living as a horn dog in college. Finkle was the stuff of all-star come dreams, a muscle-bound defensive lineman with a repressed bum.

The day before finals I returned from Milner Library in a self-absorbed mood, ate some cereal and went directly to my room. I closed the door and met with Finkle's huge bottom lying in full view, placidly awaiting my inspection.

My 6-foot-3, 225-pound fraternity brother—a huge hunk of rough college meat—was relaxing on my bed *in the nude*. He was right out of the shower and reclining his head on my pillow, watching sports. I should have been suspicious seeing him in my room at all, since he lived further down the hall, yet something told me he had a clever excuse.

"The shower in our room is broke," he said, grinning, brawny, and several times my weight. His naked backside lounged upright in the damp air. "I needed to wash the hide. Don't you use a towel?"

"Everything's in the laundry," I said.

"That's OK," he said, appreciating the opportunity. "I'll just lie here and air-dry."

His buttocks were larger than life, two critical targets for my desire. They appeared rock-solid, with no creases, and unsoiled. My eyes measured them: a foot long, a foot wide and two and a half feet across. Spread out, they filled my bed, with Finkle's leg hanging over the edge. Each mound of meat appeared undomesticated but begging to be disciplined.

"Mind if I get changed?" I said.

Finkle didn't answer. He turned his head, resting it more comfortably on my pillow, and watched me remove my clothes. His eyes were somewhat sleepy, while mine were wildly impressed by the curves of each rear cheek. Young guys rarely complain when other guys disrobe; they just watch in silence as if every garment removed means one less for them to tear off in a fight. The true test was if Finkle minded my stinky feet! But he didn't comment, so I stripped of everything but my boxers and felt I was making real progress impressing my straight friend.

"You want to smell my ass?" he mumbled, using his most undemanding voice. He pressed his hams together, making air kisses with his cheeks.

I hadn't expected him to be this up-front, pose in my dorm room and pursue a sexual encounter with me. He was not in a relationship, so I expected he was just being horny, maybe teasing, not serious. This was the only way for him to get off: ass talk with another guy, casual and discreet. By offering the appeal of his exposed butt, he hoped to elicit company in shooting off a load.

"If you don't," he continued, attempting not to act solicitous, "then I'm going to sleep. Wake me up when your roomies come home."

Finkle turned his head and buried it in my pillow. He spread his legs out—not completely, but wide enough for me to see the pink hole winking at the base of his crack. It kept pinching, calling to me, asking me if I was interested.

It didn't take a spy to grasp the meaning of this clue.

Tucker Sr. always said that parents were the first diplomats, lovers the next, then roommates and, lastly, college friends. Tonight was pre-finals Study Fest at Harriet House, where all the fraternity guys made cheat sheets off their girlfriends' notes. Should I tell him? Perhaps he already knew. I didn't have a girl, nor did Finkle; and neither one of us bothered with cheat sheets, since I knew my material and Finkle's teachers had guaranteed his coach he'd pass his classes.

I turned the frosted tortoise lamp on for mood and shut the TV off.

Sensing that we were in agreement, Finkle reached a hand

under his belly. His hips shifted slightly off the sheets. He began to grope his cock. I sat by his thigh, which was folded over the bed, and let my hand caress his thick flesh. His legs were strong lover's legs; I imagined them bent over me, propelling his hips forward as he screwed my ass. Thick beads of moisture clung to his cheeks. I wiped his buttocks dry. His hams were rounded like two volleyballs bunched together. My fingers led my lust over the sprouting hair until my touch met his crack. Long blond hairs, like spider legs, reached out from the crevice, protecting his hole. Gently, my fist punched each cheek to test its resistance.

My full-bodied friend murmured. His hand dug deeper beneath his belly as my index finger caressed the shallow gap between his firm mounds. He uprooted his chest from my bed and pushed his dick from hiding under his waist. Finkle's tinkler flipped out from underneath his big balls. It lay hard, with drops of precome lathering the head.

I leaned forward and kissed his haunches naughtily, smelling the clean aroma wafting from his seat and tasting the sweet hide that wrapped his posterior muscles. His ass rose in the air, a mountain of hind meat leading my kisses over the canvas of skin.

Acting quickly, I slipped out of my drawers and jerked my cock to erection.

My lips paid homage to his football frame. I wanted to kiss him all over, between his legs, on his cock, up his navel, over his man boobs. Then across his neck and onto his lips. I wanted to wrap my body around him like a wet towel and make raucous love in the fraternity house like we were indiscreet boyfriends, pet frats mating. But Finkle began snoring lightly, teasing me, letting me know that he wanted action, not passion. His ass wagged in front of me, asserting its hunger. I lulled him to patience by sniffing his crack loudly and munching on the hole.

Finkle toppled headfirst into my pillow like a pacified kitten as the first sensations of a tongue in his anus ripped through his body. He was a butt boy, a natural receiver. He wanted to get fucked. I pulled his cheeks apart and chowed down on his tight end, his virgin chute, scented and delicious. Slowly, my finger inched around his opening, smearing the saliva, rubbing the circle, and dove in.

Finkle sat up and groaned. His dick swung between his legs, ready to dart into a pussy and do the duty. He grabbed his cock and pummeled its length while his hips fell back on my finger, fucking me. He was equipped with a thick cock, heavy like a bull's, with bull balls and a bull head. It progressed to striking manhood and was good to plow any hole; but his psyche loved to be humbled, pummeled, screwed, to swallow another jock's dick or finger or toe while his Finkle hammer pounded in his palm and shot his load.

"I gotta come!" Finkle cried out.

His ass banged my finger. I shoved the middle finger in too, really fucking him. This stiffened his ride and made him curse as he came. His anus tightened around my fingers, nearly breaking them into pieces as he shot his juice over my sheets. White seed smothered my pillow. He growled and kept humping my hand. His huge hips swelled, shadowing my crotch; he repeatedly heaved his heavy cock through his fists.

I stood up, yanking my ass cracker in one fist while fucking his hole with the other. I wanted in. Finkle's hand reached behind his hip and made a perfectly round hole with that hand for my dick to fit in. *OK, pet, I get it.* I obeyed his masculine wish, his need to remain sexually pure, and squeezed my cock through his clenched fist. It was wet with come, Finkle come, white and hot. Immediately he gripped me, clutched me roughly, and didn't release.

Had he done this before, in the locker room, with Dunster and Martin?

Like this I hammered Finkle against his thigh, my dick in his take. My two fingers explored the cavity inside him, giving my fuck all the fire it needed. His fist tightened into a smaller hole, strangling my long prick. The sound of spanking dick in a sweating palm grew intense, too loud, but I couldn't stop. I pulled my fingers out of his butt, groped his balls, and shot my load against his side. Come flew everywhere. I kept tugging his testicles, stretching them, milking them while mine freed huge amounts of semen, future loads, which canvassed his ribs until my balls were dry.

Finkle let go of my meat. My swelled dick collapsed against his leg.

I couldn't tell if he wiped his hand on my sheets or smelled the come first.

I released his balls and slapped his ass.

He crashed onto his side, pleased, his energies depleted. He watched me and didn't move, quiver, ask to smoke, nor reposition himself on my bed to make room for me. His bulk lay there, emotions sealed, enjoying the vigor of fratsex coursing through his body.

There was something in his blank stare. Like he was thinking carefully. Did he know who I was? Tucker the Spy? Agent of Ass? Had he read all my notes about Walter, Martin, and Dunster? His eyes slowly fell to my dripping cock. Had he been spying on me?

Nervously, with the scent of moist come hanging in the room, I put on my boxers. He watched me, waited, and then sat up like he was awakening from a long nap. He smacked his lips apart and looked around. The clock in the corner gave him an excuse. He lifted from my bed and stood to go. A shed of hesitancy flashed over his face. He didn't want to leave just like that, screw then go. So in typical fraternity fashion, he extended his hand and jabbed me roughly in the chest.

"I'll see you in class," he said.

"Sure," I responded. "See you."

He stepped back, observing me closely. I furrowed my brows and returned his blank stare as if to say that nothing more than small talk had transpired in my room. He nodded and vanished, ass and all.

Though I didn't understand his exit, I didn't forget our meeting either, not Skin Boy. Finkle had graciously exposed the ins and outs of his broad behind to another fraternity boy. Even when he didn't return to Henry House the next fall, I never relinquished the success of spying and finding a big jock ass to hump. The young athletes in my fraternity, while careful in their closeted attempts to conceal their goods, were no match for Tucker the Spy. As I advanced in my junior and senior year, so did my talents. Ask Martin. Ask Dunster! With the alchemy of my desires I secretly attracted the moments when naked fraternity flesh revealed itself unexpectedly and to me alone. After that Finkle night, I soon realized the ultimate purpose for my presence on campus, at the fraternity house, in life: to find all varieties of males and make love to their masculine butts. Large or small game, it's no matter, as long as they are firm and respond with a wild go up the ass! A spy can see this in an initiate's eye.

A spy knows.

The Sweetheart of Sigma Queer

Simon Sheppard

"Suck my cock," I said, and he did. Not the best I've had, but good, very good, and anyway the whole situation kind of excited me. He opened wide and took my dick as far down his throat as he could. I moaned. His tongue did a little dance on the underside of my shaft, and this time I moaned for real.

"That's it," I said. "That's a good, hungry cocksucker." He nursed on my flesh a little more, then pulled away, raised himself up, threw his arms around me, and kissed me on the lips. I kissed back.

"Hot," he said when the kiss had ended. "Really hot."

I like to know the guys I have sex with. It's a stupid trait, one that's gotten me into trouble any number of times, but there it is. "How'd you get into—"

"This?"

"Yeah, this," I said.

He lay back, one hand lazily stroking my damp hard-on.

"In high school I always felt like an outsider, and a queer outsider at that. So when I went off to college, I wanted to feel like I belonged. I suppose I still do." He smiled up at me. "My dad had gone to the same university, and I really wanted to join the fraternity he'd been in. So I felt real lucky when, after the bid party, I was invited to pledge. The fraternity brothers were a bunch of straight guys, a lot of them jocks, and though I wasn't exactly that, I guess I passed."

He'd taken his hand off my hard-on. I guided it back, and he jacked me off as he continued.

The Sweetheart of Sigma Queer

"There'd been a hazing scandal a couple of years before—somebody had nearly died—so the stuff we pledges were put through was more humiliating than anything else. You know the kind of thing: 'Turn around, drop your pants, and bend over.' It's a funny thing about mooning: It can be read as a sign of contempt, but it's also submissive behavior, proffering your ass to an alpha male."

The guy was an intellectual, no fucking doubt about that. I got my fingers wet with spit and reached down to his ass, proffered or not, and began to rub his softly puckered hole.

"Should I stop talking?"

"No, keep going," I said. What the hell.

He smiled and snuggled up to me, his hand still working my cock. "After the trou-dropping, the brothers brought out a box of women's lingerie and had us pledges strip down and put it on. We had to walk from the fraternity house to the quad that way. And back. I can remember what I had to wear: a silky black slip and matching panties.

"I guess I looked good in lingerie; I was accepted into the fraternity. I moved into a room with my Big Brother, Tony. He was a business major and kind of a jock, but not offensively so, and we got along just fine. In fact, the whole fraternity thing was pretty good. Sure, I was surrounded by straight boys and sure, some of them could be assholes, but most of them were actually nice. Of course, they didn't know I was queer. I was really closeted then, and I wasn't about to let on to the brothers that I wanted to suck their dicks."

"There wasn't a gay fraternity on campus?" I asked.

"Honey, this was the Deep South, OK? Ten years ago."

"OK." My fingers were pressing into his moist hole now. I wanted to fuck it. I wanted to fuck him.

"Then one night we held a big kegger. I admit it—I was pretty drunk. We all were. Over in one corner, Tony and his girlfriend were having what seemed like a heated argument; it looked like he wasn't going to get laid that night. Everybody else was dancing or groping or, like me, just chugging down brews. And a few of the brothers had stripped off their shirts, including this guy named Bret, all muscles and chin.

"I really had the hots for him. OK, he was pretty much an irredeemable straight jerk, but with Bret I didn't want discourse, I wanted intercourse. With all that sweaty, liquored-up flesh around, I found myself with a fairly unmanageable hard-on, so I excused myself and went up to my room. I had just gotten down to jacking off when the door opened. Apparently, I'd been too blasted to properly lock it. It was my Big, Tony, and he'd caught me with my pants down. Literally.

"I didn't know what to expect, but I was a bit surprised when he just stood there with a big drunken grin. Then he locked the door, unzipped his pants, and slurred, "Do me instead. I'm so fuckin' goddamn horny." I'd seen him naked of course, and I knew he had a nice cock, but I'd never seen it hard before. Now it was standing up like an open invitation, and it didn't take long for me to accept. Tony stood there for maybe a minute while I knelt, sucking him off, and then he gave a grunt, started pounding into my mouth, and came down my throat. I was still on my knees when he zipped back up, looking down at me with what probably was a smile—they do say that straight guys are the biggest fans of getting blown. Then he headed back to the party, leaving me and my hard-on to fend for ourselves."

He paused and looked at me uncertainly. I really wanted to put my dick inside him, but I also was a bit curious what happened next. "What happened next?" I asked.

"Oh, Tony treated it like one of those 'Boy, was I drunk last night' things. But then I started servicing him on a regular basis. We never discussed it—I just sucked him off when he needed it. I hadn't had much sex before that, so it made me nervous, excited, and a bit ashamed, all rolled up into one. But I sure did like the fact that my roomie wanted to fuck my face.

"Then one night, shortly before Christmas break, when Tony had gone north on a weekend ski trip, there was a knock at my door. It was Bret, smelling like the Heineken brewery. 'Listen, Rick,' he said. And then nothing; the hunky guy was tongue-tied. At last he got it out: 'Don't get the wrong idea, OK? I'm straight, but…well, Tony says you give the best blow jobs he's ever had.'

"I fucking almost fainted. I couldn't believe that my Big had told anyone about me. After all, it seemed like self-preservation would have meant his keeping quiet, right? But then I realized that if I was just a mouth to him, a mouth he could fuck, then he could get his rocks off and still keep his straight credentials intact. He could think of himself as a totally het boy who just liked being sucked off by another guy, and who knows, maybe he was. And now here was Bret, the muscled object of my fevered affections, and he wanted to be serviced too. I know—if I had a shred of self-respect, I probably would have said no. But…well…you know…"

"I think I do," I said, twisting two fingers inside his ass. Just how long was this story anyway?

"I didn't say anything, so Bret must have figured—rightly, as it turned out—that I'd be happy to suck him off. He held out a gym bag he'd brought. 'Listen, can you put this stuff on? It will make it, um, easier for me,' he said, sounding more like a little boy than I'd have expected. Inside the bag was the black slip I'd worn during hazing. Not the black panties, though. The ones he'd brought were light-blue jobbies, very sheer. I couldn't believe it.

"See, what Bret couldn't have known, what I never would have told anyone, was that I'd found wearing lingerie exciting. Hazing was the first and only time I'd put on women's stuff, but I'd barely been able to keep my hard dick in those panties on that walk through campus. And in the months since I'd pledged, I'd often jacked off to thoughts of being naked except for silky underwear, surrounded by straight guys with hard dicks.

"So when Bret held out the lingerie, I eagerly stripped down, pulled on the slip and powder-blue panties, and got down on my knees. 'That's it,' Bret said, 'suck me like you were a girl.' Bret's dick wasn't as prepossessing as the rest of his body, so even with my minimal experience I had no problem deep-throating him. He grabbed my head, muttered 'Eat it, bitch,' and shot his load in my mouth. And that was that; I'd sucked off the man of my dreams. 'Put the clothes back in the bag,' he said. The slip was light as a cloud in my trembling hands. The crotch of the panties was soaked through. 'And don't,' he warned, 'tell anybody about this.' Like I would. After Bret left, I jacked off so hard my dick was sore all the next day."

He spit on his hand and went to work on my cock. It felt so damn good that my growing impatience vanished. Almost. But he wasn't finished talking yet.

"That was that. I didn't see Bret again before I left for winter break. I figured that he'd gotten himself some pussy and forgotten about me. But only a few days after I got back to campus, he came over to me, looking a little shy—which on him looked just plain strange—and said, 'Want to go for a pizza or something? My treat.' And so he started using me on a regular basis, in my room when Tony was gone, his room when his roommate was out. Once I even sucked him off in the men's room at the library, but without the lingerie it wasn't as good. Tony kept fucking my face too—I guess when he couldn't get otherwise laid, but it was Bret I really wanted. It wasn't because of who he was, really, it wasn't even his looks. It was because of, well, me. I needed him. I wanted to be pretty for him. I wanted to be pretty so someone would love me."

He looked in my eyes with an expression so pure, so vulnerable that it made me ache. It made me want to come. It made me want to screw him.

"Finally, one night, it happened. Tony was spending the night at his latest girlfriend's house, so I invited Bret over. He brought a fifth of Cuervo and a teddy, garters, and stockings. 'I want you to look like a whore,' he said, then took a big gulp from the bottle.

" 'A pretty whore,' I told Bret, hardly believing I was saying it. 'Your pretty whore.'

"Bret took out a condom. 'Don't want to catch anything from some faggot, do I, slut?' he said. I couldn't get words out. I just shook my head. And then he pulled his foreskin back, unrolled the rubber, and lubed up. 'Fag, I'm going to fuck you good,' he said. And he did.

"I hadn't been fucked before, and it hurt at first, hurt pretty bad when he shoved his cock way inside me as I lay there on my back, big strong Bret between my stockinged legs. But I managed to take it, threw my arms around him, and his strokes became less brutal. That's when he looked at me blearily and said, 'I love you.' I couldn't believe it. 'I love you, Rick.' Just like that. I felt, well, I felt so damn pretty."

I was beginning to get more than a little annoyed. I wanted to fuck Rick, just like Bret the fratboy had, but the story obviously meant a lot to him, so I lay there, him in my arms, my fingers up his ass, as he continued.

"That was the only time he said that. In fact, he started to seem more distant, and we had sex less frequently. But then it's hard to have a secret affair with someone who's in the same frathouse. I can't say I really loved him, not even a little bit. Even then I didn't think so. But I couldn't shake the feeling that I somehow belonged to him, or at least a part of him. Hell, I don't know, maybe I did love him in a way.

"And then one night I was at the pizza place. I overheard some guys a couple of tables over, talking. I really wasn't eavesdropping; they were loudmouths. 'So ever since that girls underwear stunt, some guys have been calling your house Sigma Queer,' one of them said. And then the reply, 'Dude, it's not the house that's gay. Nobody knows that better than me. It's just this one brother, a guy named Rick. He's nice enough, I suppose, but he's a real big faggot.' I recognized the voice; I didn't even have to turn and see who was talking, though I did look. It was Bret, his back toward me, and the other guys at the table were all laughing and grinning. I ran out in the street, a slice of pepperoni pizza still in my hand.

"A few days later Bret showed up at my door. I shouldn't have let him in, I guess, but I did. I put on the slip he'd brought. He shoved me down onto the bed, got me on all fours, and pushed the lacy hem up around my waist, and I let him fuck me. I wanted him to fuck me, and he used my ass hard. Somewhere in the middle Tony came back. He sat there watching until Bret shot his load, and then he fucked me too. After it was over I lay there in the dark, wanting someone to love me and crying myself to sleep. But that didn't stop me from jacking off the next day when I remembered being fucked by both Tony and Bret.

"Finally, a week or two after that, I kind of realized I'd had enough. I was having a snack in the kitchen of the house when

The Sweetheart of Sigma Queer

Bret showed up with another fraternity brother—a senior, a husky dude who always acted real tough. His name, if you can believe it, was Jimbo. He looked at me and said, 'I'm fucking horny and I hear you'll let anybody fuck your ass.' I couldn't stand the guy's attitude. I told him, 'You heard wrong.' 'Bitch,' Bret said. And then Jimbo spat on me, actually spat on me. And that was it. I decided it was time to move out."

And I'd decided it was time for Rick to put out. Enough. I had let him tell his story, and now my reward was past due. I pushed him back on the bed and climbed on top of him.

"All I wanted was to be pretty," he said.

"You are pretty, " I said, and I meant it. I ran my hand over his legs, over the black mesh stockings, up to the garter belt. He moaned and spread his legs. My fingers moved to his silky red crotchless panties. My dick was as hard as it gets. I reached over for a rubber.

"You don't have to use that," he said, but I did use it. I didn't want to bring something home, not from a whore like him.

I pushed his legs in the air, my hands against his stockings, his taut muscles beneath. His bigger-than-average dick was stiff against his belly, leaking precome. I slapped some lube on his hole, so wet it was soaking his crotchless panties, then positioned my dick head up against his pussy.

"Pretty," he said. "I want to be pretty for you."

And I slid all the way inside him and started fucking his cunt. His insides felt great, all warm and yielding and wet. I reached under his slip, grabbed one of his little nipples, and tweaked it hard. He closed his eyes and licked his lips. Like a slut. Slut. I rammed into his hole, banging him, making him squirm and moan.

"Hurt me with your dick."

"You bet, you little fucking bitch." And I screwed him as hard as I could.

Pretty. He was so pretty. So pretty and fucked-up and willing. And good sex, such a good fuck.

Much better than my wife.

The Last Pledge Task

Steve Soucy

Why do young men pledge fraternities? Different reasons, to be sure. Some must enjoy the instant gratification of having dozens of brand-new close friends and supporters following initiation. Others might do it for the quick hookups with sorority girls at mixers; wearing certain Greek letters on campus can be a key to unlocking the door of getting laid nonstop during college years. For me, I was betting on the law of averages holding true: It was my quest to find those brothers in the fraternity that would be inclined to a little same-sex exploration.

I'm happy to say, I did not come away from my fraternal tenure disappointed.

I pledged Sigma Phi Epsilon spring semester of my freshman year at a state university in upstate New York. When I rushed during the first week of February, I went to many informal events and met with the representatives of several fraternities. It became clear quite quickly that Sig Ep was to be my number 1 choice. I didn't care for every brother in this fraternity (56 in all) but seemed to have enough in common with a majority. Most of the guys were cool, and there was a good mix of athletic types, partyers, and the intelligent set.

Bids were offered two weeks later, and on the appointed evening, just after midnight, four inebriated guys who lived on the same Quadrangle as me were standing in the hallway outside my door. I stood there with a slight erection in my underwear, which is always the case when I'm roused from sleep. One of them secured a pledge pin to the area of my shirt just above the heart, they all welcomed me, and I was in.

There was something about standing in front of them, almost naked, that gave me a complete hard-on after I closed the door and heard them walk away. One of the guys, Nick Whitman, was a lacrosse player that I met at summer tryouts in July. I had seen him naked in the shower a few times, and he'd provided ample inspiration for several follow-up jack-off sessions. His excitement for the organization was infectious, and he was the one who suggested I come check things out.

Once I was pinned and after I met my nine pledge brothers, the activities began. Our Pledge Master was a malevolent junior from Manhattan who played the part well: He was at all times scowling, angry, and treating us with immense disrespect. I was truly frightened of him until we were invited into his room for a meeting and found him playing the latest release from the Communards, a group fronted by the falsetto-singing Jimmy Somerville. It was such a gay CD with Jimmy singing about his latest homosexual breakup, there was no way to fear the guy after that.

For the most part, the pledge period was fair, and although we had to participate in a few meaningless activities (like being locked in a room and made to finish two bottles of tequila and half a keg of beer), almost all the events promoted solidarity, friendship, and reliance on your peers.

Another important ideal I took a keen interest in was that a pledge always helped another pledge through a moment of need. Enter Sean O'Toole.

Sean was a 6-foot-2 rugby player with blond hair and bright blue eyes. He looked like he should've been attending the sunny campus of UCLA and surfing the waters of Malibu every evening after class. He had pectorals and biceps that bulged without a flex beneath his clothing and a look that caused young women to swoon and become awkward before him. There was something in the way he carried himself, though, that made me choose him to be my partner on those few nights when brothers gave us mandatory sleepovers to promote pledge unity.

Sean's girlfriend went to Mount Holyoke in Massachusetts, and because of the distance between them he had "needs" that required frequent tending. I was just the guy to help him out.

It was 2 in the morning, and our conversation took a dangerous turn to how long it had been since we'd had a really good blow job. He, somewhat embarrassed, mentioned that once when he was drunk "beyond comprehension" he let a rugby buddy go down on him, and shockingly, it was the best he'd ever had.

Well, this got me started, and with all the curious innocence I could muster, I asked if I could give it a shot.

We were on the floor in his room, and his hands were behind his head in a pose of absolute bliss and relaxation. He thrust his hips in a slow, rhythmic motion and whispered that my mouth felt great on his dick, which disappeared and reappeared, glistening with saliva. He told me to use my tongue on his balls, and I did. This sent him into throes of ecstasy that made me want to come as I stroked my own dick.

I had to take a break and jump away when we heard his roommate stop snoring in the adjoining room. But once the fear of being caught subsided, we went at it again and I was relentless in my effort to bring him to climax. When he was on the verge, he said he wanted me to swallow his load and attempted to hold my mouth on his dick, but I pulled away at the last second and watched as his come shot all over my face.

This exemplar of brotherly love happened every night Sean and I were alone.

During our 12-week pledge period we were all required to interview and perform a task for every brother on the fraternity roster. Hell Week was only two days away and I realized I had 10 interviews and tasks to complete. I worked strategically and finished all on-campus brother interviews first and then started taking the purple-and-white campus bus that ferried students from the uptown campus downtown, and met with the rest.

Brother Eric Cavaliere was an upperclassman who lived off campus and was to be my final interview as a pledge. He was one of the 12 Founding Fathers of our chapter. Many of these seniors were not as active or visible as us younger members; when I spotted his name on the master list, I knew I'd never seen or met him.

The rumor from a few of my pledge brothers was that Eric preferred to be interviewed on campus and that he met during a break between his psychology classes in the campus center. I was also told that his pledge task was one of the less complex ones: wait in line, order his sandwich, and deliver it to him with a Coke. After which he'd give an abbreviated interview and take off to study in the library.

Piece of cake, but the clock was ticking, and I had to secure his answers to my questions within 24 hours.

Brothers had differing opinions on Eric, and although they would never speak negatively in front of a pledge, I got the feeling he was "tolerated" rather than admired. I heard he made only occasional appearances at the weekly Sunday meeting on campus and that he was quiet. If he had fit in with the group at one time in the past, he seemed to prefer being on the sidelines now.

I called Eric on the phone and the conversation went something like this:

"Hello, Brother Eric. I'm proud to be a Sig Ep pledge. My name is Drew Alexander."

"Yeah?"

"Um. I was wondering, sir—you're my final interview, and I was hoping you might be able to meet with me tonight or tomorrow morning?" I was tentative in my request. We were supposed to give brothers sufficient notice for an interview.

"I only meet pledges on campus" was his reply.

"Yes, sir, I understand that."

"And I won't be on campus until Friday morning."

"I understand, sir, but I need to obtain this interview before midnight Thursday," I said.

"Sounds to me like you should've had your act together and called before now."

He hung up.

At this point in the pledge program I was in no mood to deal with an annoying, uninvolved brother who could stand in the way of my acceptance. I was becoming tired of showing respect for these guys who were essentially my equal, but since I wanted what they had—brotherhood and to be let in on the secrets of fraternity—I reminded myself that I had to complete these simple requirements. So I bit the bullet and, armed with my best kiss-ass voice, hit the redial button on my phone.

Eric picked up.

"Brother Eric?"

"Yes." He sounded annoyed.

"I regret that I have upset you, sir. I will do whatever it takes to secure this interview. Name your task and I will complete it willingly—*anything*." I waited for him to say something. He didn't.

"I can meet you at your apartment or off-site, in the middle of a desert, wherever or whatever is most convenient for you. Just, please, don't deny me access to you or I won't be eligible for Hell Week."

"Why are you wasting your time with this nonsense?" was his reply.

There was silence on the line, but my plea must have appealed to his sense of responsibility for my fate. It was highly irregular, but he agreed for me to come to his house.

"I'll sign your pledge book and then you can go. Don't worry about the task."

I thanked him and said I'd take the first bus downtown.

The ride took about 20 minutes and I got off at the last stop: the corner of Washington Avenue and Lark Street. Eric lived on Dove, which was a block away from the South Mall, an area of buildings that make up most of the city skyline.

I walked down a tree-lined street and passed two-story brownstones until I saw the polished gold numbers 968 that announced I'd reached my destination. I found two names above the doorbell for apartment number 2: ERIC CAVALIERE & CHRISTOPHER FISHER. I pressed the doorbell and waited for either the buzz that would allow me entrance through the locked door or the intercom to carry Eric's voice through its speaker.

The intercom crackled with life.

I climbed the stairs and came to a landing at the second floor. As I was about to knock on the door it swung open. Eric didn't look like I'd imagined. He was slightly shorter than me, but his body was solid and stocky, well-defined. He was Italian and obviously spent a considerable amount of time in the gym. His shoulders were broad and his back V-shaped; he had dark hair and dark features.

He wore a dress shirt and khakis, which gave him a grown-up, professional look that I wasn't used to seeing on other brothers. He looked me in the eye as I shook his hand, and his grip was strong, powerful.

The Last Pledge Task

I was immediately attracted.

I made a quick glance into the interior of his place and saw that it was immaculate, decorated with quality furnishings. In no way was it your typical college-male apartment: no beer bottles in view on a puke-stained carpet. I got the feeling there were no *Playboys* scattered on the living room table or behind the toilet.

I started with the customary greeting: "Hello, Brother Eric. I'm proud—"

"That's OK." He cut me off and stepped away from the door to allow my entrance.

He closed it and turned around to face me. I could tell he was checking me out in the lamp-lit room, sizing me up, wondering if he should simply sign my book and send me away or whether he should extend a courtesy to have me stay a little longer. He had a bold look about him, and his gaze made me nervous.

"I brought my pledge book," I pulled the steno pad from the backpack I'd been carrying on a shoulder, "but I really would like to get your interview. Are you sure you can't spare a few minutes?"

"Your name's Drew, right?" He motioned to the couch and I sat down, nodding.

"I apologize for leaving this to the last minute, Brother Eric, and appreciate you making an exception to see me."

"Don't sweat it. Today was a tough day; I sort of took it out on you."

"I'm a pledge, I'm supposed to be abused."

He laughed at that.

"Actually, this'll be good. You'll be my study break." Eric looked over at a desk that had several open books surrounding a computer. "I have a psych-stats paper to finish for tomorrow."

"I won't take up much of your time."

"The standard interview questions?" he asked, sounding bored.

"I try to keep it interesting."

The sleeves of his dress shirt were rolled up to his elbows, and his forearms were massive and covered with dark hair. I imagined unbuttoning the shirt and unzipping the pants to reveal a trail to white briefs.

"Before we start this thing I'm gonna change. I'm still in my work clothes."

"OK."

"Help yourself to a drink. There's Molson and Rolling Rock in the refrigerator."

"You want one?" I asked.

He thought for a moment then said, "Why not?"

My heartbeat accelerated. I had a raging hard-on that was straining to be let out of the confines of my pants. I readjusted myself as Eric disappeared down the hallway and didn't get up from the chair until I heard him slip into the bathroom.

I turned the overhead light on in the kitchen. The refrigerator had two magnets that held photographs on the door. One was close-up of Eric and two adorable little girls, most likely his nieces. They were sitting on the floor together in front of a Christmas tree. The other featured Eric and a handsome guy who looked to be in his late 20s. They were standing very close, each with an arm around the other, on a balcony with clear azure water in the background. They looked like they'd been laughing—their smiles were radiant.

I took out two bottles of Rolling Rock. I needed a bottle opener but didn't want to rummage through his things, so I waited for Eric to return. My dick was semi-hard and a little obvious in my pants. I kept willing it to go down.

"Where do you keep your bottle opener?" I called out.

He entered wearing a pair of sweats and a T-shirt. His body was perfectly toned.

"Here." He pulled it off the wall, where it hung from a nail in clear view. "I was always losing it."

Back in the living room, I stood at a window and looked out. The sun had gone down and Eric had a nice view of downtown. I took a hefty swig from my beer bottle then turned to face him. He settled where I'd been sitting on the couch.

"Where was that picture taken?" I asked, as I sat on the floor against a wall.

"Which one?" Eric threw me a large pillow. I placed it behind my back.

"The balcony shot."

"Cancun. Spring break last year."

"Looks beautiful. I went to Fort Lauderdale with my pledge brothers. Can you say 'shithole'?"

He laughed. "Yeah, we've all done that kind of a trip—you're still young."

"Not that young," I said defensively.

"To someone who's 21, 18—you are 18, right?"

"Nineteen."

"Nineteen feels like a lifetime ago."

I knew Eric had a story to tell. The challenge, or so I thought, was in getting him to open up.

He took a larger-than-average mouthful of his beer to finish it. He got up and asked if I wanted another. I tried not to stare at his dick—the outline of which was clearly visible in the tight-fitting sweatpants.

I accepted.

Once he'd handed me my second and sat down again, he said, "Let's cut to the chase, Drew."

"What do you mean?"

"If I gave you the opportunity to ask only one question, what would you ask me?"

I stared at my leather Timberland shoes.

"I'm not sure I understand."

He explained: "I don't have time for this interview. So I'm proposing to change the rules. If you could ask me one question—one question that would decide where this night is headed—then we can get on with it."

"One question," I echoed, certain I knew what he was driving at.

"I'm the Brother, you're my pledge," he leaned forward—his eyes were intense. I felt a little flustered. This night was not turning out as I'd planned.

"You get one question. Make it count."

I thought for a second or two and blurted out: "Who's the guy with you in the picture on the refrigerator?"

"My ex-boyfriend, former roommate." He said this like it was the most natural state of affairs in the world.

"You live here alone?" I couldn't hide the excitement in my voice.

"That's two questions. You were only allowed one. Now it's my turn. Why are you pledging Sig Ep?"

"The guys are cool, it's a good group."

Eric looked at me like he was waiting for something more. For some reason I couldn't refuse him the information he was after.

"I also got into a fight with one of my roommates. My living situation had challenges," I continued.

"Hmm."

I finished my second beer and so did he.

"Another?" Eric asked.

"Yeah."

He left the room and I took a deep breath. He came back with two more opened bottles.

"Why were you fighting with your roommate—what's his name?"

"Tim."

"What was between the two of you?"

"Nothing."

He stared at me hard and I stared back. I was the first to look away.

"How do I know I can trust you?" I asked. "I don't know you at all."

"Isn't that the purpose of this meeting—to get to know each other?"

I took two more gulps from my beer bottle and made a decision. The maxim *Nothing ventured, nothing gained* was running through my head. I don't know why or what it was, but something about Eric let me tell him my secret.

"I met Tim last year while I was still in high school. He blew me away. We were inseparable throughout the summer and then one night we were sleeping together in his bed, the temperature had dropped, and a window was open. We woke at exactly the same time. He got up and closed the window and climbed back in, under the covers. His foot brushed against my leg and our bodies just sought the warmth of each other and then our mouths. We kissed, had sex, and that changed everything."

"Was it your first time?"

"No."

We both laughed at the abruptness of my answer.

"Third," I confessed, "I was sexually active at an early age with two of my neighbors."

"When did it end with Tim?"

"October."

There was silence as we both adjusted to the new intimacy between us.

"How are you doing now?"

"Well, I still live in the room. My other roommates always favored Tim to me, so I'm something of an outcast right now. And a little confused. You're the first person I've told. It feels good, though."

Eric nodded as if he understood exactly what I meant.

I asked: "Are you gay—I mean *really* gay? Because I'm not sure about me."

"The guy in the photograph in Cancun, his name's Chris. We were together for two years. Things didn't work out. He took a job in Boston about a month ago. I'm definitely gay. It's something I've just admitted recently, but yeah, that's what I am."

"This is the last thing I was expecting tonight."

"I know. I opened the door and was looking forward to signing your stupid book and sending you on your way."

"Why didn't you?"

"Because I could tell you were interesting."

I smiled and looked down at the ground, embarrassed. I looked up when I heard Eric move to the floor and watched as he made his way to me. He put his hand behind my head and pulled me in for a kiss. I was frozen on the spot. He ran his hand through my hair, and the kiss seemed like it would go on forever. But then he pulled back. I stared into his green eyes.

He stood up, and I could see the head of his dick pushing out the top of his sweatpants. He pulled his shirt down to cover it and offered me his hand. He gave me a slight pull and we were standing in front of one another. We kissed again and this time I let my hands wander. His whole body was firm and tight. I moved to his ass and found that he wasn't wearing underwear. He shuddered when my finger traveled down.

I could feel his dick. He kept pushing against my own while his body made slight gyrating motions.

He pulled away and held my face in his hands. He stared at me, intense.

"Are you sure you're OK with this, Drew?"

"Yeah," I said, breathless.

"Do you find me attractive?"

"Not at all," I said, and he laughed again, flashing the smile that was captured in the photograph on his refrigerator. "Is this allowed, a pledge brother hookup? I don't remember reading about it in my code of conduct book."

"It's probably not the first time it's happened," Eric said. I couldn't help thinking of Sean O'Toole. "I can keep a secret, can you?"

Eric never let go of my hand as he led me from the living room to his bedroom. He sat me down on the mattress and pulled my sneakers off. Then he stripped me of my jeans, socks, and shirt, leaving me in my underwear.

He took his T-shirt and sweats off. His dick stood out a good nine inches from his body. All I wanted was to put my mouth on it, but he made me wait, and we just lay there on his bed and kissed for a while. He was on his back, and I climbed on top of him and we stayed like that, holding one another and letting our hands run.

Eric pushed my head down and into his crotch, and I took him in my mouth. He arched his back and pushed his dick till it was going down my throat, causing me to choke.

"You'll get used to it," he said.

I couldn't help but catch (and like) the future implication in that statement.

After a few minutes of me sucking him, he moved us into a sixty-nine position and sucked me until I had to push his face away. I was getting close.

He asked: "Did you and Tim ever?" He touched my ass with a finger.

"A few times."

"When was the last time?"

"It's been like seven months."

"I love doing that. Do you?"

Eric's fingers found the entrance to my hole. I could feel the weight of his body against mine when he repositioned himself so his dick was rubbing against the crack of my ass.

"Was Tim's dick as big as mine?"

"Not by a long shot."

"Wanna try?"

"I don't know." I couldn't help but think his dick would rip me apart.

"What if I told you you had to? That it's your pledge task." He showed off a sinister grin that reminded me he was in charge here and that I should play this game.

He kissed me. He used his hand to guide his dick to my hole. He pushed, but I was completely dry. His arms held me tight, and I could tell he was dying to do it.

"Do you have K-Y?" I asked, hesitantly.

He got up from the bed and crossed to the bathroom. He returned carrying a white tube of lubricant, two condoms, and a hand towel. He propped a few pillows and sat with his back against the headboard.

"I'm gonna need some help here."

The Last Pledge Task

Eric smiled and handed me the Magnum condom—still in its wrapper.

I opened it and slipped it on as he held his dick straight up. When I was done he brought my head close to his and kissed me. I pulled back.

He had me straddle him.

"Just relax," he purred, then closed his eyes.

I tried to sit on it, but it wasn't working. Without a word he turned me over onto my stomach and laid himself down on top of me. He kept whispering and moving his tongue in and around my ear. The heat of his breath was driving me crazy.

Little by little, I relaxed. Eric was completely patient. He pushed the head of his dick in, and it felt all right. He went slowly and I was surprised that I could take him inside of me. Then ever so gently, he started moving his dick in and out. Once he thrust deep and I felt a jolt of pain; he acknowledged it and was careful not to hurt me again.

Then he started to move his dick faster, and it felt a little uncomfortable. He moved faster, and faster, until our sounds became loud. He told me to hold my dick in my hand—he was getting close. I did what he said and could feel and hear the weight of his body slapping against mine. He pulled out, slipped the condom off, and climaxed. He let out a load that landed all over my back.

Eric quickly wiped me off with the towel and rolled me over. I jacked off as he kissed my mouth and hit the wall behind us when I shot.

We laughed again, and then collapsed, exhausted. I put my head on his chest and he kept his arm around me.

"I have to admit, that's the hardest I've had to work for a pledge task."

"Who said you were finished?" He smiled and kissed me again.

We lay there for a while until Eric spoke: "This is going to sound awkward, but I hope you'll come back, Drew."

I held him tight and listened to the sound of his breathing. We eventually got up, took a shower together, and had sex again.

I could sense our evening was coming to its inevitable end. He had that paper to write, and I had homework to complete as well. When I was about to leave Eric's apartment to catch my bus, he asked, "You hungry?"

"Starving."

"What do you say we walk up to Amazing Wok and grab some food. Then I'll drive you back to campus?"

We walked the short distance to the restaurant. We talked more about our backgrounds, families, things you're supposed to reveal before you consummate a sexual relationship. With Eric it had all happened so easily—just like with Tim. But this time there was nothing tentative about our coming together. We seemed to move into this with both eyes open.

We stood inside the warm take-out lobby where the smells of Chinese food swirled around us and looked at the menu posted on the wall above.

I turned to Eric—he was in profile.

He turned to me and asked, "So what'll it be?"

Initiation Night
(and Everything After)

Clark Anthony

"You haven't called a brother in a while."

His right hand gripped my wrist. I nodded.

"But here we are, about to graduate, and I get this message on my machine..."

What could I say? I needed it again. I had held off for as long as I could, but I needed to try it again. His left arm pressed firmly against my abs. It felt good.

"'C'mon, Charlie, can we get together? Let's do it again. You remember freshman year..."

Well, he did remember, and I sure hadn't forced him to come over. His rod ground tighter against my ass, ready. Yeah, he needed it too.

"I remember getting all over your butt. I guess you just want some payback. It's your last chance."

He was baiting me, just like always. I knew not to respond, but it was tough with his mouth hovering right next to my ear. I just let him trash-talk for a while and thought about our freshman year.

I go to a small Southern school, and most everyone's kind of repressed when they get here. Not me and Charlie, though. We were both city kids—Charlie from D.C., me from around Philly. Not the mean streets, but not some candy-ass prep school either.

We both rushed Sigma Chi and had no problem getting

accepted. Rush requirements had been silly crap—reciting poems in praise of brothers, stealing Honor Code signs, stuff like that. All the brothers are scared shitless that the college administration will nail them for hazing, so they keep all the real craziness on the down-low. It's kind of agreed that the college will look the other way on initiation night, though. Sig Chi is famous for coming up with bizarre rituals to fill that final night. You gotta weed out the weaklings sometime.

The Sig Chi fraternity house stood just a block away from campus—innocent-looking white clapboard. A gray-haired neighbor lady clutched a rake, smiling benignly at the festivities. "You boys have fun tonight," she clucked from across the hedges. All eight of us new brothers milled around the lawn, waiting for something to happen.

The Sig Chi president, a senior named Lee, waited until all the brothers had arrived and then launched into a canned speech about how bloody honored we should be to join such a distinguished bunch of shitkickers as Sig Chi. I sneaked a look at the old lady. She leaned on her rake and grinned like a simpleton. *Such upstanding young men, these college boys.*

We shifted from foot to foot until Lee finished, then got hustled up the worn brick steps and inside. Two brothers, one on each side, practically launched me over the threshold and into our poolroom, lit only by the dimming sunlight. To my left I saw Charlie get shoved up against the table, then just a glimpse of red as someone yanked a bandanna over my eyes. Unknown hands shoved me, blindfolded, toward the stairs.

"So, you do this all the time, I bet?"

The question jolted me back to reality, me on my hands and knees with Charlie pressed to my back. "No, man, this is the first time since freshman year…"

Initiation Night (and Everything After)

"You're shitting me!"

"Fuck no." I hadn't, either. I know what I want, and I didn't feel like dealing with the closeted head cases roaming this campus.

"Damn, man, you could have had whatever you wanted." I could tell from the tone of Charlie's voice that he thought I was nuts. His left hand strayed from my abs toward my crotch. "Not even with Sean?" he asked, forefinger stroking my balls. "He wanted your cock."

I started, and he laughed, pulling his hand away. I hadn't fucked Sean, but hell, how did he remember after three years?

After practically breaking my legs going down the stairs and slamming against a doorjamb, I realized there was now only a single brother guiding me. With one hand on my neck he pushed me through a door and clicked it shut. His hand trembled fiercely.

"You can take off the blindfold now."

I pulled it away from my face and spun around to find Sean, a cute redheaded sophomore. He looked like a young Boris Becker, with the same ice-blue eyes and lanky, muscular body. But he stared at the floor and his body seemed limp.

"Take off your clothes," he mumbled.

I was hoping he might do the same, but Sean didn't move, so no such luck. The trembling, the mumbling: I knew he was either straight and embarrassed or gay and scared. I wasn't leaving the room without finding out which. My nose is a little crooked from a baseball that crunched it when I was in Little League, but everything else is in place and pretty good-looking. Six feet tall, 165 pounds, muscle straight through, and a nice year-round tan. If I take off my clothes, people notice. And hell, this was a direct order from an older Sig Chi brother on fraternity initiation night. Like I'm gonna disobey?

I yanked the white T-shirt I was wearing over my head and noticed that my nipples were rock-hard. This little striptease I was gonna perform had me hot, but what about Sean? I looked up from the sneakers I was kicking off, and Sean jerked his head away, avoiding my eyes. His face, usually so pale and composed, looked purple. Maybe it was just from the heat in the stifling basement or the bad lighting, but I was starting to think that "gay and scared" was the right description for Sean.

Well, if they were going to make us do this, I might as well have fun. Shirtless and barefoot, I unbuckled my belt, then snapped it out of my jeans. The sudden noise got Sean to look up, and he kept staring. I unzipped the jeans nice and slow. I wished Sean would make his mind to help me get naked, but he just stood, wide-eyed, like some amazed little kid.

By now my cock was raging. It shoved the band of my boxers slightly away from my stomach, exposing the light trail of hair below my abs. I figured if Sean got just one look at that cock, the fun would begin. I stepped out of the jeans. But when I started to lower my boxers, he snapped.

"Leave those on," he barked, suddenly gruff, like the man he wished he were. "Come on, let's go." He threw open the door and shoved me into the main basement room.

The basement was massive, and couches full of Sig Chi brothers were ringing three sides of the room. About a dozen 30-packs of cheap beer sat on a table. Most of the other initiates were lined up against the one bare wall, all stripped to their underwear. I was headed toward them when Charlie came down the stairs.

If it had just been Charlie and me in the room, I would have gotten on my knees. He was a specimen, really fucking built, with lean calves, flaring thighs, and tight, rounded biceps and pecs. His skin was hairless and gleamed like he'd been oiled. He saw Sean staring at me and snickered. Charlie knew I was only looking at him, and flexed his abs. He didn't seem to mind my staring, and took his place next to me in the line, shoulder to shoulder. It took some willpower to keep myself from going down on him right then and there.

"So," Charlie hissed into my ear, *"are we gonna get it on or not?"*

"So," Lee shouted, "are we going to get this going or not?"

Everyone was happy to make us stand there—probably since most of us were hot—but the brothers laughed assent. They wanted to see some action.

Lee was in fraternity-president speech-making mode. "We know you all are smart, but Sigma Chi has also got to ensure the physical fitness of all new brothers. So we've brought you here. There's a tourney starting right here. Pair off. You're going to wrestle. Matches end when the brothers think one of you has won."

The idea of wrestling with Charlie had me hot immediately. I sneaked a glance at him. He caught my look and smirked, then paired off with a wiry freshman named Darren. The Sig Chi brothers whooped and hollered while we split into four pairs. When we got into a line again, Charlie and I were on opposite ends. I was just going to have to win a couple fights to get my hands on him.

Lee made Charlie and Darren fight first. They both got into a crouch, and the brothers laughed their heads off. Charlie was about three times Darren's size. The match was quick. Darren went for one of Charlie's legs and tried to trip him, but Charlie wrenched him into a side headlock and forced him to his knees. They could have called the fight right then, but I got the feeling the brothers liked looking at Darren's skinny, tight body wrenched into submission. Charlie rolled him onto his back and pinned him, his knees on Darren's chest.

Everyone chanted, "One…two…three!" Charlie let Darren up. Then, so quickly no one could react, Charlie reached for

Darren's boxers and tore them straight down the side. Darren stood for a second—humiliated, his face bright red and his long, thin cock curving and hard—and the basement exploded. Brothers screamed approval. Jody, a football player, slammed his arm into the couch, yelling and laughing simultaneously. I noticed Sean stare hard at Darren, then turn his head away sharply. Charlie just walked over to the six-packs and popped the top off a Beast, drinking some and pouring some over his head, like pinning Darren had taken all his energy and he needed to recharge.

I felt sorry for Darren, embarrassed by all these closet queens, but when I looked at him again he had a small smile. He knew they wanted him, naked and hard, and he sat proudly against the wall. He kept his legs spread as he sat, his cock sticking straight up. I started to think it was going to be a beautiful night.

"Yeah, we get it on as soon as you shut up, Charlie."

"Cocky little son of a bitch, ain't you? Remember what I did to you on initiation night, man. Let's go."

I remembered. It had been a long time, but we were set. I tensed my body.

The next two matches were a blur. The Sig Chi brothers howled and shouted their way through the matches while I watched Charlie. I promised myself that if I could get my arms around Charlie's neck, if I could get to those oiled thighs and pecs, I'd drive him into the ground. He looked strong, but I could be stronger. I wanted my hands on his body.

The third match ended with the brothers screaming and knocking back beer. Lee had chugged too much, and he wasn't able to make a speech. He just grunted at me and my opponent— a tall, built freshman named Jed. We walked to the center of the room and took on a crouch posture, like real wrestlers. I used the

few seconds before the match began to take stock of the guy. Jed
was a farm boy, with corn-silk blond hair and the kind of broad,
sinewy shoulders that come from pitching too many bales of hay.
Stripped to his boxers, I noticed that Jed's legs were scrawny and
his feet too small for his upper body. I had to go for his legs and
avoid getting trapped in a headlock.

Lee was standing behind me and yelled the order, "Wrestle!" I
dropped low and dived forward before Jed could react, taking
him out at the ankles. He fell to the ground with a thump. I
grabbed one foot in each hand and struggled to my knees, getting
leverage on him and driving his legs apart. He tried to yank away
from my grip, but I kept his legs spread long enough to do what
I had to.

Praying I wouldn't make such a beautiful kid a soprano before
his time, I dropped down between his legs, aiming my elbow at
his crotch. It connected with his package and he grunted in pain.
I thrust my hand into his boxers and grabbed hold of his balls,
twisting them. I felt Jed's gigantic cock beat against my hand and
almost lost my resolve, but kept twisting. I threw my whole
weight on top of his upper body. His head smacked against the
floor and I pinned his shoulders.

This match was over. One down. One more till Charlie.

"You sure you're ready?"

*One last taunt. With Charlie there always had to be one last
taunt. I arched my ass back into his crotch and felt his taut cock
return the pressure. That was all the response I needed to give.*

"Yeah, OK, man. You're ready."

Barry was the next one to go up against Charlie. Barry was built
like a linebacker, but so slow he could never have gotten to the
quarterback. Every fraternity has one of these guys: a big, slow kid
who isn't very smart and isn't very nice but gets initiated anyway

because sometimes, if a fraternity brother gets into trouble, it helps to have a guy who's stupid and mean on your side.

Charlie came out of the crouch so fast Barry had no time to react. He took the fat slob by the head and jammed Barry's chin into his shoulder. Barry staggered back and Charlie tripped him. The room shook with the *thud* of Barry's fall, and Charlie was on him, snatching one arm into a lock. He twisted the arm around and behind Barry's back. The big kid howled abuse, so Charlie yanked it again. Barry was like fucking pudding, a total wimp. Jody, the Sig Chi football player, jumped off the couch and shouted that the match was over just to shut up the baby and end the embarrassment. It wasn't a wrestling match—it was a slaughter.

I had no problem with the next match. Bryce was a decent-size guy who probably could have given me a fight. But as we grabbed each other around the shoulders and I started to overpower him, he whispered to me, "Just don't go after my balls like with Jed, man, and I'll let you win." No one could have heard it over the brothers' screaming: half rooting for me, the other half rooting for Bryce. Bryce let me push him to his knees and drive him onto his side. From there I thrust him onto his back. Slipping an arm under one leg, I pushed up until Bryce's shoulder blades were pinned to the floor. The Sig Chi brothers groaned; they'd been expecting a longer match. But no one questioned that I'd won, and I knew who was next in line.

"On three, man," Charlie hissed. "You do the count."

The brothers had almost finished off the Beast. Lee grabbed Charlie's wrist in one hand and my wrist in the other, lifting them above our heads. "The winners!" he laughed drunkenly. "Now who will be the champion? Come on, wrestle!"

I gave Charlie a look and he gave me a sneer. I'm sure he drew stares all the time. I wasn't the first, I wouldn't be the last. I adjusted the waistband on my boxers and got in my crouch. Charlie stomped around for a few seconds, then bent at the knees and leaned slightly forward at the waist, his hands forming a loose V in front of him: a perfect wrestler's crouch. I found myself wondering whether Charlie had wrestled in high school. If so, the best I could do was put up a better struggle than Darren or Barry.

Lee started the count, but Jody, who was one of the other fraternity leaders, jumped up and shouted to stop him. He'd been knocking back the beers all evening, and even at his size, they'd had an effect. "Nah, nah, shit, man," he slurred. "They've been in that damn position all evening. Make 'em really fuckin' wrestle, man! Make 'em get on the ground or something. C'mon, I used to wrestle, I'll show 'em what I mean!"

Jody started toward us, but Charlie stopped him. "I know what you mean," he snapped. He grabbed me by the shoulders, and I flinched. His hands were like a vice. "I used to wrestle too," Charlie said. "Get down on all fours, man." I got down on hands and knees, and Charlie shifted behind me. He knelt and leaned on top of my back, right hand on my right wrist, left arm around my stomach. His thick cock pushed at our boxers and against my asshole. I pushed back. I glanced up and caught the look on Sean's face. He looked frustrated. He looked fascinated. He looked horny.

"C'mon, we're ready," Charlie shouted. "Count to three, man."

"One...two...three!"

"One...two...three!" Lee shouted, and the room exploded again. Before I could move, Charlie yanked up on my wrist and flipped me on my side. I just barely managed to slide onto my stomach so he couldn't pin me right away, and we were wrestling.

I had learned something in three years. I reached and grabbed Charlie's left arm, where the wrist met my stomach, throwing all my weight up and backwards. It flipped Charlie off my back and gave me time to shift until I faced him. I grabbed the arm with my whole body and tried to yank it behind Charlie's back. He stopped the move and broke the hold. We separated. "Shit, man," he spat. "This year you're a wrestler."

Charlie sat on my back and pulled my arm behind me. I shifted, one shoulder pressed hard into the floor, just trying to keep the hold from being too painful. My hair is short but wavy, and he grabbed it in one hand, pulling my head around. I saw his pecs, nipples solid and erect. I knew what I had to do. Before Charlie could start another hold, I wrenched away the arm he held and shifted my body around to face him. I drove my face forward and bit at his nipple. I didn't do more than graze it, but Charlie shouted and shoved my head away.

I wasn't in the mood to listen to Charlie give me shit. I hurled myself forward from my knees and decked him. I landed on top of him and pinned his shoulders just long enough to finish what I'd tried three years ago. As Charlie struggled beneath me, I thrust down and bit one of his nipples. He groaned, and his struggling seemed more like writhing. I bit the other nipple, just a little bit, before he shoved me off him.

The nearly successful assault seemed to take the steam out of Charlie for a minute. I got a pretty decent half nelson on him and drove his head down to the floor. With my other hand I stroked one pec and rubbed against his abs. Winning was not my top goal for the evening. Our bodies were pressed too close together, and we were moving too fast and hard for the drunken brothers to notice. I slipped my hand beneath the band of his boxers and felt something spring against it. Curling my fist around his thick, hard cock, I gave it a few quick strokes. My hand jerking on his dick gave Charlie new life. He flexed his shoulders and twisted.

Initiation Night (and Everything After)

Quickly I found myself knocked onto my back, and Charlie was on top of me.

It was my turn to taunt. "You know you like it, Charlie. Why you pushing me off?"

He grinned, and I lunged forward again. He bumped me away and seized me in a side headlock. His bicep, curled around my neck, cut off almost all air, and I found myself unable to move. He shoved one hand roughly into my boxers, sliding it over and down my smooth ass. I jerked convulsively as his fingers probed my asshole, rubbing the edges and sliding shallowly into me. I tried to break the lock, but Charlie was too strong. Then his hand left my ass and took my cock, pumping it. I gave into the motion as he pumped me harder and harder. I felt come bursting toward the head of my cock, but he stopped too soon and threw me aside. Disoriented, I barely felt Charlie thrust me onto my back and straddle my waist.

I'd had the air knocked out of me by the force of Charlie's hit. The Sig Chi brothers all appeared upside down, still hooting and screaming. A couple had torn off their shirts in the hot basement. One guy in the corner looked like he was jerking himself off, but maybe I didn't see it right. Charlie was sitting on my abs and smashed my upper body into the ground once or twice. I didn't resist as he pinned my shoulders.

The brothers counted me out: "One...two...three!" Lee went fucking berserk, practically bouncing off the walls and screaming over and over that Charlie had won. Charlie gritted his teeth and pushed himself up into a squat, but he wasn't done with me. He reached down and grabbed me by the hair, driving me until I was kneeling in front of him. Then he thrust both hands into the air in the posture of victory. He looked down on me, conquered, and grinned. I could see his rod just a few inches from my mouth, raging to be free of his boxers. If it were only the two of us in the room, I would have taken it down my throat. He looked, he grinned, he knew. I guessed we had passed initiation, but I wasn't done with Charlie.

Charlie must have pinned me, because the next thing I knew, I was naked and on my knees in front of him, one of his hands grasping my hair. He had already torn off my briefs. Charlie released my hair, but I stayed kneeling. He had won again, and again thrust both hands straight up. This time, though, I wouldn't be stopped.

I reached forward and jerked his boxers over his stiff rod. It sprang free, and Charlie grabbed my hair again, this time in both hands, guiding my mouth onto his thick cock. I put my hands on Charlie's ass and he thrust his hips forward. His cock slid back and forth over my tongue, and I opened my throat, taking it all the way until my face was buried in his smooth, rock-hard abs. I yielded to the rhythm and let my hands sink down to my own cock, stroking it. Holding my head steady, Charlie slowly fucked my face, his rod driving into my mouth and down my throat again and again. As I felt his rod swell, I speeded up on my own cock, which by now was close to the edge. Charlie gave little grunts of pleasure as I tightened my lips and tongue on his rod with each stroke. We both drew to the edge. I pulled and stroked on my cock until come burst over my hands. Almost simultaneously Charlie thrust even deeper, then exploded, come filling my mouth and sliding down my throat.

I'd held off for a long time. Not anymore. Charlie's the better wrestler, but he wasn't the only winner tonight.

Hard College Days

M. Christian

"Who put a giant condom on the clock tower? Who, every year, makes their pledges run naked through the library? Every Halloween, jockstraps are mailed to all professors. *Used* jockstraps. Every spring the toilets are plugged with dildos. *Used* dildos," the Dean said, standing at the window, looking out at the afternoon quad. His hands were crossed behind his back, but his shoulders and arms were locked tight. Firm. Rigid.

"You're talking about Gamma, sir," Greg Shimkisst, the Head of the Student Body, said. A head many staff, students, and professors knew was firmly up the Dean's ass.

"No shit, Sherlock. Of course I'm talking about Gamma. They're the worst of the worst—the bottom of the barrel—and I've had it with them," he growled, rumbled, not moving from his position at the window. "They're about to get their asses kicked, and I'm the foot that's going to do it."

"Yes you are, certainly you are. Absolutely, sir," Greg said, nodding, nodding and nodding again.

"Primo ass kissing, Greg. Sure you don't want to make it your major?"

"Well, I have been reevaluating my educational plans, sir—"

"Just get Gamma in here, you asshole!"

"In all my years as a educator—" the Dean said.

"Since dinosaurs ruled the earth," Ramrod said in hoarse stage whisper. The perfect jock, the archetypal muscle boy: all planed muscles and chiseled pecs. Buzz-cut hair like the warthog's back. Looked like he could bench-press a Buick, punch out a marine. He also sang show tunes like a pro. His "There's No Business Like Show Business" was incredible.

"—I have never seen such deplorable, reprehensible behavior—"

"Doesn't get out much, does he?" Trojan echoed, grumbling, also in a low voice. Studmeister. Dick dueler. Pole-vaulter. Flagpole climber. If it was long and hard, he wanted it, usually got it—if it stood still long enough. Could also give as well as get. The joke around the Gamma Alpha Epsilon house was that not even the mouse holes were safe when Trojan was in a 'mood.' Get him drunk enough, though, and the Master Stud of the Universe got all weepy about hoping to find true love some day.

"—that threatens to undermine our years of hard work—"

"Both of them," Hardware hissed between falsely smiling teeth. If it ground bits and bytes, then Hardware was its master—and its slave. He was responsible for the house's huge telecom and power bills, but also for putting microcameras in all the campus men's rooms. His slicked-back hair smelled of ozone and lube, his face was sprinkled with resilient acne, and his pant legs hovered almost a foot above his two-tone wing tips. But just the other night he had his other brothers enraptured as he lyrically discussed the beauty to be found in an beautifully scripted piece of software.

"—if not the entire fabric of this great society—"

"Polyester or rayon-blend?" Queenie muttered with a quick flip of his blond tresses. *Does this go with this? How do I hide this? How do I make this bigger?* If it had to do with color, light, shade, or fabric, Queenie knew about it. He could turn a linebacker into Cher, or Ramrod into Madonna—which he frequently did, only sometimes with permission. Down deep, though, he was the duckling who hoped that one day he'd graduate into swanhood.

"—you complete and utter *assholes!*" the Dean said, still at the window, broad back to them all.

"Um, sir, I get the impression that you may have found our collegiate antics a bit aggravating—" Hardware said, nervously straightening the pens, pencils, and slide rule in his pocket protector.

"Yeah, man, chill out already," Trojan said, absently adjusting his running shorts.

"Boys will be boys," Ramrod said, straightening his wifebeater T-shirt.

"Somebody sure got up on the wrong side of the bed this morning," Queenie said, flicking a piece of lint off his cashmere sweater.

"If that wasn't enough, your idiotic pranks are not only giving this school a bad name but are seriously fucking with even the whole *idea* of gay fraternities. You fucking faggots are just shooting yourselves in the fucking foot!" The Dean said, turning away from the window just enough to fume and spit at them. His neck was corded and his eyes bloodshot.

"Fuck you!" Trojan said, beginning to take an angry step forward but catching himself at the last moment.

"Creepy fag basher," Ramrod sneered, curling a tension-white lip.

"Oh, dear," Hardware said. "I do think that would be considered a very clear example of textbook institutional homophobia and more and possible grounds of a civil suit—"

"Bitch!" Queenie said, hissing like a ruptured boiler.

The Dean sighed, seeming to shrink. "Look, boys, I was young myself once. I know what it was like. Hell, I even did my own share of stupid fucking pranks. I'd even consider some of what you you've done to be pretty damned clever…" The Dean stopped, took a moment to stare out the window a bit more, as if marshaling himself. "But this last stunt was just so damned over-the-top…"

"Thanks for the compliment, even if it is coming from a homophobic, irresponsible authority figure such as yourself," Hardware said, with a grin wide enough to show off his braces.

"Fucking A! Gamma Alpha Epsilon *rules*!" Ramrod whooped, punching the office air with a tight first.

"Thank you, Sir, may we have another?" Trojan said, crossing his arms and smugly smiling.

"Well, that's very nice of you to say!" Queenie said, blushing as he touched chin to chest in mock embarrassment.

"Shut the fuck up!" roared the Dean over his shoulder. The room was suddenly library-silent. "Look, you fucking faggots, I don't know how the hell you managed to get it, or get so damned much of it, but did you really have to fucking spike the faculty lounge water cooler with fucking Viagra!"

"We just thought you all needed it, dear," Queenie said, giggling delightfully.

"Actually, it wasn't all that hard. All we had to do was entertain a few premeds—well enough, that is, to get them to get their hands on it. The next step was a bit harder, since it's not a compound that's water-soluble. But we also managed to entertain a few physics and biochemistry majors—and they were *very* eager to solve our little problem for us," Hardware said, making a show polishing his short-bitten nails on his shirt.

"God knows you limp dicks couldn't have gotten it up by yourselves," Trojan said, grabbing his half-hard dick through his shorts.

"Just consider it a competitive edge," Ramrod said, thrusting his pelvis out, fucking the air.

"You fucking faggots!" the Dean roared like a mad bull, swinging away from the window. As he turned, he knocked his sterling silver water pitcher over (gift from the 1975 graduating class), and soaked his desk (gift from the 1988 graduating class). He knocked it over without touching it or the desk with his hands (courtesy of Gamma Alpha Epsilon house).

"Fucking A!" Ramrod said, staring with eyes wide and mouth shocked open. "Holy Fucking A!"

"My goodness!" Hardware said, eyes gaping as well. "Such a prodigious member!"

"Talk about higher—and harder—learning," Trojan said, licking his lips. "Hard college days—definitely hard college days!"

"You shouldn't keep something like that covered up," Queenie said, grinning wickedly. "Highlight, dearie—highlight!"

The Dean hung his head, cupped himself—but he couldn't hide his length, girth, and hardness. "It's horrible! My wife came to have lunch with me, but she took one look and ran away! I have an alumni dinner in three hours, but I can't leave my office! I don't know what to do!"

"I think we might be able to help you out," Trojan said, grabbing his own stiffening cock.

"We do have a flair for such things, after all," Queenie said, reaching around to grab hold of, and playfully part, his ass cheeks.

"We do score very high in manual dexterity and problem-solving abilities, Sir," Hardware said, starting to play with his own zipper.

"We're Number 1—we know how to score!" Ramrod cheered, slipping thumbs into his shorts.

"You're not fucking with me, are you, boys?" The Dean said, looking up, a suspicious look on his normally dignified face. " 'Cause if you are, I'm going to fucking bury your asses! You'll be out of here so fast your heads will spin! It'll be the end of you and your fucking fraternity!" Blustering and fuming, the Dean let go of his dick and slammed both hands down on his desk. Freed, his cock stabbed out, knocking painfully on a drawer. "Fuck! Crap!" he moaned, jumping back and grabbing hold of himself once again. "Well, don't just stand there, you fucking pussies! Do something about this."

"Well, hate to say this, Dean, but we are going to fuck with you," Trojan said, kicking off his shoes and yanking down his jeans. His was a cocksman's cock: a tool of many mouth and asshole victories. It looked polished, like his too-many-fucks-to-count that purified it down to the perfect essence of dick. Even his balls were smooth and hairless, ready for action. He was also dramatically, perfectly, absolutely hard: always ready for action.

"Fucking A, bubba!" Ramrod said with a leer. "We're gonna be burying into your ass, man!" Gym shorts down, Ramrod's rod was a hairy, bristling beast, like something the school mascot would have between its legs. His balls looked like they were hanging from a thornbush and his cock as like a piebald baseball bat. He was also powerfully, totally hard: always ready for some extra curricular activity.

"It's your head that's going to spin, darlin'," Queenie said, elegantly slipping off his Italian shoes, shimmying off his tight jeans, pulling off his sweater, unbuttoning and neatly folding his silk shirt. Naked, Queenie was a sleek and hairless statue, smooth and white as imported marble. His cock was narrow and long, dropping almost to his knees. His pubic hair was deftly and neatly trimmed. Slowly, ominously, he got harder and harder until he bobbed and dipped: up, willing, and able for some sweet loving.

"Funny you should call us a 'fucking fraternity,' Dean, because we are extremely adept at homosexual sexual activity, especially anal intercourse," Hardware said, pulling down his own polyester slacks. He forgot, however, that his shoes were still on, so he had to quickly sit down and slip off his ugly tennis shoes, and then his pants, and finally his baggy Y-fronts. His dick was a fireplug, squat but very thick, capped with a plump, juicy head. His hair was twisty and wild, like a briar patch from which his badger's head of a dick poked out. He was determinedly erect, logically hard, and smartly ready for some experimentation on the property of propelling matter through a variety of biological tubes.

The Dean jumped up and back, hands again slapped over his chemically induced boner. "What? Wait a minute—that's not what I meant!"

"I believe that was the framework of the assignment," Hardware said, wrapping a pudgy hand around his cock. Stoking himself to even more impressive dimensions, he grinned and started to walk around the desk.

"Gotta give it the ol' college try," Ramrod said, grinning like he'd just scored a touchdown. His meaty mitt was tight around his Casey the Slugger special, and as he walked up to the Dean he stroked it roughly, working himself even harder. At the tip of his bat a glistening drop of pearly precome grew and dripped onto the fine Persian carpet (gift from the 1963 graduating class).

"It's the least we can do to restore the fine name of the school," Trojan said, slowly sensually licking his palm and wrapping it around the head of his own big dick. With a leisurely circular movement he coated the bulbous head until it was slick and shiny, all the time walking toward the Dean.

"And we love to do requests!" Queenie said, slapping his dick up against his belly. As it went *splat* against his smooth skin it got even harder, tensing until pale-purple veins showed against his alabaster cock shaft. He drummed his fingers along its length, tapping out the opening bars of an old disco tune as he also walked toward the Dean.

Watching the main men of Gamma Alpha Epsilon approach him, dicks and cocks hard and at the ready, the Dean stepped back and back and back—until he slammed up against the window. Words didn't seem to be possible. He just stood, his ass against glass, shaking his head in denial.

"Come on, Dean, just consider it an education," Trojan said, walking up to him, mixing both their furnaces of body heat. He reached down, grabbed hold of the Dean's left hand. At first he resisted, his arm tight against his side, but then he seemed to relax, relent a bit—at least enough for Ramrod to take his gently quaking hand and wrap it around his own über-studly big dick.

"You're in good hands, sweetie," Queenie said, nimble fingers dancing at the Dean's belt buckle, working his dexterous magic. The Dean momentarily freaked, spreading his legs to keep his pants at least partially up, but Queenie was too good, too quick, too…something…and soon slacks and boxers were down—all the way down.

"This is supposed to be an institution of higher learning, after all," Hardware said, sliding next to the Dean and starting to rub his fireplug against the older man's thigh. At first the Dean tried to inch away but—perhaps trapped, or just simply resigned—he stopped. In fact, after a few moments he actually began to learn back against the student's energetic thrusts.

"Give it up for the team, man!" Ramrod said, standing on the Dean's other side. He reached down and, with his wrestler's glove, his football player's fist, his baseball player's mitt, took the Dean's other hand and clamped it around his throbbing cock.

The Dean's dick was handsome, almost elegant: dark skin, almost tan, perfectly smooth except for a darker ring of scar where he'd had his foreskin. His pubic hair was a salt-and-pepper thicket. Hidden among the tight curls were a pair of fat balls, like furry plums.

The Dean's was a good cock, a big cock—and a very hard cock.

"We have lift-off!" Hardware said from behind the Dean, his smooth hands caressing the older man's equally smooth and peachy ass cheeks, the head of his thick, short dick flicking up and down the crease, leaving behind a shimmering trail of sweet precome. Up and down, up and down, hesitating just a bit, just a fraction of a very aroused second to pause over a dark, hairy asshole.

"Tastes like school spirit," Queenie said, wrapping his silken lips around the Dean's quivering cock. Holding the Dean's cock head in his mouth, he washed around the head with a warm, firm, hot tongue. Carefully, dedicatedly, he explored and tasted the corona, the shaft, the veins…every little inch of the many-inched hard dick. Queenie was a maestro, and this was one of his finest performances: sonata in D major for big cock in wonderful mouth.

"Give it up for the home team!" Ramrod bellowed like a bull in heat (which he was) as the Dean's hand grabbed his cock. In return, the tight-end, power-hitting broad-stroker gave the Dean's fist full-hipped, hammering fucks—fucking the Dean's mitt with every ounce of his rippled, zero-body-fat jock's body. Sweat, silvery precome lubed the action, giving his thrusts a *slick slick slick* sound to accompany his powerful strokes.

"You're wasted in admin; you're a natural, man." Trojan said, his words playful but his tone sultry, seductive. As the Dean's fingers worked his big dick, he tickled his own long and sensual fingers over the Dean's knuckles—like fingertip kisses—guiding him, helping him in knowing how hard to squeeze, how fast to stroke, how long to go, when to slow. Like kisses—or a dance partner giving the right taps on the shoulder: With Trojan's guidance, the Dean's hand became a perfectly controlled mouth or asshole, the ideal socket for Trojan's very eager, very hard, very hungry cock.

The Dean had a cock in his right hand, a cock in his left hand, a cock pushing between the cheeks of his ass, and his own cock was in a very hot, very eager mouth. He didn't say anything, he didn't have the words; he just made a very deep, very satisfied *mmm* noise.

"Touchdown!" yelled Ramrod as his cock jet spewed, shot white, and hot, so thus white-hot, come. His eyes flickered as he rocked back and forth, his tree-trunk legs finally betraying him as he crashed backward to sprawl across the Dean's desk (gift from the 1988 graduating class). "Oh, man," he mumbled as he lay splayed on the hardwood. "Oh, man…"

"Oh, yeah, come to Mommy," said Queenie, sucking on the Dean's dick as it suddenly jerked, stiffened even more, and dumped a cup of come down Queenie's eager and very willing throat.

"That's the answer!" cried Hardware as he gave his dick a hard shove between the Dean's ass cheeks—perfectly, neatly slipping into his ass. The virginity as well as the welcoming tight warmth snapped him into a spastic come that knocked his own legs out from underneath him and filled the Dean's ass.

"That's my stud…oh, yeah!" Trojan crooned as his own come came—his hot jism flying from his throbbing cock, splattering across the Dean's thigh and all over the rug (gift from the 1999 graduating class) in a sticky white Rorschach test. Before he collapsed, he managed to stagger up, grab the Dean by the cheeks, and give him a big, wet kiss. "Thanks!" he whispered when their lips separated.

"How'd it go with Gamma, sir?" Greg Shimkisst said a few hours later. When the Dean didn't immediately respond he added a querying "Sir?"

"Hum?" The Dean said, shaking himself from some kind of internal revelry. "I'm sorry, Greg, did you say something?"

"Um," Shimkisst said, disarmed. "I…I was just asking about how it went with Gamma Alpha Epsilon, sir. You know, the disciplinary hearing?"

"Oh, that," the Dean said. "Don't worry about it, Greg. Had a nice little chat with those boys, worked the whole thing out. Nothing you need to worry about," he said with a light, dismissing wave.

"Um, right…" Shimkisst said, suspiciously. "Whatever you say, sir."

The Dean looked at Shimkisst for a long minute—long enough for the handsome young man to blush and look a bit uncomfortable. "Actually, Greg, there is something you can help me with—something that's come up that has a lot to with that whole situation with Gamma."

"Certainly, sir—anything you need, sir. I'm here for you, sir."

"Right," said the Dean, smiling widely. "I like that about you, Greg: a willingness to please. Now let's get started, shall we? Oh, but before we get going, do me a little favor and lock the door?"

Pledge-napping

Christopher Pierce

My cock was hard at the thought of what my frat brothers and I were about to do. I dropped my hand to my crotch and felt my dick hardening through the denim of my jeans. With my fingers I gently rubbed the shape of what was getting longer and stiffer by the second, and it felt fucking good.

"Come on, man!" one of my brothers, Sean, said to me, "Stop playing with yourself, we gotta get going!"

I snapped out of my momentary sex trance.

"Sorry, dude," I said, "I'm just about ready."

"Let's check you out," Jake, our other brother in the room with us, said.

I pulled my ski mask over my head and adjusted the eyeholes so I could see clearly through them. Turning to face my buddies, I knew I might as well be looking into a mirror—we were all dressed identically. Boots, jeans, sweatshirts, and ski masks.

Tonight we were going to see just how willing our pledges were to do whatever it took to join our fraternity.

"Looking good," Jake said, and Sean gave us the thumbs-up signal. "Let's go."

We left our room and went down the stairs into the frathouse's common room. Some of our brothers were there, sprawled on couches, watching TV and playing video games. James, our house president, stood up when he saw us.

"You good to go?" he asked.

"We're ready," Sean said.

Pledge-napping

"Know where you're heading?"

"Dexter Hall," I said, "on Sixth Street. Room 301. All three of them live in the same apartment."

"That makes things easier," James said, reaching to pick something up off a nearby chair. "Don't forget your PBs," he said as he tossed each of us a man-size canvas sack. Jake, Sean, and I caught our "Pledge Bags" and slung them over our shoulders.

"See you later," he said. "Good hunting!"

We headed out.

The frat's van was ours for the night, so we piled in and drove the three blocks that separated our house from the dorm that was our destination. It was 2 A.M., and the campus was pretty empty. We knew from weeks of tracking our target's movements that they would be fast asleep at this hour.

In other words, ripe for the taking.

We pulled the van up in front of Dexter Hall and shut the engine off. I looked back from the passenger seat to see Jake stuff some of the last of the gear we'd need into a black backpack, which he slung over his shoulder along with his pledge bag.

"OK, is everyone clear on the plan?" Sean asked.

"I got it," I said.

"Piece of cake," Jake said. "Or is it ass?"

I grinned, even though I knew my brothers couldn't see it through my mask.

"Why not both?" I asked. "Let's have our ass and eat it too." My buddies laughed.

"Let's go." Sean said.

We got out and closed and locked the van's doors. We wouldn't be here long enough to get ticketed; we were just going to go in, take what we wanted, and leave.

When we reached the main entrance of the dorm, it was locked, as we'd anticipated.

"Jake," Sean said.

"I'm on it" was Jake's answer as he pulled a Dexter Hall resident access card out of his pocket. He swiped it through the reader mounted on the wall, and the door opened with a loud click.

For some reason that clicking sound made me very horny again. Anticipation of what was coming had made my dick hard as a rock. My brothers and I entered the dorm lobby and got in the elevator heading for the third floor.

When we got off the elevator, the hallways were empty. We made our way silently to room 301. The three of us stood outside the door and exchanged a final glance.

"Ready?" Sean asked Jake and me.

We nodded.

"Let's do it," I said, and Jake pulled a key out of his jeans pocket. He used the key to unlock the door, and he pushed the door open silently. Inside, room 301 was dark and quiet. We went in and closed the door behind us, after making sure no one saw us go in.

We knew the standard layout of our college's dorm rooms, so we found the bedroom quickly and silently.

The three sleeping young men looked serene and peaceful.

But not for long, I thought with a mental smirk.

On Sean's silent signal we pounced, one of us on each one of them. The boys woke up instantly as my brothers and I pinned them to their beds.

"Hey!"

"What the hell?"

"Holy shit!"

Pledge-napping

"Shut the fuck up, cocksuckers!" Sean roared at them.

"What's happening?" one of them asked in a terrified voice, and I heard the smack of Jake backhanding him.

"Cooperate with us," Sean said in a lower voice, "and you won't get hurt."

"Who are you?"

"Lambda Tau Delta," I said.

"Jake!" Sean said, and Jake opened his pack and took out three pairs of handcuffs. He tossed one pair each to Sean and me and kept the third.

"On your stomachs, pledges!" Sean said, and the boys reluctantly obeyed. We yanked off the blankets covering them. My boy and one of the others were naked, but Jake's had underwear on. Jake pulled a switchblade out of his pocket and shredded the flimsy fabric.

"But why?" one of the pledges asked.

"You all signed release forms that said you'd do anything to get into our house," Sean said.

"We're giving you the opportunity to prove it," I said, as I yanked my pledge's hands together behind his back and slapped the cuffs on him. The metallic clicking sounds I heard told me my brothers were doing the same.

"This isn't what I thought."

"Thinking isn't your job!" Sean yelled at the boy. "Your job is to shut up and do what we tell you."

"Hey," Jake said to me, tossing me a short coil of rope. I caught it, unwound it, and wrapped it around my pledge's ankles, knotting it tightly. Then we tied black scarves around their heads, blindfolding them so they couldn't see anything.

"What are you going to do with us?"

"You're coming with us," Sean said. "Now stand up and *shut up!*"

Shaking with fear, the three young men stood up on their beds with some help from us.

"Bag 'em," Sean instructed Jake and me. Slipping my PB off my shoulder, I opened it up and spread it in front of my pledge's feet.

"Take one small step forward," I told him, and he obeyed silently, stepping into the bag. I grabbed the sides of the sack and pulled it up around him until it completely enclosed the young man from head to toe. I closed the bag over the top of his head and pulled its drawstrings tight into a knot.

This guy wasn't getting away, no fucking way.

I heard a quiet moan of fear from my bag.

"It's OK, man," I whispered through the material, "just do what you're told and everything will be cool."

The young man in the sack didn't answer, but he stopped moaning.

"Load up," Sean said, and I jumped down off the bed. I grabbed my bagged pledge and pulled him forward until I could hoist him over my shoulder.

"Don't struggle," I told him when he squirmed, and he stopped. I turned to see my brothers, each with their own pledge bags full and slung over one shoulder.

"Ready to move out?" Sean asked.

"Ready," Jake said.

"Let's go," I said.

We carried our captive boys out of their dorm room and locked the door behind us. No one saw us as we took them down the hallways and into the elevator. Luckily, none of the pledges weighed more than 150 pounds, so it wasn't hard to carry them.

It was important that the guys got tied up, bagged, and carried—it robbed them of their control, made them helpless, submissive, just as they'd be if they were accepted into the frat. They'd have to prove they would do anything for their brothers, and this was their first chance to do it.

When we reached the ground floor we lugged our pledges out of the elevator and back to the dorm's entrance. My brothers and I were out the door and almost down the steps when a campus security officer rode by on his bike.

He saw us—three young men, each with a stuffed and squirming man-size sack over one shoulder—and stopped.

"What's going on here?" he asked sharply.

"Don't say a fucking word," Sean hissed under his breath to the pledges. Then he told the guard, "Official fraternity business," and the officer relaxed.

"Oh," he said, "pledge-napping, huh?"

Sean grinned and glanced at Jake and me.

"Yeah," he said.

"Did they sign release forms?" the officer asked.

"Yes," Sean said, "we've got them at the house."

"Fine. Go ahead, then," the officer said. At a nod from Sean we went down the rest of the stairs. Jake fished the keys to the van out of his pocket with one hand, holding his captive's legs in place with the other. He unlocked the van's side loading door.

"Guys?" the officer said as he started riding away.

"Yeah?" Sean said.

"I don't know what y'all do with those pledges, but Lambda Tau Delta is a fine fraternity. Make 'em show you how bad they want to join."

"Yes, sir!" Sean said, and I gave the departing officer the thumbs-up sign.

"Let's load 'em," Sean said, gesturing for Jake and me to go first. My brother leaned into the van and let his pledge sack slide off his shoulder down onto the mattress and pillows we'd cushioned the interior floor with. The boy inside let out a little yip of fear, like a puppy, and all three of us laughed.

I patted my pledge's butt through the canvas of the bag and said, "Don't worry, little pledge boy, you just do exactly what you're told and nobody'll get hurt."

After Jake stepped out of the way I took his place at the van door and let my sack fall onto the mattress.

"That's right," Sean said, "we don't want to hurt you—we just want to have a little fun with you."

Sean dumped his bag in the van with an evil-sounding chuckle. "But we *will* hurt you if you give us any trouble." Then he gave us our assignments—Jake driving, himself in the passenger seat, and me watching the pledges.

I climbed through the door into the back of the van and Jake slammed the door shut, locking it. I sat on one of the bags, ignoring the grunt of protest that came from it. Stretching out, I rested my legs on the second sack and propped my feet on the third. Sean and Jake got into the front and Jake started the ignition.

"Everything cool?" Sean asked me over his shoulder.

"Everything's great," I answered. "I think we got ourselves some choice pledge meat here, guys."

Sean grinned and turned back to face the front.

My dick was hard. Having these captured young men in our power was really turning me on. I rubbed myself through my pants, then unbuckled them and pulled them down enough to expose my stiff rod. It popped out, ripe and ready for action.

I couldn't wait. I had to sample some of what we'd caught. Reaching forward and raising my knees, I grabbed the bagged boy under my legs and pulled him up until the top of the bag was near my groin.

Pledge-napping

I untied the drawstrings and opened the sack. The boy's head popped out and I recognized him instantly—it was Trevor Jacks, a hot blond freshman I'd been watching for weeks. I untied his blindfold and let it fall off his face.

He looked up at me and his eyes went wide when he saw me all in black with my ski mask covering my face.

"Who...who are you?" he asked.

"It doesn't matter," I told him.

"But—"

"Shut up," I said, slapping his face. "I've got a better use for your mouth than talking." I grabbed the back of his head and pulled it toward my hard cock.

"What the fuck?" he said.

"Show me what a good cocksucker you are," I said.

"Fuck you!" he barked at me. "I'm no fucking faggot!"

"It doesn't matter what you are," I told him, pulling his head until my dick was pressing against his tightly closed lips, "and it doesn't matter what you're not," I continued. "Do you want to get into this frat?"

"Y—" Trevor started to say, and I forced my cock into his open mouth.

"Then suck my dick, little pledge boy." I finished with satisfaction. Trevor grimaced with disgust but obeyed me. It felt so fucking good to have my cock in his mouth. I'd been anticipating this for days, and now it was finally happening. Three young men tied up in sacks, at our mercy, totally in our power, ours to do with as we pleased.

Trevor wasn't a very good cocksucker, but that was OK. Just having my dick in a soft warm mouth was all I needed right then. In fact, I was so horny and it felt so good, I was just about ready to come already.

I used both hands to hold the pledge's head in place and started fucking his face. Trevor grunted in protest, but I held him tight and didn't give a damn.

A few seconds later I was ready, and as my orgasm exploded within me my dick shot its load down the boy's throat. Trevor convulsed in disgust, but I was stronger than him and kept him in one place. He made sounds like he was trying to throw up, but it was too late—he'd already swallowed another man's semen, and there was no way to undo it.

Then the pledge made moaning sounds like he was going to cry. I let my cock slip out of his mouth, and I stuffed it back in my pants and buttoned them up. Then I petted Trevor's head, like I would a pet's, and tied his blindfold back on.

"It's not gonna hurt you, man," I said quietly. "Don't worry about it. Just remember that everything that happens tonight is for the frat. It won't make you a faggot. But it will make us want you to be our brother, and you'll get in. Just remember: For The Frat."

"For The Frat," Trevor whispered as I gently pushed his head back down into his sack. I tied the drawstrings tight when he was in, feeling a little affectionate possessiveness for him. It looked like he was accepting what was happening, and was ready to do whatever it took to get into our fraternity.

The van slowed down and stopped. I looked up as we were in the driveway behind the frathouse. "We're here," Sean said as Jake shut the vehicle down. "Let's get them inside."

I got up off the two bags I'd been sitting and resting my feet on, and the guys inside groaned in relief. Sean and Jake got out, came around to the side of the van, and opened the loading door. I jumped out to join them. When Sean reached for the sack that had Trevor inside, I stopped him.

"That one's mine," I said.

Pledge-napping

"Whatever," Sean said, and grabbed one of the other bags. One at a time, Jake and Sean and I pulled each bagged pledge to the door, then leaned over and hoisted the sack up and over one shoulder.

Jake locked up the van and we headed inside. We went through the rear door into the basement of the frathouse. Our brothers were waiting for us when we got to the big windowless recreation room we'd been instructed to bring the pledges to.

They were all standing on the edges of the room against the walls.

Candles burned in holders mounted on the walls, filling the dim room with eerie illumination. The floor had been cleared of everything, except for three objects in the center. The objects looked like combinations of sawhorses and exercise equipment. They actually were wooden and metal racks, shaped like inverted V shapes, the V points softened with thick padding.

"Welcome back," said house president James, stepping out of the shadows to greet us.

"Thank you, sir," Sean, Jake, and I said together. We knew that this was now our fraternity's ceremony room and all formalities were to be observed while we were in here. Language and manners were ritualistic here.

"Your mission was a success."

"Yes, sir."

"Prepare them."

Wordless, we set our burdens down feetfirst so the young men could stand inside their sacks. Sean, Jake, and I opened the bags and released the pledges, then removed their handcuffs and the rope binding their ankles. We left their blindfolds on. To their good fortune, the pledges didn't try to fight or run. They just stood there, a little dazed, and didn't speak. Trevor almost lost his balance, but I straightened him so he didn't fall. Sean, Jake, and I took off our ski masks.

"Pledges," James said, walking around them in a circle, "you have all indicated that you would like to be accepted into this fraternity. Know now that this frat is not just a club for guys who want to get drunk, party all night, and fuck easy pussy. We are a brotherhood, a sacred trust. Our bond between each other is unbreakable. To us, this fraternity is all-important—more important than school, more important than girls, more important than family. Tonight, you have a chance to prove your intention to us. We, the men you say you want to call your brothers, are going to show you what commitment and devotion means."

He paused significantly. Sean, Jake, and I, along with the rest of our brothers, started rubbing our cocks through our jeans and shorts. Then James continued.

"If you are willing to do anything for this fraternity, you have your first chance now. Anyone not willing to face this trial—speak now and you will be returned to where you were taken from, no questions asked. However, you will not be allowed to join us this time, and any future applications to do so will be rejected immediately."

He stopped again, facing the kidnapped pledges.

"Do any of you wish to be released?"

There was dead silence in the room for a few seconds. Then my pledge, Trevor, spoke up.

"No, sir," he said, "I'm ready."

I grinned, congratulating myself on picking a promising pledge. The other two boys answered quickly in the same manner, no doubt not wanting to look like pussies in front of their buddy.

James nodded to us, and again Sean, Jake, and I hoisted our

captured pledges up and over our shoulders and carried them to the center of the room, where the V-shaped racks were waiting. Feeling Trevor once again over my shoulder, mine, made my cock even harder. I forced myself to be patient; it wouldn't be long now.

We put the young men down onto the racks, each one slung over them so his ass was up in the air, easily accessible. We slid their ankles into the restraints that had been built into the rear legs of the racks, then fastened their wrists into the front leg restraints.

The pledges did not protest, but they were visibly frightened to be put in bondage. Trevor, despite his determination earlier, was shaking. Sean's boy had started sweating, and Jake's was whispering to himself in a frantic mantra.

I think they knew what was coming, but despite their fear, they were ready to do what it took to get into the frat.

"Line up," James said, and our brothers silently divided themselves into three groups, forming a line behind each bound pledge. James produced a jar of lubricant and dipped his fingers into it, then used them to slick up the captive's assholes. The pledges gasped when he touched them in that most private and intimate of places. The first man in line behind each bound boy jacked his cock to full erection, then stepped up to their pledge's butt.

"Now," James said, and out brothers shoved their hard dicks into the captives' assholes. One of the boys screamed in pain and shock. One burst into tears. Trevor just grunted in surprise, and I felt something like pride. I knew then that I would recommend him being accepted into our fraternity, and if he was, I would keep my eye on him, maybe take him under my wing.

My brothers started fucking the pledges then, thrusting their cocks in and out of them with passionate precision. The boys struggled, but they were bound securely to their racks and could not escape. The brothers in line behind the ones doing the fucking watched hungrily, jerking their own cocks and waiting for their turns.

Sean, Jake, and I waited to the side of the lines, knowing we would be the last to rape the pledges. While the young men were mercilessly fucked, James spoke to them.

"Pledges," he said, "listen to me. Being penetrated by us does not make you weak. Being penetrated by us makes you strong. It does not make you a pussy, it makes you a man, because only a man can endure it. A boy will scream and cry like a girl, but a man will take it, take it as long and hard as he thinks is possible, and just when he thinks he can't last any longer, he finds new strength inside himself. If you want to join this brotherhood, if you want to enjoy its privileges, its pleasures, and its protection, you must let us claim you, take you, rob you of your manhood, and then let us give it back to you."

He paused.

"You must find strength you don't know you have—the strength of your true manhood. No one outside this room will ever know what has happened here tonight. Do you want to join us?"

"Yes, sir!" all three pledges said together, through their tears.

"I'm gonna come!" said the guy fucking Trevor.

"Me too!" said the guy next to him.

"I'm there!" from the last one, and together the three men climaxed, groaning gutturally as they shot their loads of semen deep inside the pledges. When they were done, the guys pulled their cocks out of the boys' butts and stuffed them back in their pants.

"Next," James said, and the lines advanced forward as the men who had just finished stepped aside.

"Again?" one of the pledges asked fearfully.

"Not again?" the other said.

Trevor said nothing.

The captives got their questions answered when the next frat brother shoved his dick up their ass.

James, Sean, Jake, and I watched as the pledges got fucked over and over again. When each man finished, he went back to stand against the walls of the room, watching silently as they had when we'd first arrived with our captives over our shoulders.

When everyone in the lines had had his turn, it was time for our house president to take his share of the spoils. He fucked each of the pledges quickly, ruthlessly, hard, fast, and mean. I don't know where he got the energy or the juice, but he shot a load into each of the boys, one right after the other.

James put his cock back into his pants and stepped away from the racks. He and everyone else looked expectantly at me and my fellow pledge-nappers.

Sean, Jake, and I looked at each other and grinned. It was our turn. Sean and Jake took their places behind their pledges, but before I did, I leaned over far enough to speak quietly into Trevor's ear.

"It's me," I said.

"I'm glad," he whispered. "Is it almost over?"

"Yes," I said, "but I'm going to fuck you first."

Trevor took a deep breath.

"I'm ready," he said.

I stood up to see Sean and Jake looking at me curiously.

"Let's do it," I said, and the three of us dropped our pants. Our cocks, hard and dripping, jutted up like swords, and together we impaled the pledges with them. The boys still gasped in shock, despite having already been raped by all the other guys.

Trevor's ass was still amazingly tight even after getting plugged by the guys before me. The other pledges must have been the same, judging from the groans of appreciation coming from Jake and Sean. For some reason this fucking was better than the other times I'd pledge-napped. Somehow it was hotter, more intense. It must have been the connection I felt with Trevor.

Before, it had always been hot to kidnap the pledges in the middle of the night, take them back to the house, and fuck them, but it was never…personal, I guess. It was just me, acting for the house, doing my duty as a member of the fraternity.

But not this time.

This time it was all that but more. I didn't know Trevor. I'd only met him a few times when he was applying to the house. I'd never been alone with him, never really talked to him. But this was more than just a brother fucking a pledge.

It was I, specifically, fucking Trevor himself, not some random pledge.

That must have been why it felt so fucking good to plow that ass, why it felt like my balls were on fire and my cock a rifle about to shoot off.

It was so hot I did something I'd never done before, something I didn't know whether any brother had ever done. I slumped forward onto Trevor's back, repositioning my arms so that my hands were out of sight between his legs.

To my surprise and delight, his cock was hard. I took it in my hand and squeezed it, and the pledge moaned softly. Kidnapped pledges were not supposed to get any pleasure out of their ordeal. Their comfort was not important, and their enjoyment was not even considered.

But this time was different.

I wanted Trevor to get off on this as much as I was. But my brothers couldn't know about it. They wouldn't understand.

Pledge-napping

Blending the movement of my hand with the thrusting of my body so my brothers couldn't see what I was doing, I started jerking Trevor off. His whole body tensed up with surprise and excitement. "Shh…" I whispered softly to him, and he heard me and kept quiet. So I jacked my pledge while I fucked him, and it was my favorite night of pledge-napping ever, so far. For a few seconds it was almost like we were alone, just the two of us, instead of in a crowded room surrounded by men watching us. My dick was so deep inside him I could feel it hitting his prostate gland with each thrust inward, and Trevor moaned quietly every time it happened.

Sean and Jake were groaning with passion.

"I'm close, man!" Jake said.

"I'm gonna come," Sean added.

I was nearly there myself. I whispered to Trevor one last time. "You ready?"

"Yes, sir," he said, then: "For The Frat?"

"Yes," I answered, "and for me."

My pledge exhaled deeply, and I knew he understood. My cock was about to explode in Trevor's butt, and his cock was pulsing and quivering in my hand.

It was time.

"Guys," I said to Sean and Jake, "let's go for it!"

"Yeah!"

"You know it!"

And the three of us shot our loads, even though with Trevor it made four, but no one knew that but him and me. As my orgasm sent bursts of pleasure through me, I angled Trevor's cock up so his spunk would hit his abdomen and chest and not the floor. Jake, Sean and I let out grunts and groans of carnal bliss, and I used my left hand to cover my pledge's mouth so he wouldn't make any noise and give us away. Our semen spurted inside the captive young men, joining that of our brothers before us, so hot it burned them from the inside out. It was incredibly hot, the best and most intense orgasm I'd had in months.

When Sean, Jake, and I were all finished, we slowly pulled our cocks out of the pledges' assholes and stuffed them back in our pants. The boys lay on their racks, breathing heavily, exhausted. James stepped back out of the shadows, three chloroform-soaked rags in his hands.

"It's done," he said. "You've done well, pledges. Your reward will be acceptance into this fraternity. Congratulations."

"Thank you, sir," each pledge said weakly.

James walked up to Trevor and clamped one of the rags over his nose and mouth. Already fatigued emotionally and physically, the pledge breathed in deeply and was knocked out within seconds. The other two did the same when James covered their noses and mouths with the rags.

"Return them," James told us.

As our brothers filed out of the room, talking quietly about the night's events, Sean, Jake, and I released our pledges' wrists and ankles from their restraints. We retrieved our pledge bags and helped each other to stuff the young men back into them, then tied off the tops of the sacks before we put our ski masks on one last time. Then we hoisted the bags back up over our shoulders and headed out. It was really late now, probably between 4 and 5 in the morning, and the campus was still deserted. We drove in the van back to Dexter Hall and silently returned the pledges to their room.

Sean and Jake dumped their captives down onto their beds, but I carefully slid Trevor off my shoulder and took him gently

Pledge-napping

out of his pledge bag. I set him down on his bed and covered him with his blankets. He looked happy, in blissful sleep.

Sean and Jake were already out the door and ready to head back to the house to get some sleep as I stood there looking at my pledge.

"Dude, let's go!" Sean whispered to me.

"Coming," I said, then took off my ski mask, leaned over, and kissed Trevor very softly on his lips.

"Welcome to Lambda Tau Delta," I whispered to him.

Then I tossed my empty pledge bag over my shoulder and went to join my brothers.

Do Unto a Tight Ass

Troy Storm

"OK, pledges, the Compliance Committee has called you dorks together because—"

Senior Brother Michael looked around at his fellow committee members sitting with him behind the beat-up desk. The new pledges had been rousted out of bed to gather in the fraternity basement rec room in the middle of the night—always a sign of trouble. The other two senior Compliance Committee members nodded sagely as he cleared his throat.

"Because we've come across a little problem with your sex life—more important, which affects our sex life—and we wanna set you young studs on the straight and narrow."

My fellow initiates shifted uncomfortably, sleepily cutting each other puzzled glances, wondering what the fuck the Compliance Committee was but somehow knowing, whatever the hell, it was it was going to adversely affect our ragged butts.

And our ragged butts were exactly what it was going to affect.

"As you know," Brother Michael continued, "one of the fine traditions of this fraternity—though not an official one, and sure as hell not written down—is that of the older brothers welcoming the younger members into our close-knit fellowship by allowing the pledges to bestow sexual favors on their senior brothers."

The 20 pledges instantly stopped shifting around and focused their attention sharply on brother Mike.

My freshman dick instantly pumped in my PJs. Finally. There had been a lot of talk on campus about how hot this particular group of horny frat guys were, but so far I had seen precious little evidence of it.

"It has come to our attention that some of you young gentlemen are not exactly proficient in according us our sexual needs. You give pretty good blow jobs, but the butt-fuck thing is a pile of shit." He gave us a smart-ass, shit-eating grin. "If you'll excuse my somewhat gross terminology."

The pledges waited apprehensively. I steamed. Up to now no brother had ever asked me for a blow job. Obviously, on the stud meter I ranked zilch.

"So we're gonna have a practice session," brother Mike announced brightly. "Right now. Strip. Jammies, boxers, jocks, whatever. Drop 'em." One of the committee brothers leaned over and whispered in Mike's ear. "Oh, yeah, well, OK, we're gonna be practicing nipple play too." He gave his fellow committee member—a good-looking stud whom you never would have thought was a Tit Lover—a weird look.

One of the reasons I had pledged this particular frat was it was noted for harboring all kinds of kink. Cool.

After a few seconds of hesitant, muted grumbling, the 15 or 20 new pledges stripped, as the committee members wandered among us, making cracks.

"Hot ass, Sonderson, though I hear you can't take a pencil shoved up it."

"Good-looking dick, Malcome. It better shoot as good as it looks."

They got to me. "Ah, Always Hard," senior Michael said, smugly, "the frosh pledge who tries to live up to his name. Why don't we start with you? Get up front." He slapped my ass and sent me scurrying to the raised platform where the desk was.

A few guys snickered. Brother Mike snapped. "Listen up,

shitheads: Believe your sorry asses, you're all gonna have come coming out your ears before we get you shaped up into decent sex objects. We're fed up with hearing your screams of agony. Anybody else with a boner, get their butt up there with EverHardon."

Five or six guys joined me on the platform. I was pleased to note I wasn't the biggest—man, that can really get you razzed in the showers—though I did seem to be the hardest. My dick head was practically kissing my belly button.

The Southern kid, Bradley, outhung us all. Mansfield had the biggest knob and Parker the fattest nuts. My tamped testicles were practically nonexistent, they were clutching the root of my bone so tightly.

"OK, line up according to how big your dick is. Left to right." We shifted around, bumping into each other. With all that raw male flesh rubbing up against mine, upping my blood pressure, and upping my bone measurement, I found myself standing next to Bradley. He grinned at me and glanced at my meat. "Glad to see I'm not the only freak around here."

I had to swallow to clear my mouth of saliva. "I think of us as heavy-loaders the rest of the pledges strive to emulate."

Bradley laughed. "Right fucking on, smart mouth." He reached over and gave my meat a friendly backhanded swat, causing it to unleash its load of precome, which I tried to staunch to keep from making a mess.

Which annoyed Senior Brother Mike.

"OK, wiseasses, we'll start with you two dorks. Which one of you has bottomed? Don't shit me now."

Bradley dropped his eyes and his ears got red. I had never had anything up my ass. And certainly never had the pleasure of shoving anything up anybody else's.

Do Unto a Tight Ass

"I shoulda known," Mike mumbled. "The big mothers are the fastest to flop on their backs and fan their fucking ears. I don't know what the hell it is. You cherry, AllHard?"

Shit, did it show? "Everhard, sir."

"We'll fucking see about that, won't we? OK, show your fellow shitheads your butt hole." A couple of the other committee members threw a ratty blanket on the beat-up desk, laid me down on my back, and pushed my legs up. The Nipple Lover Committee member got in a quick pinch of my tits before the other brother slapped his hands away.

Moving aside to let Senior Brother Mike inspect my bung hole, the two committee associates proceeded to pull boxes of condoms and tubes of lube out of the desk drawers.

"OK, you turds," butt inspector Mike announced, "gather round." He started the demo. "If you're faced with a tight-assed cherry hole, this is what you do not do."

He rammed a finger up my butt. I screamed. My legs shot out and slammed him in the chest, knocking him bass-ackwards into the group of pledges gathered around. The place broke up, whooping and cheering. I jumped up, appalled at what I had done, and my butt in pain.

One of the smirking seniors helped Brother Mike up, who was gasping for breath, as the nipple-loving one pushed me back down into place, stroking my tits.

"You sonofa—" Mike started for me. I winced, and Nipple Lover jumped in between us, crouching in a Ninja Turtle attack pose.

"Touch those tits and you're oatmeal, bro. We told you to take it fucking easy with the cherry holes." He turned and gave me a wink, quickly cruising my nips. Cute dude. Cool dude. Marshall something, I think his name was.

"OK," Mike pulled himself together and continued his lecture. "That's one reason you don't use a finger to ream a tight butt hole open. Gimme the fuck sticks, guys." He snapped his fingers, and my Ninja protector pulled a box of small plastic bumpy rods out of a drawer. Mike grabbed a handful and flung the rest to the assembled pledges.

"Anal probes," he announced clinically, wielding a fluorescent-orange gel rod about six inches long that looked to me like a Popsicle gone way wrong. He bent it almost double to show its flexibility.

Smiling benevolently and standing to one side, he swung his arm in a big arc and jammed it up my butt. I jumped and Ninja Turtle lunged forward, but after a couple of seconds my ass adjusted to the shock and it felt pretty good.

Satisfied I wasn't going to mule-kick him in the chest again, Senior Mike announced, "Pair off and ream each other out. I wanna see those tight asses loosened. We're coming round to check."

He shoved the hunky Southern dude, Bradley, between my legs. "Start ripping 'er open," he instructed, indicating my hole.

Pulling a rubber glove on, Mike held his raised arm in front of him like a surgeon and started into the crowd, his three middle fingers clutched tightly together and held high. Bradley's big bone, I noticed, was rock-hard. Mine had died when Senior Mike slammed his damned finger up my butt.

Bradley grinned and extracted the knobby plastic out of my bunghole, one bump at a time. Weird, but cool. Then, squirting lube all over it and getting it greased up good, he gently pushed the sex toy back in, bump after bump after bump gently prying my anus open and pushing deeper inside.

Whoo. My dick bounced as each bulge of the probe pushed

through my gulping O ring. Cooler and cooler. I wiggled my butt to let Bradley know he was treating my asshole right. Grinning, he began to stroke the probe in and out. I was on the point of blowing a wad. That was the most awesome feeling that had ever happened inside my ass.

Keeping the rhythm going, he stuck the fuck finger of his other hand in his mouth and got it good and wet with his spit. Reaching over to press it to my lips as he worked the probe around in my ass, he said, " 'Keep your nails trimmed and do unto a tight ass what you'd want done to yours.' My finger has always worked just fine." He added another finger, then another to stroking my lips as I opened my mouth and sucked in the group.

"O-o-oh." He gave me a look that said he really liked that.

Reaching for his chiseled pecs, I stroked my palms across his nipples. His heavy lids drifted down, shading his big blue eyes. The corners of his full lips curled up. He worked the probe in my ass in wider and wider circles, pressing it outward toward my anal opening and dibbling it around inside my ass. I scrubbed my hands over his chest, ironing over his solid pectorals, riding the butt of my hand over the hard planes, and then plucking at his eraser-size nubs.

That seemed to really make him feel good. "I'm gonna make you so fucking happy," he muttered.

I came.

A shot of my come hit me in the chin, another sprayed over my shoulder, then a splatter of milky blobs covered my chest. Bradley cranked the anal probe around in my ass. I could hardly breathe, it felt so fantastic. My chest thundered. My gonads thumped. The small, delicate hairs circling my butt tingled.

I pinched and tugged on Bradley's pronglike titties, wanting desperately to put my hands on his dick, but I couldn't reach it.

Snickering wickedly at my lack of control, he pulled my hands off his pecs and, holding my wrists, scrubbed the come into my chest with my open palms, rubbing them in tight circles over my own tits. I was floating about a foot off the desk, my butt hole sniffing hungrily at Bradley's monster meat.

Brother Mike appeared from nowhere and gave my butt a stinging slap!

"OK, you assholes." He smirked at us and then turned and yelled at the group of groaning and gasping guys spread out over the broken-down couches scattered around the rec room. "You get the idea. Stop diddling each other. It's time to fuck butt!" he shouted, shaking his hard dick at the assembly. He was a hard-nosed asshole, but he had a dick to make a man bend over and grab his ankles.

I had a quick vision of being bent over, taking all Brother Mike had to offer and watching him through my legs, breaking out in a hot sweat as my asshole cut his swaggering ramrod down to size.

But something new and amazing was happening in my hole to break my reverie. My dick blurped out another blob of cream. Bradley, who had moved closer to shield my ass with his big body when Brother Mike popped my butt and started yelling at the other plebes, smugly showed me the anal probe. It wasn't up my ass. He had replaced it with a handful of flexing fingers. I came again.

This time he scooped up the come coating my pubes and smeared it on his rubbered-up dick. He moved to aim his load at my hole.

Brother Shithead Mike pushed him away. "Not yet, fuckface. OK!" he yelled. "This is the way you guys are gonna do it. Group up. Littlest dick fucks first, then the next biggest, then the next." He was sweating and paying a lot of attention to Bradley's huge meat.

"Us Compliance Committee members will come around and check to see that all you guys can take it from now on, and we're gonna fuck each and every butt to be sure. OK, now go to work."

My dick was drooping again. Brother Mike was not a romantic soul. I could imagine him being a brutal fuck. Ninja Turtle didn't even look that interested in creaming ass. All he was waiting for was to get his hands on guys' chests.

At least the third senior committee member looked like he was going to treat us pledges' asses right. And he swung a very nice hammer.

Bradley grabbed a group of cute guys and lined them up between my legs. The first guy eagerly pushed his boner into me. "Take it easy," Bradley instructed, standing by. He slipped behind the guy, rubbing his giant bone up and down the guy's crack. "Remember, this is eventually going up that." He nuzzled his dick against the pledge's hole. The guy gulped. "You want me to be gentle too, dontcha?" Bradley purred. The pledge gently fucked my ass. I loved it! I decided I was a natural bottom, built for bringing happiness to men who needed a hole to hump.

Each guy brought me off. Proudly and eagerly. I loved my fellow fuck buddies. My butt couldn't wait for the next-size dick to drill into it. I was having such a good time working my way up the size ladder, for a moment I was afraid getting fucked by Bradley wouldn't be the amazing experience I had been looking forward to.

I was wrong. It was. And more.

His huge meat slid inside and filled more of me than had been filled by the previous five guys altogether. And when he told one of them to fuck his butt while he fucked mine, his massive meat ballooned even bigger inside me.

Slowly he pulled the thing out and solidly he pushed it back in, over and over, faster and faster, while the other guys swarmed over us. One pledge stuck his dick in my mouth and another crammed his head into my crotch to suck me off while Bradley balled my butt. I felt hard-ons shoved into both hands, and while I jacked my fellow pledges off, a pair of lips suckled my tits—hey, it was Ninja Tit Lover, giving my nubs his all.

The guy behind Bradley came, grunting and groaning, and was replaced by another pledge who was just getting started good when Senior Brother Mike showed up to yank him away and ram his ordinary eight-incher up Bradley's ass.

What a Southern gentleman Bradley was. He grunted and cussed as if Brother Mike was giving him the greatest fuck ever. It got me so hot—along with the dick in my face and the two in my hands and my bone being serviced and my tits tongued—that I came again.

And so did most of the other guys. Hot come dripped all over me and Bradley. And, obviously, Bradley's ass was what Senior Brother of the Compliance Committee Michael needed to calm himself down from having to handle all the randy pledges. I thought we were going to have to go to the dining room for breakfast with him stuck up Bradley's butt.

Eventually, though, Brother Mike noticed what was happening to me and decided he wanted that kind of action himself. All three seniors did. We fucked and sucked and shot our loads right past morning chow, when the other senior members began to wander into the rec room and want some of the early-morning wake-up action themselves.

Somebody ordered pizza and soda for us pledges so we could keep right on sucking and fucking and getting sucked and fucked.

Most of us missed class that day, but when the dean of men

heard that our frathouse had been making a special effort to educate the new members on proper sexual health, our fraternity got a commendation, and the dean got an invite to attend an orientation session. The dean is a very hunky, middle-aged gay stud, and it is much to our frat's advantage to keep him happy.

Which we did.

The fraternity nominated the Compliance Committee as Outstanding Frat Dudes of the Month.

And Bradley and I moved in together.

Drinking Contest

Michael Rhodes

I went to college at Alabama State and pledged with Sigma Delta Phi fraternity. I can't say it was really my choice. I got a lot of pressure from my Dad to join—he said being in a frat was the best part of college. I was pretty leery about hazing. Even though it had been outlawed by the university for years, I knew it still went on.

One of the things that made me feel less nervous about Delta Phi was learning about their unique "initiation" system. Each freshman pledge was hooked up with a senior member at the beginning of the first semester. The idea was that the senior would play a kind of mentor role and help the pledge learn the ropes. I pictured it kind of like having a big brother, and being an only child, this really appealed to me.

My first night there, though, I learned that the arrangement wouldn't be quite as idyllic as I'd thought. The house leader, Connor, organized a small welcoming party in which he told us he'd be announcing our pairings. He told the pledges, though, that he first wanted them to understand that every Delta Phi member had to earn his place. The seniors to whom we would be assigned had the responsibility of certifying to the frat whether we were worthy.

"You're going to have the first semester to prove yourself," he said. "Each senior will be devising his own way of testing you. You pass his tests, you're in the frat. You don't, you're out. It's just that simple."

Drinking Contest

My heart pounded as Connor began to recite the matchups. I looked around at the seniors, many of whom were on the football team and were already starting to get rough with their pledges. One of them grabbed his match in a headlock, threw him to the ground and sat on him, pounding his chest like an ape. I was only 18 but looked even younger, with a small build and weighing a lightweight 135 pounds. If any one of these guys sat on me, I'd be history.

Finally, we were at the end and I began wondering if I'd be forgotten. That's when Connor looked at me, smiling. "Devan—you're with me." My heart sank. If there was anything worse than being stuck with one of those football team monsters, it was winding up with our bright, savagely funny leader. Surely he was going to force me to do something truly awful to set the tone for the rest of the crew.

Later that night Connor approached me and said, "Let's go for a walk." I nodded nervously and followed him out the door into the 90-degree humid night. As we walked (with me meekly staying behind him by several paces) I noticed he was carrying a small paper bag. He led us into the woods behind campus, asking me some questions about where I was from, what classes I was signing up for, etc. After we'd gone a ways we came to a fallen log. He sat down and patted a little area next to him.

"Have a seat."

I sat down and he started talking.

"So listen, Devan, here's the deal. Your initiation is going to involve a series of drinking contests. Five, to be exact. In each one of those, I pick the poison, and we start with equal amounts of whatever it is. Basically, the trick is, you gotta keep more down than me. I'll give you a fair shot with each, but you only get one shot. You've gotta win three out of five or you're out. Got it?"

I sat dumbfounded. How on earth could I compete in drinking with someone like this? I had never been a big drinker. I didn't even drink at high school graduation, when all my friends were getting completely ripped.

"Yeah, I...I guess so."

"Cool," he said, and opened up the bag, pulling out two giant plastic cups and a bottle. "We're gonna start with a little vodka." He filled up a cup and handed it to me, then filled his own. Holding his up to mine, he asked: "Look even?"

"Yeah."

"OK, listen up. You get the first drink. You down the whole thing, you've won. You get half of it down, I get a shot. If I don't get it all down, we go back to you again. First one done wins. You spit it out or puke it up, you've lost. Ready?"

"Yeah."

"Go for it, dude."

I stared at the vodka. The quantity looked enormous. No way was I going to get all this down in one swallow. I told myself my only objective should be to get past the first swig without hurl-ing—at least I'd be guaranteed some measure of dignity. I brought it up to my lips and began drinking. The liquid burned as it went down my throat. I heard Connor whispering words of encouragement. I got about halfway through before I felt like my stomach was flipping upside down. I stopped, closing my eyes tightly as I willed my stomach to settle. Connor laughed.

"Hey, not bad, Devan. Not bad at all."

He lifted his cup to his lips and began drinking. As I watched the muscles in his throat ripple with each swallow, I began despairing that the contest would be over just like that. Suddenly he stopped, cheeks puffing out. He swallowed hard, then belched loudly. "Oh, fuck!" he exclaimed. He tilted his cup toward me, smiling devilishly. About a quarter cup left. "Still got one more chance, Devan."

I sighed loudly. "There's no way," I said softly. He continued grinning as I lifted my cup and started again. This time I did less than half of what was left before my overwhelmed stomach, already battered by being so nervous earlier in the evening, gave a definitive revolt. I spit the last swig in my cup and held my stomach hard. I felt tears being squeezed out of my tightly clamped eyes.

"Oh, dude!" Connor cried, shaking his head. "Good try. Good fucking try." He patted me on the back roughly, which I futilely tried to prevent with a wave of my hand.

"Sorry, dude. You're oh and 1. You get an A for effort, though."

I shook my head. "I'll never survive this. What's next, scotch? You might as well toss me out of the frat now."

He chuckled some more. "Naw, dude, you can do it. You can do it." He tapped my cup with his. "Bottoms up," he said, and downed what remained.

After the wave of nausea left me, I felt the first wave of a better feeling hit. "Wow," I said. "I'm starting to feel better about losing."

He laughed again and we talked for a little while. He poured a little more tequila in his cup, and I even took a few little sips out of mine, which was as much as my stomach could handle.

At one point he stood up and stretched his arms into the warm September night. "Damn, it's so fucking hot!" he said, whipping off his shirt. "I'm sweating like a pig!" His perfectly chiseled, hairless chest was indeed dripping with sweat. My timidity and caution weakened by the alcohol, I found myself stupidly staring at him. He noticed.

"What are you staring at, dude?"

I shook my head, looking down. "Nothing, I'm just a little buzzed."

"Yeah, me too." He kicked my toe with his. "Dude."

"Yeah?"

"Listen, I hate to see you lose the first round. It puts you at such a disadvantage for the rest of it, most of which we'll be doing in front of the other guys."

My eyes shot open wide with horror. "Oh, no!"

"So look, I'll give you a chance. Right now, this minute, you think of some way to earn your wings, and I mean really earn it. I'll give you a shot to redeem yourself."

I thought hard. "I can't down any more of that stuff, I'm sorry."

He moved a step closer. "So think of something else."

I could feel the heat of his body against mine and found myself, crazily, staring again at the glistening beads of sweat on his chest. I shook my head in drunken slow motion. "I've gotta earn it, right?"

"Yeah," he said.

"Gotta drink something, right?"

"Yup."

My eyes darted around. I swallowed hard again. "How about…something kind of gross?"

He lifted his eyebrows. "Like what?"

"Like…I don't know. Like what if I have to lick up all that sweat on your chest?"

He burst into laugher.

"That's fucking sick!"

"Well," I said. "Yes, it is. But it would show, you know…how much I want to stay in this frat. That I'd, you know, do anything."

He looked at me with a wicked smile, then stepped closer. "I like the way your mind works," he said. "So show me."

I leaned forward, trying hard to avoid staring at him too

revealingly. I saw little beads of sweat everywhere on his chest, including around his nipples. I looked up at him one last time, then closed my eyes and rolled my tongue quickly over the center of his chest. His skin was hot, the taste salty. I looked up for approval. He seemed fascinated.

I turned back to the task at hand. Sticking out my tongue, I brushed it some more over the center of his chest. Then I began to lick up drops of moisture with doglike upstrokes, first cleaning up the center of his chest, then moving over to the right side. When I licked across the flat, brown circular patch of his nipple I heard a barely perceptible, tiny rush of air escape his lips. Despite the tremendous amount of alcohol washing through my blood-stream, I felt something happening between my legs.

I kept licking, with bigger and broader strokes across his chest. As I cleaned above his left nipple, he lifted up his muscled arm. I saw a patch of coarse, black, glistening hair inside his armpit and caught a powerful whiff of heady odor.

"Clean that up, dude," he whispered. "And you have the victory."

Too eagerly, I rushed at his arm and buried my nose and mouth into it. I licked at it hungrily, and for one brief, humiliating moment could hear myself breathing in the rich, manly aroma. Then I pulled back and sat back down on the log.

"Dude," he grunted. "You'll do anything to win, won't you?"

I shrugged. He pulled his shirt back on. "Guess we outta get back."

"OK."

He hesitated a moment. "Wait—gotta take a piss first." I expected him to walk away, back behind a tree or something. Instead, still facing me, he unbuttoned his pants, lowering them just a little before reaching down and yanking out an enormous, almost fully engorged penis. It looked like it was 10 inches long.

I was mesmerized. I'd never seen another guy's erect penis, certainly not that close. I knew he was watching me. Suddenly I saw a trickle begin to dribble down onto the ground between his feet. I looked up and saw him staring at me again. I heard the trickle turn into a powerful, steady stream, splashing onto my feet and ankles. I spread my legs out quickly to avoid getting wet.

He grabbed the base of his dick. Horrified, I realized that he was moving the stream steadily closer to me, until it was almost at the base of the log. Raising it up just a little would make the stream splatter all over me unless I moved quickly. Was this another test? I kept my eyes focused on his. Slowly I brought my legs back closer together. I felt his warm drops sprinkling on me again. If this is a challenge, I thought—*fine*.

The stream moved no higher, gradually pulling back as his bladder emptied. When he had finally forced the last dribbles out, he thrust his massive tool back in his pants and smirked at me.

We walked in silence back to the house, where he announced to the others that I had emerged victorious in the first round. I received a generous round of masculine approval, including backslapping, shoulder-shaking, and hair-mussing. Gratified, I moved quickly up to my bedroom, where I feebly attempted to jerk off before passing out.

In the days that followed I found myself awkwardly attempting to strike up conversations with Connor, without success. There was no further hint of the strange and surprising intimacy of that first night. Indeed, I felt essentially invisible around him. I slowly began to find my place in the tribe but without his help.

Our next contests took place in October. As promised, they were public affairs. The first was a tequila shot-glass contest. In honor of the occasion, it was fiesta night at the frathouse, complete with nachos, guacamole, and margaritas. I tried not to eat too much of the fatty stuff before Connor and I faced off with lime, salt, and Cuervo. I had no illusions that I could beat him at this. My stomach was already jumping up and down at having to do this in front of everyone, and I hated tequila. I just wanted it over with. Right as we were getting ready to sit down, though, Connor snapped his fingers: "Darn—I forgot something." The other guys hooted. "Dude, come with me a sec."

He took me by the shoulder and hustled me upstairs into his room. Opening up his closet, I saw an enormous, flowery red dress.

"Oh, no."

"Oh, yes."

"Oh, my God, please, no."

"Dude," he said, coming over to me. "It's Cinco de October. Don't spoil the party."

I buried my head in my hands. "I can't! I just can't!"

He grabbed both my hands, then lifted them both high up in the air. "Dude," he said. "You don't have a choice." With a quick motion he grabbed my shirt and pulled it over my head. My arms fell back down as he just as quickly unbuttoned and unzipped my shorts, pushing them down enough so they fell around my ankles. I realized my heart was beating. Was it fear of my pending humiliation? The fact that I was being undressed by him? Or maybe it was just that, for the first time since that night in the woods, Connor was finally paying attention to me.

He knelt down in front of me, lifting up a leg roughly and slipping my sandal off my foot. "Got you some heels too," he said. I moaned and rolled my eyes as he took the other sandal off. He went over to get the dress, handing it to me. "Put it on," he said. By the tone of his voice, I knew it was pointless to resist. As I tried to figure out how to put it on, he slapped his head. "Dang! Forgot something else!"

He went to the closet and pulled out a plastic bag. Inside were a pair of red women's panties. My mouth fell open. I shook my head in panic.

Calmly, without hesitation, he walked over, grabbed the dress, and dropped it on the floor. Then he put his thumbs inside the sides of my underwear and yanked my BVDs down to my thighs. With complete embarrassment, and no alcohol as my excuse, I watched as my semi-boner popped out between us.

"See," said Connor. "Looks like you're going to enjoy this after all." He slipped a foot out of his sandal, stuck it between my legs on top of the underwear, and pushed them down. Losing his balance a bit, he stumbled forward a step, and I stumbled back, out of my underwear. My dick was even harder by this point, and it bounced up and down awkwardly. I covered it with my hands and closed my eyes.

I felt his breath next to my ear. "Everyone's waiting, Devan," he whispered. "You've got three minutes to get dressed." I heard first a rush of air, then the door open and close.

Quickly, in panic, I put on the panties and threw the dress over my head. He'd said I had heels but, gratefully, I couldn't find them, so I just left.

The chorus of jeers and catcalls that greeted me as I descended the stairs can only be compared to the din I imagine awaits sinners when they parade into Hell. Connor played some Mexican folk music as accompaniment. Although the other pledges, many of whom had endured similar humiliations, were grinning, I could still feel their sympathy.

The contest was a joke. I was required to do a quick Mexican hat dance before each shot. Connor easily paced me after four rounds, and by the time I got to the fifth, even the lemon and salt were making me feel barfy. I sipped just a little before spraying a fine tequila mist over my pretty red dress. The other guys howled and crowned Connor king. Feeling just a tad looser, though, I did a quick curtsy before rushing upstairs to change.

The third game happened several weekends later. The alcohol was beer and the game was a kind of modified version of quarters and the board game Taboo. Each of us was given two team members. Each team took turns popping quarters into a beer-filled glass, but if you made it, instead of making your opponent drink it, you had them pull a Taboo card and act out the charade. If your team members guessed in time, you didn't have to drink the beer; otherwise, you did. This one was kind of fun, actually, and I even thought I might have a chance at winning. But Connor was a much bigger ham, and though I stuck it out for 45 minutes, in the end I had to run into the bathroom to avoid retching.

Down two to one, for November's contest I knew I faced sudden death. Connor's latest stroke of madness was a wine and cheese contest, in which he invited members of a campus sorority and once again turned it into a party. The emphasis for this game was actually more on the cheese. Each of us was blindfolded and given various cheese samples. If you guessed incorrectly, you had to down a glass of wine. Depending on which cheese you screwed up on, you would be given either a white, blush, or red. Lucky for me, I actually like wine and I really love cheese. Also, all my screwups resulted in red-wine penalties, and Connor had chosen a very smooth cabernet. I was probably also helped by the fact that Connor had tied one on the previous night. Still, when he finally capitulated I had not a hint of nausea, and actually had the full attention of several partygoers fascinated to learn that one can actually "bruise" wine.

In the interim, Connor continued to be as distant as ever. Whereas I'd noticed that seniors and their pledges seemed to be forming tight and friendly bonds in the other pairings , Connor was routinely dismissive of me. The only times it seemed he warmed up to me were during the brief moments of our contests. I thought often of the strange overtones of our two experiences and wondered to what degree, if any, Connor was conscious of the sexual dimension. In truth, I was barely conscious of it myself. I'd never really fantasized about sex with other guys before, and I wasn't really fully thinking through what was fascinating me about these experiences. It was like I got to a certain point of thinking about it, then just stopped. Maybe Connor was doing the same thing.

Anyway, December 5 was our final contest. Everyone knew that, like the first contest, the last one was going to be just the two of us off on our own. Mano a mano. I was, in a strange way, looking forward to this. I wanted very badly to stay in the fraternity, and I certainly felt like I'd already earned my place. Whatever the contest, I was determined to have victory. I prepared for it by clandestine, periodic bar outings in which I focused on bourbons and liqueurs, figuring they were the most likely candidates.

When contest day rolled around, Connor told me in the morning to be ready at 6 P.M. to go for a little drive. "Bring a sleeping bag," he said. "We're not coming back tonight."

My mind raced with possibilities for where we might go. At the appointed hour I was fully prepared with a hastily purchased sleeping bag and some toiletries. Connor was already packed up, and when he honked the horn for me to come out I left to a surprisingly warm, heartfelt round of handshakes and wishes of good luck.

Predictably, Connor said almost nothing as he took us onto a highway that stretched into the green hills. After almost 2½ hours, we ended up at a small cabin tucked away in the forest. The night was chilly. "Grab your stuff," he said coolly.

Inside he immediately set to work firing up a wood stove. I asked him whose place it was.

"Belongs to my folks. Been coming here since I was a kid."

I wondered what on earth we'd be doing that we had to drive this far to do it. In a little while he went out to the car and returned with first a grocery bag, then an ice chest. He opened the bag up and pulled out a variety of food items: bread, chips, doughnuts. Then he pulled out a bottle of vodka. My heart sank. More vodka.

But then out came a bottle of tequila. And a merlot. My eyes opened up wide. He flipped the top off the ice chest. Inside it was stocked with lunch meat, steaks, potato salad, cheese—and beer. He twisted the caps off, handed me a bottle and grinned ferociously.

"This is gonna be a best-of, Devan. You've come a long way. You've really held in there, and I'm proud of you." I felt myself blushing in appreciation at his recognition. "First we'll have a little warm-up." He raised his bottle, and I returned mine with a clink. We took a sip.

"So why don't we have a little dinner first?"

We finished our beers as he cooked the steaks over the wood stove. He served us each a glass of wine with dinner. Without him saying I needed to, I found myself carefully matching his every sip, and we finished our glasses at almost exactly the same time.

We talked about the other guys, life in the frathouse, classes. He asked me a few questions about girlfriends. I told him I hadn't dated much in high school.

"Your girlfriend's pretty, though," I said.

He nodded politely. "Thanks."

After a while he began staring hard at me for a few moments. "OK," he said. "Time to begin."

He brought over all the alcohol and four glasses. "Here's the deal," he said. "This last contest is about winning and dignity. You're gonna have to decide which is more important to you. We're each going to take turns drinking each of these in order: a shot of tequila, a shot of vodka, a glass of wine, and a cup of beer. We're just going to alternate. But you can skip a drink if you remove parts of your clothes, but there's only four: shirt, pants, shoes and socks, and underwear. You get past those and the other guy gets to think of something…", and he hesitated, trying to think of the word, "…undignified to do. But it's gotta relate to drinking. First one who says he can't do it, or first one who can't drink the next drink, the contest is over, he loses."

I had to hand it to him. He was a fucking genius. I nodded.

I decided to be bold on my first try and down the beer. "Gutsy," he said as he removed his shirt. Then I settled down a bit and took off my shirt. We both took off our shoes and socks, and it was his turn to be bold. He drank his beer.

I didn't like the idea of stripping down to my underwear so soon, so I had my glass of wine. Then he had his. I had the vodka, and he followed. Same with the tequila.

My stomach began to churn a little. I debated, then leaned forward and drank another cup of beer. As my stomach roiled, he leaned forward and drank down his. He set the cup down contentedly and smiled at me.

I wanted to drink more, but I couldn't. Reluctantly I slipped my pants off. Quickly and calmly he downed another glass of wine. It was still too soon for me. To buy more time, I stood up and slowly lowered my underwear. Once again, I was embarrassed to see my penis much larger than it should be in front of another guy. Before I'd even slipped the underwear all the way off my feet, he was kicking down his own pants.

"Your turn," he said mockingly. "Drink or dignity?"

I stared down at the wine glass. My stomach still felt funny, but I couldn't stay this far behind. I knelt down, picked it up and closed my eyes, choking it down. For a second I thought I'd lose it, but I held the last gulp in my mouth long enough to let the feeling subside, then swallowed.

With an air of complete confidence he removed his pants. I shook my head in futility.

"All right," I said thickly. "You've got me. Tell me what I have to do."

He eyed me with an amused, contemplative expression. "Hmmm," he said. "OK, I got it." He stood up and walked over to the Coke bottle. Grabbing another plastic cup, he poured it about a quarter full of soda. Then he brought it over to me. As he stepped close I could feel myself becoming even more erect. Instinctively I began to bring my hands together to cover myself. He slapped them away with his free hand.

"You'll need to have that thing out for this little dare." He brought the cup just below my penis. "You've got 60 seconds to piss in this cup and drink it."

"Fuck no!" I cried.

"Fine," he said. "Then the game's over."

"Shit!"

"Fifty-five seconds."

I sighed heavily, contemplating.

"Fifty seconds…45."

"Damn it!" I grabbed my cock and pointed it into the cup. Since I point upward when erect, this wasn't easy. As Connor counted down five-second intervals, I tried to force some piss out. I'm shy peeing around other guys, though, and it's always hard to pee with an erection. Especially down. Into a plastic cup.

"Twenty-five seconds."

I closed my eyes and forced myself to think of something else. I tried to recall some factoids I'd learned in my Civil War history course. I pictured blue and gray soldiers pissing on the countryside after a hard day's battle.

"Fifteen seconds."

Suddenly I felt a little tinkle of piss come dribbling out. The sound of it started to freeze me up again, so with sheer will I forced out one giant shot. I looked down and saw the yellow liquid, then up at him for approval. He nodded. I reached down and gripped the cup with my hand, lifting it up, then hesitating.

"Eight…seven…six…"

"Aw, shit!" I cried, and with one quick motion threw the sweet, salty mixture down my throat. I clamped my eyelids down so tight I could feel tears coming out.

Connor busted into laughter. "*Dude!*" he howled. "You are such a *stud!*"

I began coughing and gasping. "Oh, fuck, man, you are evil. Totally evil."

I gave a final wheeze, then opened my eyes and looked into his. With new confidence I told him, "Your turn!"

Still grinning, he walked unsteadily over to the drinks and sat down. He reached for a shotful of vodka, but then his grin softened a bit. He swallowed hard—I could see it was finally getting to him. Then he rolled back and pushed down his underwear. I got a glimpse of his hairy asshole as he clumsily pushed his underwear off with his feet.

"Yours."

Drinking Contest

I knelt down and grabbed the wine glass. I told myself, *Nothing can be worse than what I just did,* and downed the glass. But my stomach now was in full revolt, and I had to kneel very still for several long moments to suppress my gag reflex. I knew I was coming to the end of my rope.

Then he grabbed the vodka and with an equally quick motion drank it down. He grabbed his mouth for a moment.

"Almost," he whispered like a weary prizefighter, refilling the shot glass. "Almost, but not quite. Your turn."

I looked again at the glass. There was no way.

"All right," I said. "Hit me with your best shot."

He laughed. "Funny you should say that…'specially 'cause I got to take a piss now too."

"Oh, you are so sick, man," I said. "So fucking sick."

"Lie back," he commanded.

I slowly lowered myself onto my back.

"Open your mouth."

My heart was pounding in my chest.

"I fill it up, you swallow."

If I hadn't been so wasted, maybe I would have quit right there. But you drink that much that quickly, you get kind of fearless. With all the courage I could muster, I opened my mouth. He looked down at me wickedly. Several long moments passed. I could see he was having to concentrate too. Then I saw a thin little stream begin raining down on my belly. It was warm, but surprisingly, I didn't flinch. As the stream grew it began to move up my chest. Then with a quick motion he aimed it straight into my mouth. His piss splashed on my face but began to quickly fill up my mouth. When I could feel it spilling down my cheeks I closed my mouth over the salty liquid and swallowed it down. Connor stopped peeing. My stomach did a few somersaults, but with an incredible feeling of exhilaration I realized I'd done it. I'd done it!

Connor shook his head at me in amazement. Then he let out another giant stream of piss on my neck.

"Hey!" I yelled in protest.

"Oops! Sorry!" he said, giggling drunkenly. He tried stopping, but he was so wasted and, obviously, had to pee really bad, so every time he giggled he'd pee, and every time he peed he'd giggle. Finally he grabbed his dick and ran into the bathroom. I saw him erupt in two spurts on the floor as he bumped his way into the bathroom. Then I heard a loud, pounding stream into the toilet. When it was over he let out a giant "A-a-ahhh!" And started laughing hysterically.

I began laughing too as he emerged, doubled over. "Dude," he said. "I'm so fucking...I couldn't stop..." he said, clutching his side and falling down to the floor. "I couldn't stop!" He rolled onto his back, lifting his feet onto the couch.

When the laughter subsided, he cleared his throat and said, "OK, I owe you big-time for that. It's your turn now. Do your worst."

I pondered. What was left? How much nastier could this get? But as I looked at him with his feet up, I got an idea. A truly awful idea.

"Grab that beer," I said. "Come over here."

With gratitude I saw him swallow nervously. I lay down on the floor, resting up on my elbows.

"Here's the deal, Connor. In about 10 seconds I'm going to roll all the way on my back and lift my legs over my head. I'm going to rest them on the sofa. You're going to take that beer and pour a bit on my ass. If I can pull it off, my asshole is going to be open and some of that beer's going to go up my ass. Then you're going to have to put your mouth on it and suck it down and clean up my asshole. You'll have about 15 seconds from when I say go. You can't do it? You lose."

Connor's face turned white and he shook his head. "I can't put my mouth on another guy's asshole."

"But you can make him drink your piss. What's the difference? Anyway, I don't care. That's the challenge, take it or lose."

He looked at me in awe. "You have learned much, young Jedi," he said. "I accept your challenge."

I rolled back and positioned my legs directly overhead, resting my toes on the couch. When I had gotten my ass to be level, I stretched my hole open with my fingers. Then said: "Go."

Connor began pouring the beer on my ass. That was the easy part. I could feel my hole burning up and realized I'd given far too much time for this. I began counting down rapidly.

"Ten…nine…eight…seven…"

"Dude!" he squealed. Then he leaned over and I felt his mouth surrounding my ass. I heard a sucking sound as he slurped up the spicy juice.

"Clean it up! Four…three…" He licked me all around my asshole, then stepped back, exhausted.

"Oh, God, that was *so gross!*" he yelled. But as I rolled forward I noticed that his cock was rapidly hardening. "Dude, you are so going to pay for that!"

"If it was so gross," I said, "why are you popping a big-time boner?"

He looked at me strangely. I had the vaguely uncomfortable feeling that I'd crossed a line here. The playful grin vanished from his face and he moved toward me with steely determination.

Quietly, but firmly, he said: "Drink or dignity."

I knew I couldn't back away from this now. I stared at him levelly. "Dignity."

He stood for a moment, breathing heavily.

"Here's the deal," he said. "This is sudden death. I'm gonna put victory on the line for both of us with this one." I shuddered at this—what could top what we'd already done?

"You're going to roll on your back again, in that same position you were in. You're going to grab your prick and start jacking off. You'll have 60 seconds to come. All of it, every drop, has to land in your mouth. But that's not all. You've got to keep your mouth open and hold it there. See, I'm gonna be jacking off too. I'll have 10 seconds after you come to come myself. I've gotta get every drop in your mouth too, or I lose. Every drop. Then you've gotta swallow it, dude. A big mouthful of your come and mine. Swallow it down and keep it down, or you lose, and you're out of the frat. But you swallow it all, I'll give you the victory."

I stared at the ceiling for a moment. This had gotten so bizarre. Were we going too far? Was being in a frat worth this perverse game? But then I looked down and saw how hard I was. The truth was that I was so fucking horny I was going to explode. I needed to come. So did Connor. I'd come this far—I wasn't going to back down.

"Sixty seconds," I said, rolling back. "Wait till I get in position."

Connor chuckled. "You mean wait till you get your dick in position." I wiggled my torso to get my genitals hanging directly over my mouth, resting my feet again on the couch. Only a few inches separated my lips and dick. Coming this quick would be easy, I thought. My throbbing penis was dying to be stroked.

"Sixty seconds," said Connor. "Go!"

I began stroking rapidly. So did Connor. "Fifty seconds, dude," he said.

Drinking Contest

Even though I was horny, I could tell the alcohol was having an effect. I began stroking harder. "Forty seconds," said Connor.

"Fucking drank too much…" I panted. Connor smiled. Then with my minute ticking down, he shocked the shit out of me. He licked his hand, reached over, and grabbed my dick. The slickness of it, or maybe the fact that it was his hand, made my cock feel like it was bursting with sensation.

"Oh, God," I said.

"What is it, Devan?"

"Ahh," I moaned. "You're…you're rubbing my dick for me."

"Yeah," he whispered. "I'm rubbing little Devan's dick for him. How does it feel, Devan? How does it feel?"

"A-a-ahhh, it feels good."

"Yeah, I know. It feels so good, doesn't it? Wait till everyone hears about it, Evan. Wait till the guys find out that we made little Devan jerk off in his mouth. Wait till they find out he swallowed down his own come. What do you think they'll say?"

"I…I don't know. Maybe you better…you better stop."

"No, I'm not gonna stop. I don't care how long it takes. You know why?"

"*Why?*"

"Because I want to see your little dick squirt in your mouth. I want to see you fill up your mouth with your own come."

"O-o-ohhh…Ga-a-a-hhhd…my dick…you're rubbing my dick…"

"Yeah, Devan."

"You're going to make my dick…make it squirt…"

"Yeah, you got it, baby."

"You're gonna make it squirt in my mouth…"

"Oh, yeah."

Connor leaned forward and forced my dick within an inch of my lips. I could feel his cock pressing against my thigh. "Oh God, please...please make it squirt...please squirt come...in my mouth...A-A-AHHH!"

I felt my body shake violently as the first wave of my orgasm propelled a thick, massive ribbon of come out of my dick lips and into my gaping mouth. Connor held me down tightly as he started to slow-pump more creamy explosions. My mouth was filling up quickly with jism, and I fought hard not to swallow. Connor pumped away until I could feel come on my lips, my teeth, drowning my tongue. Finally there was nothing left but a big sticky blob on the tip of my dick. Connor scooped it with a finger, then wiped it off using my front teeth. Incredibly, I was sure I'd gotten every drop. Then, abruptly, he threw my legs down and parked his incredible, massive member directly over me. He slathered his hand up with more spit and began grunting and jacking off like some desperately horny ape. His dick, which pointed more down than mine, was easy to position right over my mouth. I would have returned his kindness and whispered a few words of encouragement, but I had a soup bowl full of come in my mouth.

Suddenly I heard him shouting "Oh, fuck, yeah" as he practically stuck his dick in my come-bucket mouth. I could feel the vibration of his shooting streams of liquid goo entering me, as I was now filled to overflowing. He let out one final, wild groan and squeezed a last few drops, then let go, cupped my chin with his hand, and closed my mouth shut.

I closed my eyes, feeling the hot, sweet cream swirling around my tongue. "Come on, dude!" he cried. "You can do it." With a giant swallow, I forced down the whole load, so fucking much it made my throat hurt. Then I opened my mouth, choking and sputtering.

Drinking Contest

We sat quietly for several moments, with each of us slowly getting our breathing back to normal. Connor finally turned to me. "Nice work, dude."

I took a few deep breaths. "Jesus! Thanks for the assist."

"Well," he said, grinning again. "Now you know I'm not such a bad guy after all."

I smiled back. "Yeah. So. Your turn now."

He looked back incredulously. "Dude, you've gotta be kidding. You've won."

"Nah, too easy." I said. "Far as I can tell, there's only one thing left to drink." I lifted myself up and crawled over to him. I gathered a little saliva on my tongue, then opened my mouth slightly. I pointed my finger at his mouth, raising and lowering my eyebrows quickly. "So what do you say? You ready to swallow some of my spit?"

He stared into my eyes as I slowly moved my face closer to his. My lips parted again, and I could see his parting too. My tongue flicked out, just centimeters away from his own. Then abruptly he closed his mouth and leaned back his head.

"Dude," he said. "Let's just…let's just say you won."

I pulled back, and suddenly felt a strange kind of longing and disappointment. But I faked a smile and lay back down on the floor. He did too. As much as we'd had to drink that evening, it didn't take long for both of us to pass out.

In the morning we packed up and headed out. We talked freely about lots of things, but nothing of the prior evening. When we got back to the frathouse, Connor told everyone I'd won a tropical drink marathon after he'd ended up hurling on one too many mai tais. I received a round of congratulations and happily took a permanent place in my new home.

Connor became like kind of a distant older brother. He never did completely warm up to me in any other way, and we never messed around again. Eventually I came out, but he ended up marrying right out of college. I always thought that was kind of sad. In the end, I guess, I won the biggest victory of all. But I still have him to thank for it.

The Frathouse Blues

Colt Spencer

I live in a fraternity with 11 other guys. It's never easy, but you get used to it. The brothers are fun to hang around and can generally throw a pretty good party, even if they do tend to get out of hand sometimes. They're a cocky bunch of bastards, I have to admit, but cocky is good. We all make our way in this world being somewhat arrogant in our youth, especially in college, when we think we know everything. But as I learned while living in the frathouse, there was an awful lot that I didn't know yet.

My story begins on a Friday just like any other, when—without warning—a piece of mail in a plain manila envelope was delivered to our door, certified. It was addressed to "The Boys of Aetta Betta Pie," which was the nickname some of the guys had come up with for our fraternity. Get it? Hey, it wasn't *my* idea, OK?

Curious and already slightly amused by this mysterious delivery, I opened the envelope. It looked like a story of some kind, but I didn't know what to make of it. It was called "The Men From the Boys," and there was a note that had been paper-clipped to the manuscript. It read:

Dear Boys: I wanted to share this story with you. For some reason, I thought you might enjoy it. A Friend.

I shrugged. What the hell was this all about? I glanced at the clock and saw that it was just about time for my afternoon classes to start. Shit! I threw the story down on the coffee table and grabbed my books. As I ran out the door and jogged across campus, I forgot all about the mysterious package.

But I was soon to find out that it was not so easily forgotten.

Biology class was pretty boring that day. Our teacher, Mr. Peters, kept droning on about dinosaur DNA like the class actually cared, and I was becoming restless. As I doodled a biohazard symbol on my notebook, I became aware of someone's eyes on me. I looked to my right and saw this guy kinda staring at me. Or maybe not. I looked back to my notebook and continued with my scribbling for a few moments, then casually glanced back in the guy's direction. Sure enough, the dude was still checking me out.

What the hell was this guy's problem? I wondered. Then he kinda smiled at me and winked quickly before turning back toward Mr. Peters and his dino DNA theories.

Fuckin' fag, I thought, irritated by the guy's attention. Did he have to be so fucking obvious about it? I mean, couldn't he do that shit in the campus restroom where all the other fruits apparently met up after hours?

I looked back over at the guy and again caught him looking over at me. This time he motioned toward Peters and rolled his eyes. As if I was supposed to encourage him. As Peters finally called an end to class for the day, I gave the fairy a dirty look and walked right past him. As I did, I couldn't help but notice his look of disappointment. *Ha,* I thought as I walked out the door and started across the quad.

As I kept walking, though, I started to feel a little awkward about my behavior toward the guy. I mean, after all, it wasn't like the guy grabbed my dick in the shower or anything. I guess I should have felt flattered instead of offended, but for some reason I just couldn't shake the feeling of unease the guy's attention had brought up in me.

My thoughts were diverted, though, when I heard my name being called out by Kathy Keefer, who started waving at me from across the quad. I smiled and waved back but kept on walking toward the fraternity house. I had a party to prepare for.

When I got back from my class and walked in the front door, something felt a little bit weird on fraternity row. Some of the guys were hanging out in the living room, making quite a bit of noise about something or other. They all looked up to see who it was coming in, and they all had these weird looks on their faces, like they were startled by my arrival.

"Good," said Johnny, the undeclared "leader" of our frat pack who was also undeniably the most book-smart. His grades were among the best on campus. "It's just you." He looked relieved to see me.

"Thank God," said Marcus, the rough-and-tumblin' soccer captain who was also my roommate.

"What's goin' on, fellas?" I said, tossing my books down.

"Did you read this crap?" asked Steven, the not-too-bright football player with a thick neck and blond crew cut to match. His roommate Kyle was also sitting in the room, though he seemed to be keeping pretty quiet.

"What is it?" I asked, not remembering our afternoon delivery.

I could feel all eyes upon me as I took the pages Johnny thrust at me and began to read. My eyes must have bulged right out of my head as I perused the first page.

My favorite part about being in college is being able to watch all the other guys in my fraternity in the showers. They make me hot for them. I often think about them as I jerk off at night, lying in my bed, jerking off quietly so my roommate doesn't hear, thinking of sliding my mouth up and down Billy's cock, or eating Jake's ass. When I come, it's always the best, better than the time before. I love my brothers. I just wish they knew how much...

I stopped reading, suddenly feeling very warm. I could feel my face turning red. I looked up at the other guys, and they were all staring at me intently, waiting for my response.

"Who sent this?" I said.

"Whoever it is," said Stephen, "he's one sick motherfucker. I'd like to beat the shit outta him, and I will if I ever catch the faggot."

"Now them's fightin' words," said Johnny, laughing. "And you were the one who popped a woody when you were reading this."

"Fuck you, cocksucker," Stephen challenged, grabbing his crotch for effect.

Johnny kept Stephen's glare for a few moments, then shrugged it off with a casual "Whatever." Still, there was definitely tension hanging in the air, and, always the diplomat, Marcus was the first to step in and smooth things over.

"Let's just forget this ever happened," he said before crumpling the story up and tossing it in the nearest trash can. The other brothers agreed, but I could tell there was still a lot of nervous energy in the room. I couldn't help but think something was not right anymore. Every one was trying to act like it was no big deal, but I could tell that it was. It irritated me. It was probably that little queer back in biology class, I thought to myself, as I started up the steps to my room. He must have found out which fraternity I was in and had the damned story sent to us. I didn't feel so bad about giving the little faggot a dirty look anymore. But it wasn't just the presumptuous actions of a lovelorn sissy that was irritating me. That was just part of it.

The Frathouse Blues

As I turned the doorknob of the room I shared with Marcus, I realized that for some insane reason I couldn't quite comprehend, I had an erection.

Later that night, I had just gotten out of the shower and was getting dressed when Marcus came into the room. He didn't say anything to me; just went to his bed and sat down.

"Hey," I said, pulling my shirt down over my chest. It looked for a moment like Marcus was kinda checking me out, but I shrugged the idea off. Marcus just sat there, quiet as hell, and I could tell that he was really jumpy about something.

"Is something bothering you?" I finally said.

"Huh?" he said, his tone strangely defensive. "No, why would you ask that?"

"I don't know, man. You're the one who seems kinda tense."

"I'm not tense!" He looked away for a moment. "Sorry, man. Shit, I guess I am tense."

"What's up, buddy? You can talk to me."

He sighed. "I know. It's just that…forget it."

"OK then." I sat down on the bed to put my socks on, and the room became very silent. Marcus sat there for a few moments before he finally started talking again.

"OK. Look, I don't know if you know this…I never told anyone, really, but, well…my little brother is gay."

"Uhhh, OK," I said, not really understanding his point.

"Well," he said, looking at me like I was supposed to get it. "The *story*?"

"The story we got in the mail?"

"Yeah, that one."

"Well?" I said, probably a bit too curt. I was feeling quite agitated myself, and my patience with Marcus was just about at an end. "What about it?"

He turned away from me, his eyes staring down at the floor. "I don't know, man…" he said, his voice barely audible.

"Yeah you do," I said, starting to pick up on where he was headed with this strange discussion. "Or else you wouldn't be up here right now. What, because some pervert sends us a letter and your brother is gay, you're saying you're gay too?"

Marcus snapped his head in my direction and looked at me with anger in his eyes. "I didn't say that!"

"I'm just taking your cue, man," I said. "What's the deal?"

"I don't know," he said. "I always wondered…I mean, you know how they say that it runs in the genes or somethin'? Shit, I hate this."

And then I looked at him. Really looked at him. He was sitting on the edge of my bed, looking away from me. His eyes were glistened, as if he could cry at any moment. Something inside me stirred. Suddenly, I felt panic stir within me. What was I thinking? It felt like the first time I was seeing his curly pitch-black locks, the way they playfully fell in his face. It felt like the first time I noticed the way his nose turned up at the end like a ski slope. It felt like the first time I realized how chiseled his jaw looked, like it had been carved out of stone by some incredibly perceptive artist. For a moment, for a brief moment, I thought he looked beautiful.

"Dude," I said, my stomach suddenly seized by butterflies. I got up and walked over to my dresser. "I don't have time to pick your brain apart."

"I was just talkin' anyway," he said, and I could tell from the way his voice broke that he was hurt by my impatience. He got up and walked to the door. "Sorry for bothering you."

Then he left. I stood there, a bit confused by our exchange, my hands shaking for no apparent reason. My mind couldn't stop turning the scene over and over in my head.

The Frathouse Blues

Could Marcus be gay?

I wished the thoughts would go away, but that boner in my pants kept reminding me that I wouldn't be able to anytime soon.

About an hour later, after trying to study for an upcoming algebra test, I tossed my book aside in frustration. My head was all blurred, and I was a bit perturbed to find my thoughts wandering back to that story that had been sent to us earlier. I hadn't really ever thought about having sex with another dude before, and when I had read it, I was revolted by the words I was seeing on the paper. But I still couldn't deny the erection I'd gotten, and I couldn't figure out where that had sprung from.

I decided that I wasn't going to be able to get any studying in at all, so I put my books away, left my room, and walked downstairs to see what the guys were up to.

"Hey, Kent," Stephen said, looking up from a porn flick on the television. "Decided to join us after all?"

"Yeah," I replied. "Algebra was way too hard for me."

"That's not all that's hard," Johnny cracked, pointing to the TV as the other brothers chuckled.

I laughed and took my place on the couch beside Marcus and Kyle. We all sat in silence for a while, watching the flick. Just a bunch of college guys watching some stupid porno movie. Then Kyle broke the silence.

"So who's getting hard in here?" he said, laughing.

"Hell," Johnny piped in, "the question is probably more like, Who *isn't* getting hard in here. Am I right?"

Marcus was silent. I just smiled.

Kyle grabbed his package. "Yeah," he said, shaking it, "my cock is feelin' pretty good right about now."

The other brothers grunted in agreement.

"Well then," Johnny said, always taking charge. "Since we're all sitting here with boners, I say we have a little wager."

I swallowed. What was this all about?

"What kinda wager, Johnny?" Kyle said, all ears.

"Well," he said. "I'm sure we could all stand a little bit of relief, if you know what I mean. I think it's safe to say that even though we don't want to admit it, that story today got us all a little bit turned-on."

I looked around at the other guys in the room. No one said anything, but from the various shades of red washing over their faces, I'd say Johnny was on to something.

"So I say we have ourselves a little brotherly circle jerk, just to clear the tension from the air."

"Are you warped or something?" Stephen retorted. "You expect me to sit here and pound my pud in front of you fairies?"

"No one wants to suck your dick, shithead," Johnny countered. "Just some casual stroking. Or don't you think you can perform? Is that it, Stephen? Is Captain America not feeling up to speed tonight?"

"Fuck you, asswipe," Stephen said. "My cock is definitely able to stand up." As if to prove this, he unsnapped his jeans and pushed his briefs down to reveal his hard prick sticking straight up out of his crotch. "You girls wanna sit there and stare, or you gonna get yours out too?"

Always the competitor, I thought.

Kyle shrugged. "Hell," he said, "why not? I ain't gonna see what's-her-name until tomorrow night anyway. Might as well bust a nut tonight with my buddies." He unzipped and his hard cock sprang out of its cotton confinement. I noticed with some discomfort that it was fatter than Stephen's.

Johnny looked over at Marcus and me. "Well?"

I looked over at Marcus. He was looking right at me, his eyes searching mine. I broke away.

"I'm game," I said bravely, pushing my jogging shorts down and my jockstrap aside so that my prick could stand up and breathe. I looked over at Marcus again. He looked at my cock. For a moment I thought how much I liked his gaze on my naked dick, but quickly tuned this out.

He silently undid his jeans and pushed them down as well, and his uncut cock was the next to enter the arena. I found myself spending a little bit more time checking his out than I did with Kyle and Stephen. Something about that extra skin was interesting.

"Hey," Stephen said. "No fair, Johnny. Where's your randy prick?"

"Hang on. There's one more thing that we need." Johnny jumped up from his seat and disappeared from the room. The rest of us sat there, trying not to look at each other as we wrapped our hands around our cocks. Then Johnny was back, holding not only a jar of Crisco but a box of Ritz crackers. The brothers looked at each other with a bit of hesitancy.

"You guys going pussy on me here?" Johnny said.

Of course, you can't toss that kind of question out in a room full of guys and expect them to not "rise to the challenge," as it were.

"Let's do it then," Kyle said, pushing his pants down to his ankles. "Who says go?"

"I do," Johnny said, pushing his own pants down, revealing a huge cock that must have been about nine inches long and six inches around. It was a fuckin' monster.

"Yo, dude!" Stephen said. "Nice winky!"

"Thanks, stud," Johnny replied. "Yours too."

This was starting to get really weird.

"OK," Johnny said, sitting down. "Here's the wager. Last one to bust his nut has to do all of our laundry for a month. Agreed?"

No one said anything.

Johnny hesitated for a moment before adding, "And he gets another little treat as well."

We looked at Johnny, not understanding.

He smiled. "I'm gonna put this cracker in the center of the table. When each one of us gets ready to blow our wads, we do it on this cracker." He paused for effect, then smiled devilishly. "Last one to come is a rotten egg."

And then it dawned on me.

"You can't be serious!" I said.

"Hey," he said. "Rules of the game."

"Whose rules?" Stephen said.

"It's pretty common," Johnny explained. "When I went to visit my friend at his college, his frathouse did this for part of their hazing. All the brothers and pledges jerked off, and the last one left had to eat the cracker."

We sat in silence.

"We're all HIV-negative, right?" Johnny said, looking around. Everyone nodded. "So fuck it. That's gonna make us try a little bit harder not to lose, isn't it?"

I couldn't believe this. I don't think Marcus could, either.

"You guys pussy?" Johnny said.

Of course, you can't toss that kind of question out in a room full of guys and expect them to say yes.

"Let's do it then," Kyle said, pushing his pants down to his ankles. "Who says go?"

"OK then," Johnny started. "When I say 'go,' everyone start jerkin' off. ready…set…beat!"

And that's just what started.

"Wait, guys," Johnny said. "You don't have to make it go so fast. Make it feel good. Just let it progress naturally. Do it like no one else is around."

Each guy slowed down a little bit when Johnny said this, and I found myself looking around at the others in the room, not even paying attention to the movie anymore. The funny thing was, neither was anybody else. When I looked over at Kyle, he was busy looking at Stephen, who was in turn staring over at Marcus, whose eyes I could feel on me.

Of all of us, Johnny had the best technique. He was really jerking off in a way that made me take notice. He was able to use both hands, and he spread his legs as far apart as he could so that he could slide them up and down his rock-hard prick.

Kyle leaned forward and dipped his hand into the Crisco, then slathered a bit onto his cock before starting to work himself off that way. Stephen spit into his hand and used that. I looked over at Marcus, who seemed to be really into this whole thing. I grabbed the Crisco and offered it to him. He took some and applied it to his cock. I, myself, didn't need any. Having all my best buddies around me was strangely erotic to me, and precome was oozing out of my cock, acting as natural lubricant. As each guy practiced his own technique on his hard pole, I found myself getting more and more excited.

As things progressed, each guy began to get a bit more into it. Kyle started to fondle his balls, tickling them with the tips of his fingers, tugging on his hairs. Stephen started to pinch his nipples, working his tits over with his hands. Marcus was rolling his foreskin back and forth, then peeling it down and pumping it with his shaft, working his balls over as well. Johnny shocked us the most, though, when he parted his legs and slid a finger into his ass crack. I stared at him and he stared to tickle his anus, sliding his other hand around his massive pole at the same time. I had never done that, and wondered what it felt like, but I was too scared to try it in front of the other guys.

Gradually, each guy started to get really into things. You could tell, because they were each starting to grunt and get verbal.

"Yeah, guys," Johnny cooed. "Stroke those hard peckers. Think of the hottest chick you can, down on her knees, in front of your prick, bringing it to her lips."

"Ohhh, yeah," Stephen grunted.

"Yeah, come on," Johnny continued. "Think of the best blow job you've ever had. Yeah, Marcus, play with that foreskin. Yeah, that's hot. Rough those beefy pecs up, Stephen. Yeah, just like that. Mmm, yeah. You're doin' great, guys."

This was blowing my mind. I had never been involved in something so incredibly hot before. There were no women around, yet this was as sexual as anything I'd ever done with any girl before. There was something totally primal about it. And it didn't seem the least bit gay to me at all. Just guys sitting around getting off together. No big deal at all.

"Yeah, Kent," Johnny goaded. "Just like that. Beat your meat."

"You too," Marcus said, surprising me. "Hand-fuck your dick, man."

"Yeah," Johnny said. "O-o-oh yeah. I love it like this. Jerkin' my meat with my buddies. My hot fuckin' brothers."

Suddenly Stephen stood up. "I'm gonna nut," he cried.

"Yeah, man," Johnny said. "Come on. Do it for us. Shoot your load."

"Oh yeah," Stephen moaned, pumping his cock faster and faster. "Shit yeah. I'm gonna blow. Fuck, here it comes!"

And come he did, as his thick creamy wad spurted out onto the table.

"The cracker, man!" Johnny shouted. "On the cracker."

Stephen aimed his jerking pole at the Ritz cracker and splattered a thick round of jizz onto it. His shoulders shook as he grunted like a pig, sweat running down his forehead as gradually he relaxed and his convulsions subsided.

Almost as quickly as he finished, Kyle began to moan out loud as well. "Shit," he cried out, struggling to stand up. The first blast of jizz came out as he was getting up, and it landed on his jeans. He stood over the table and managed to fire off several more rounds onto the already come-drenched cracker, moaning out as he did so. "Fuck, yeah…oh, yeahhh…ye-e-e-a-a-ahhh!"

I looked over at Marcus, who was jerking intently, then at Johnny, who slid a finger right inside his own ass. That did it. I felt my balls swelling up, and I started to get up. As I did, Johnny joined me. We stood side by side, pumping our cocks in unison, crying out obscenities as we busted our nuts all over the table and cracker.

"Shit yeah!" Johnny called out appreciatively.

"Ohhh, man," I cried, throwing my head back, letting my intense orgasm rip through my body.

As I slowed my pumping action, the room stopped spinning, and I realized suddenly what was going on. And then it came to me that I hadn't heard Marcus come or hadn't seen him get up. I turned to look at him. He was sitting in his chair still, his lap full of cream, his breathing heavy.

"Sucks to be you, man," Stephen taunted. "Now you gotta pay up."

Marcus looked up. "I couldn't get up in time. I just…"

Johnny shook his head. "Sorry, man," he said. "Rules are rules."

Marcus looked up at me. I didn't know what to do. I was still trying to get over the fact that I had just got off on watching a room full of guys choking their chickens.

"Lick it first," Kyle ordered. "On your knees, bitch."

"Oh yeah," Stephen agreed. "Just like a dog."

Marcus looked so incredibly defeated; I felt awfully sorry for him. He slid down off his chair and got down on all fours.

"Ruff ruff," Johnny said.

Marcus moved closer to the table, and then he was staring at the come-covered cracker with dread. I wished I could end all of this, but it was a fraternity agreement, and you don't go back on those. But this was crazy.

Then Marcus flicked his tongue out and scooped up a wad of our jizz, then closed his mouth around his tongue. I wondered what it tasted like.

"Shit!" Kyle said. "He did it. Yeah, pig, eat that cracker now. Eat it."

"Eat it! Eat it! Eat it!" It became a chant, and to my horror, I found myself chanting along.

Marcus bent down and opened his mouth.

"That's it," Johnny said. "Receive the bountiful fraternity communion."

And then the cracker was gone, and Marcus was chewing on the soggy cracker that had been squirted with our hot loads.

The look on Marcus's face was one of sheer terror, and I don't know that I'll ever forget it. He swallowed the cracker down and stood up. He bravely faced us.

"Not too bad, you guys," he said, cracking a smile.

"Holy shit," Stephen said, slapping him on the back. "You are one brave dude!"

"Well done, brother," Johnny said, offering his hand. Marcus accepted it, and they shook.

I looked over at Marcus, who saw me looking at him. I smiled. He didn't. I felt sorry for him on one hand, but couldn't quite deny the fact that I envied him. I actually wished that I had been the one who had come last.

Though Marcus looked somewhat defeated, I realized at that moment that I had enjoyed getting off with my brothers. And I had especially enjoyed the sight of watching Marcus get off. Looking at my roommate and best friend, I couldn't help but be envious that he'd been the one to come last. The thought excited me tremendously.

Which, of course, left me even more confused than ever.

The party was a total success. We had gotten hold of three kegs, a fat bag of weed, and invited all the hottest chicks on campus to attend. It was quite an event, if I do say so myself. Four sorority girls ended up passing out on our couches, two guys got into a major fistfight that ended when campus security showed up on complaints about the noise, and Kyle threw up all over Johnny's brand-new Adidas. I got pretty close to puking myself but miraculously contained myself long enough for the moment to pass.

Yet even with all that happened during the party, nothing prepared me for what took place later that night.

I was still pretty weirded-out over the events of the day, which was turning out to be one of the strangest I'd ever had. First that story arriving, then the guy in biology class checking me out, then Marcus's semi-confession in our room. But what had me going most of all was that I couldn't get that damned circle jerk out of my head. It was like my mind was running on a continuous instant replay of all my brothers pulling on their dicks, especially Marcus.

At about 4 A.M. I left my brothers down in the living room and decided to call it a night. I went up to my room and crawled into bed. Of course, as fate would have it, sleep was not coming easy to me that night. I had too much on my mind for that.

As I tossed and turned, my mind eventually drifted back to Marcus. What was going on between the two of us these days? Ever since that damned story had arrived, nothing between us was the same anymore. I didn't want to be mad at him. He was my best friend.

Even still, I pretended to be asleep when he came into the room a little bit later and quietly crawled into his bed.

I laid there and laid there, trying to go to sleep, but it just wasn't happening. *Am I gay?* I thought to myself. *Why can't I stop thinking about all of this? Why does the thought of two guys together make me so hot? And why can't I stop thinking about Marcus?*

What's more, my cock was harder than it had ever been, or at least it felt like it. Not since I was 15 and I saw my first porn film had I felt this turned on. And almost without thinking about it, I reached down and gently started to rub my hardness. I couldn't help it. Something inside me was saying, *Fuck it, dude. Just go with it.*

I spit into my hand and wrapped it around my cock. In my mind I saw Marcus sitting on the couch beside me, stroking his hard, uncut dick in time with my own rhythm. I could still feel his eyes on me, drinking in the sight of me pounding my pud. But this time when I thought about it, the other brothers weren't in the room with us. It was just me and Marcus, and this time, instead of staying where he was, Marcus moved closer to me. I don't know how, but I ended up imagining him getting ready to plow my hole with his cock. I could feel my legs going over his shoulders, I could feel his cock head as it pushed against my virgin hole. I could see his eyes looking down into mine…I could see the passion and desire he had for me. I could see his cock thrusting into me, each thrust bringing total pleasure. I could see us coming together, at the same time, and I could hear myself calling out his name.

"Marcus! Oh yes, Marcus!"

Suddenly, I realized something, and my entire body froze. The sound of my own voice reverberated in my head. Had I just called his name out loud? Or was that part of my fantasy? I had gotten so carried away with my jacking that I had completely tuned out everything around me. My heart was beating faster than it ever had. I didn't want to look over at Marcus's bed, but I did.

My suspicions were confirmed. He was wide awake, no doubt about it, and staring right at me. There was a smile on his face. And more than that, he had his cock in his hand.

"Hot show," he whispered. "You were really getting into that shit, huh?"

My erection was completely gone, shriveled to nothing. I gulped, sure that everyone in the house could hear it.

"You were watching me?" I managed to get out.

"Couldn't take my eyes off of you," he said. "You looked so fuckin' hot like that."

I was speechless.

"Look," he said, picking up on my case of the jitters. "I just have to say this, OK, so I'm going to." He paused again, the tension hanging in the air between us. Then: "I'm gay. I guess I've pretty much always known that, but I really figured it out today. And dude…I want you bad."

I still couldn't bring myself to say anything. I was too scared to talk, not because I was embarrassed that he had caught me, but because as he was telling me this stuff, my cock had gotten hard again. And I realized in that moment that I too was probably gay. Or at least I wanted to sleep with my best friend. Whatever the hell that means.

"I'm coming over there," he said.

I tensed up again. Part of me wanted to say "Don't!" but I couldn't. The bigger part of me wanted him as much as he said he wanted me. So when he got out of his bed and walked over to mine, I didn't say a word.

He took a deep breath. "Here goes nothing," he said.

And with that he reached under my covers and found my cock. I shuddered, but suddenly something inside me broke, and I felt free for the first time in my life. His hand on my cock, holding it like that, felt right.

"Excellent," he said. "I was hoping you'd still be sporting a woody."

He slowly began to stroke it, up and down, working his hand over it like a connoisseur cocksman, which I suspected he was after seeing his jerk-off technique. I couldn't help moaning aloud as the pleasure seared through my body.

"Yeah," he said. "That's it. You like it, don't you?" As he said this, his other hand worked on my chest, massaging my pecs, flicking my nipples.

All I could do was nod yes. I did like it!

"Well then," he said. "I think you're going to like this even better." And then he bent over and his head disappeared under my covers. I sucked my breath in and tensed up when I felt his lips make contact with my burning cock, but he reached up and grabbed my hand and squeezed it. "Relax," he goaded. "I want to make you feel good."

When his mouth slid down over my shaft, I gasped out loud. The sensations were absolutely...well, fucking sensational! He certainly knew what he was doing. Right away he seemed to know my pressure points; he even knew to pay special attention to that sensitive part right beneath the head on the underside. He flicked his tongue back and forth across that area, and I lifted my hips off the bed without even knowing it. I assume he took this as a sign of approval, because he really went to town on me at that point, sucking me with a vengeance. He slid his hand under my ass and pulled me to his mouth, encouraging me to keep thrusting toward him. It felt so damned good that I was more than obliged to do so, and began to move my hips toward his mouth, meeting him thrust-for-suck.

"Mmmph," he groaned from below, his eyes closed, a look of absolute bliss on his face. It was almost hard for me to believe that someone could get off that much on actually sucking a cock as opposed to being the one receiving the pleasure. But I have to say that I was doubly curious to find out after seeing the look on my roomie's face as he went to town on my dick.

"Oh, yeah," I said. "Man, that feels so great. Where did you learn to do that?"

Marcus lifted his head from my cock. "I don't know," he said. "I guess I just know what feels good for me, so I'm trying that on you."

Made sense to me.

"I want to try it on you," I said.

"You do?" he asked, surprise edging into his voice. I could only nod. "Well," he said, "let's sixty-nine then, because I'll tell ya, I'm loving your cock in my mouth, and I don't want to stop."

How could I argue with that?

I slid down toward the bottom of my bed as he turned himself around, and I was suddenly greeted with his cock in front of my face. I could smell the sweat of his crotch, and it took me back to the locker room and the pungent smell of sweaty crotches and armpits and deodorants and colognes—the natural smell of men. But I had an added bonus here: Marcus's uncut cock, which looked so fascinating to me, with the extra layer of skin that closed over the head.

"Hey," I said, "do I have to do anything special with this thing because of your foreskin?"

He laughed. "Not at all," he said. "Just go for it, man. If you're hurting me, I'll tell you."

As Marcus slid his mouth back over the length of my rock-hard prick, I stuck my tongue out and tentatively tasted his extra skin. Hmm…not bad. I held his cock, pulsing and alive, in my hand and guided it to my lips, which slowly closed around his shaft. It felt rubbery and silky smooth at the same time. I slid my tongue around inside his foreskin, getting a taste for it. Since I had nothing to compare it to, it seemed fine to me. Musky, sweet, kinda what I figured. Pushing it back to reveal his mushroom-shaped and bulbous head to my mouth, I continued my quest for knowledge of his sex organ, which seemed to jump and twitch in my mouth as I learned the ropes.

"Oh, yeah," he said, taking a breather from sucking my cock. "You're doing fine, buddy. Better than fine. That's fuckin' great. Keep it up, dude."

"You too," I said.

"Don't worry, man," he said. "I intend to."

And back to it he went, with me following suit. I was getting the hang of it. Yum yum. I resumed sucking his uncircumcised prick, loving the feel of it. I could see why he was digging mine in his mouth so much; it did feel extra special, like it was built to be sucked. His cock seemed perfect for my mouth. Soon I was able to get all of it into my mouth and bob up and down on him without gagging at all.

The two of us enjoyed this position for quite some time, feasting on each other's cocks for at least a good 10 or 15 minutes. Each time one of us felt close to coming we would pull our cock out of the other's mouth and stick our fingers in instead. I didn't want to lose my load that quickly, but I must say that I felt like I was a kid jerking off for the first time, when you would come if you just touched yourself. Marcus brought me to the edge so many times that I wasn't sure if I was going to be able to hold off for much longer.

"You gotta stop that," I told him. "I can't take any more of it. It's too damn hot."

He laughed. "I didn't think I'd ever hear myself saying this," he said, "but I fucking love the taste of your cock in my mouth, dude."

"I like it too," I told him.

"Good. Can I try something else on you?"

"What?"

"Lie on your stomach, OK?"

I did what he said, and he immediately straddled my body, with his cock dangling down on the small of my back. He rubbed it around a couple of times, and I could tell he was leaking major precome, because it slid around very easily. Then he started to massage my shoulders and back. I must say, he gave one hell of a massage. His fingers bore into my back and shoulders, and the feeling was awesome. He moved down my body, giving ample time to my spine and the spot right above my ass. Then he moved his body down so that he was on his knees above my legs but not sitting on them. His hands went to work on my ass, grabbing my cheeks and kneading them nice and good. He pushed up them, then pulled down on them, and in the process pushed my crotch into the bed, which sent tiny little jolts through my cock. And then, before I knew what hit me, I felt my ass cheeks being spread and something wet and warm slide into my crack.

"Hey!" I said. "What's—"

And then it hit me: the pleasure. The absolute, sheer pleasure of it. I knew then that it was his tongue. My buddy was going to lick my asshole.

"You don't like it?" he said, stopping.

"No, don't stop, man. I was just surprised. Where did you learn that?"

"I saw in it on *Queer as Folk.* You like it?"

"Dude, I love it."

And that's when I had my ass eaten for the first time. Marcus licked my crack back and forth, his tongue getting closer to my asshole with each sliding of his tongue, and I instinctively lifted my ass a little bit higher for him to get to his goal. When I felt the tip of his tongue meet my hole for the first time, I grabbed hold of my pillow and moaned, "Oh yeah, dude!"

Marcus went to work immediately following that, pressing his tongue against my anus and sliding it around. I wondered what it tasted like. You have to worry about those things. But he didn't seem to mind at all, as he delectably slobbered over my hole.

"Dude," I said, "that is s-o-o fucking great. I can't even tell you how good it feels."

Then there was a loud *slap,* and a burning sensation of pain shot through my body and straight to my cock.

"Ouch!" I yelled. "You fuckin' slapped me!"

"Sorry," he said. "You just taste so good, and I got so turned-on."

I let him slide on that one. The truth was that I had actually liked that as well. The combination of pleasure and pain was extremely hot, and as Marcus dived back in to feast on my hole, I suddenly had the overwhelming desire to know what it felt like to have his cock in my ass. And that's just what I told him.

"Marcus, if you don't put your cock in me like this minute, I'm gonna scream."

The words shocked both of us, but he didn't say a word. He quickly got off me and turned himself so that he was between my legs, looking down on me. He grabbed my feet and hoisted them up onto his shoulders, his gaze locked on mine. He reached down, grabbed his pole, and placed the head right against my opening.

"You sure?" he said.

"Just do it!" I ordered, and I felt my canal being ripped open by the weight of him as he pressed into me. I gritted my teeth, hoping the pain would subside quickly.

"You OK, man?" he said, stopping about halfway inside of me.

"Just stay there for a minute."

"I'll stop."

"No! Don't. I want this. Hang on." I looked up into his eyes, and the concern there touched me. I realized I could trust Marcus more than anyone else, and it was then that I began to relax. "OK, try it again."

This time as Marcus pressed into me, I actually welcomed the sensation. "Yeah…oh…there we go. Keep going."

So he pressed forward again, and I felt his head slide right up into me. I really felt every inch of his cock as it forced its way toward its destination, and when he crushed his pubes against my ass, I reached up and pulled his face down onto mine.

We kissed for what was, surprisingly, the first time, and I couldn't believe we hadn't done it before. Our lips pressed against each other passionately, and at the same time we opened our mouths to each other's exploration. As Marcus's cock was lodged inside me, we licked each other's lips, sucked on each other's teeth, bit each other's lips. It was the hottest kiss I had ever known. His mouth tasted awesome, the scent of beer lingering from the party.

He started fucking me slowly at first, making sure I was going to be OK, then sped up as our kissing got hotter and hotter. I reached up and tugged on his hairy nipples, pulling the nubs toward me as he moaned into my mouth. I felt blood pulsing through every one of the veins in my body when he pushed into me, then pulled out, then pushed right back in. The friction of his cock in my chute was tearing me up, and I loved every single fucking minute of it.

"Is that OK?" he said from above.

"It's great! Keep it coming! Oh yeah, keep fucking me like that. Come on, harder, man, I really love it! Oh yeah!"

"I love it too," he moaned. "Your ass is super-tight, dude. It's the hottest cherry I've ever taken. Mmm, yeah! So hot and tight! I love it inside you."

"Yeah. Fuck yeah. Oh, man, you're good!"

His body rocked back and forth as he bucked against my ass. I felt like a steer must feel at a rodeo, being ridden so hard like that. As I stared up at my studly roommate, I saw the sweat running down his face. As he slammed his cock home inside me, a drop fell directly onto my lips, and I lapped it up with my tongue. He went wild.

"That's it, man!" he groaned. "I can't hold it back any longer, dude! I'm gonna come!"

He started to pull out, but I would have none of that. "In me!" I shouted.

"Oh yeah!" he cried, and I could feel his cock expand and throb inside me as I felt my shitter being filled with his hot juice, flooding my bowels. The whole time, Marcus whimpered with passion, his moans reduced to short little chirps of "Oh! Yeah! Fuck! Yeah! Oh! Oh!" and then one long "Ohhh" as he blasted his final spurt into my ass.

That did it. The next thing I knew, my cock—without me even having touched it at all—started jerking as a steady, steamy stream of come leaped from my slit and landed on my chin. The next blast hit my neck.

"Oh, *yes*," I growled, my head jerking from side to side as my climax ripped through my body. Marcus brought his mouth down onto mine again, and as the last few spasms shot through my cock, his tongue slid inside me and we kissed again.

As we lay there, panting against each other's sweat-covered bodies, I realized that I'd never felt happier.

"I can't believe we just did that," I said.

"Are you sorry we did?" Marcus asked, the sound of worry creeping into his voice. I stroked his back.

"Are you kidding? Dude, I wanna do it again!"

"Me too."

"So it doesn't bother you? What we just did?"

"Bother me?" he asked. "Dude, why do you think I sent that story to the house? I've wanted you since the first day we pledged together."

"You sent the story?" I said, barely concealing my shock.

"Of course it was me. I've wanted you since the first day we pledged together, and that was the only way for me to see how you would react to the idea of two guys together."

I reached down to grab my swelling cock. "Here's your answer," I said.

And as Marcus started to undo my jeans, I realized that I had an awful lot to learn about life after all.

You know, some people say fraternities are stupid. But I look back on this now and realize that I am lucky to have been part of my fraternity. If I hadn't, who knows who I would be today? I certainly never would have met Marcus.

Thank God for the frathouse blues.

Butt Initiation

Jay Starre

The resounding smacks of the ping-pong paddles echoed in the fraternity house basement. Even though my naked ass was one of the three getting spanked with those hard, flat paddles, I managed to push the exciting pain away for a moment to glance over at the other two dudes in the same predicament. I could see right between the wide-spread cracks of both Dean and Tommy's butts. In the glaring light I could even see their small, snug assholes. What amazed, and titillated me, was the fact that every time those paddles would land, Dean and Tommy's assholes would gape and spasm in little erotic convulsions.

I flushed all over with embarrassment, and secret pleasure, as I realized my own asshole was doing the exact same thing. Every time that paddle whacked against my squirming butt cheeks, I felt my asshole twitching with sympathetic eroticism through the sharp pain. And my dick was hard as a rock.

"Don't forget, pledges, the first to say no is out of here. Only two of you are going to be accepted into Psi Alpha Sinfonia. If you can't take a little spanking, you're gone!" Terry, the short but powerfully built dark-haired senior, was standing to the side as he observed and supervised the initiation. I could see a big bulge in the front of his jeans. He obviously had a hard-on too.

"And if none of you pukes gives in—" Bobby huffed as he landed another blow on my bare ass, "—then we just move on to the next step in your initiation until someone finally walks out of here."

Bobby and Grant were paddling us, taking turns between the

three of us without any apparent pattern. We never knew when the next blow would land. My fellow pledges were sprawled over an old ratty couch against one wall, and I was slightly to the side and behind them, bent over a workout bench. We were totally naked, having been ordered to strip the moment we had arrived in the basement half an hour earlier. Our blindfolds had been removed only after we had been bent over in our positions and the first paddle had landed on our unsuspecting butts.

I had no idea what the other two were thinking. We weren't allowed to say anything. But I was certain of my own thoughts and feelings. Every time that paddle whacked against my ass, a thrilling sensation rushed through my entire body. The pain had almost immediately become wracking, intense pleasure. The humiliation of being bent over naked in front of the older seniors had just as quickly mutated to a sexual exhibitionism that had me spreading my thighs wider and arching my back in a subtle but no doubt unmistakable signal to the others. My hard dick did not go unnoticed.

"Jay looks like he won't be the first to say no," Bobby laughed behind me. Apparently, he had noted my excitement.

"The only thing that'll disappoint that slut is if we don't give him any dick," Grant joined his friends in laughter.

I didn't care. I wanted to be a member of Psi Alpha Sinfonia, and this initiation so far was no big deal. The fact that I was loving it was merely the icing on the cake. Every time that paddle fell, I lurched and moaned between clenched teeth. I stared ahead at my friend's quivering ass cheeks with increasing lust as they became flushed and pink under the constant paddling. I could not stop staring at their pouting assholes. My dick was in a constant state of agitation, leaping and leaking continually. I could not recall ever having been so sexually excited. This was a new side to myself I had never even suspected existed.

Butt Initiation

Wham! Slap! Smack! The dark-green paddle landed directly on Dean's squirming white ass, then on Tommy's chunkier can. Pale flesh grew pinker. My own ass burned with pleasurable pain. The hiss of Bobby and Grant's breathing was loud in the silence. Their biceps bulged as they raised and dropped their bare arms in a steady rhythm. The room began to reek of sweat—and a definite sexual odor began to pervade the close air.

But all good things must come to an end. Suddenly the paddles were flung aside. What was coming next? My ass felt as if it was glowing, heat emanating from it in waves of painful pleasure. I was breathing hard and trying to gather my thoughts. I had little time for that.

"OK, no one wants to call it quits?" Terry asked. He was apparently the ringleader. He outweighed us all, packed with muscles as he was.

We said nothing. I prayed one of the others would give in, but not before I learned what else the frat boys had planned for us. I immediately found out.

"Bobby, you stick your dick in Dean's sweet mouth. And Grant, you can fuck that big hot ass of Tommy's."

Clothes were flying in every direction as the three seniors stripped with laughing alacrity. My eyes grew wide as I saw dicks appearing and balls and asses and muscles everywhere. My ass was still burning up, and I was slightly disappointed to be left out of the action for the moment, but then things heated up quickly. All three seniors wrapped their hard-ons in condoms, then Bobby shoved a big, juicy purple cock between Dean's gaping lips. It was unbelievable! And at the same time Grant was kneeling down behind Tommy and shoving his hard cock up between Tommy's flushed, spanked ass cheeks. I stared with gawking awe as a long, stiff, lubed boner penetrated Tommy's pouting sphincter.

Neither Dean nor Tommy uttered a word, as we had been warned to keep our mouths shut unless, of course, a fat pecker was filling it. I was shaking, naked, and bent over, imagining my own butt hole and mouth being stuffed with hard bone as I watched the scene unfold.

Dean and Bobby were, coincidentally, redheaded and built similarly. Dean's pursed lips gaped and slurped, and his eyes stared upward at Bobby's big naked chest. Bobby's purple meat slid in and out of Dean's mouth with steady, wet vigor. Bobby was grinning and red-faced, no doubt loving Dean's gurgling throat around his dick.

Meanwhile, Grant was impaling Tommy's plump can with his 10-incher. They were so close to me, I could actually see the lips of Tommy's hole parting and distending as Grant's dick rode in and out of it. Grant was tall and lean, his long arms holding Tommy's wide shoulders as he thrust his hips rapidly back and forth. Tommy's chunky build squirmed and twisted sexily under the anal assault, his blond head thrown back, his mouth open, and his eyes closed. My own asshole clamped in sympathy. What would that big dick feel like up there?

Terry was naked, pumping his own hard bone. He was one huge slab of muscle. Suddenly he barked out a command. "Put on new condoms and change positions!"

I don't know if they had rehearsed the scene beforehand or just done the same thing to numerous other young pledges. At any rate, they had it down. Condoms were discarded in a pile on the floor, and new ones wrapped hard dicks. Then Grant was shoving his dick down Tommy's gaping gullet, the dick he'd just had up Tommy's own ass. And Tommy took it!

But Dean was having a more difficult time. His bright blue eyes were nearly bulging out of his head, and he was biting his lip as Bobby began to poke his fat rod up Dean's no-doubt tight asshole. You could see the redheaded 19-year-old holding back a shout as that hard pole began to slide up his fuck tunnel. The big thing disappeared as Bobby buried it to the root. Dean's entire body was flushed pink and he was trembling like a leaf.

"I think it's my turn," Terry grinned, his hand slowly riding up and down his own fat erection.

I imagined, and hoped, it was my turn too. But it was not to be—not just yet. Terry strutted over to Tommy and immediately shoved his hard boner right up Tommy's lubed, stretched butt hole. Tommy gurgled around the dick in his mouth but did not give in. He took it.

But what happened next dumbfounded me. Terry abruptly pulled out of Tommy's butt hole, as if it was merely a prelude to what he had planned next. Then he moved over to Dean, who was still on his hands and knees with a dick up his butt. With a wild grin on his handsome face, Terry nodded to Bobby and they both acted in unison. Arms bulging, one dude in front and one behind, they lifted Dean right off the carpet between them. Bobby's dick was still up Dean's ass from behind. Then Terry shoved his own hard dick between Dean's legs from in front. Dean was staring down at me as he felt a second dick drive up his ass.

The look of shock in his eyes sent shivers down my spine. But there was also a look of dreamy disbelief there. Dean was taking it—and liking it! I was absolutely stunned.

The two men drilled Dean between them. I glanced over at Tommy, who was watching the action from the corners of his eyes. His mouth was full of dick, and his ass was sweaty and pink from the earlier spanking. His body was quivering all over. He had to realize what was coming.

Tommy and I both watched Dean's double fuck with apprehensive wonder. Dean's red hair fell over his forehead, dripping sweat. His body was nearly limp, dangling between the big muscles of the two seniors fucking him. He managed not to say a word, a formidable feat. The squishy sound of dicks sliding in and out of lubed asshole was loud and lewd.

Then Dean reared up abruptly. His blue eyes gaped open. His mouth was a silent *oh*. He bit back a scream as his entire body convulsed. He was coming!

That was the most bizarre development yet! Dean was shooting his load with two dicks up his ass at once! I glanced at Tommy. He was shaking. He knew it was going to be his turn. And then Dean was being tossed aside like a used tissue. His exhausted fucked body collapsed on the ratty couch where he lay glassy-eyed and watching. He had managed to keep his mouth shut so far. He would probably make it into Psi Alpha Sinfonia.

And now Tommy was getting tested. His pale-gray eyes followed the two big seniors as they approached him, their slick hard dicks jutting out in front of them. They had quickly replaced the used condoms with new ones and were ready for action. There was no question what their intentions were. Tommy squirmed and twisted under their hands as they lifted his butt and began to take turns plowing it with their hard dicks. He managed to take that, even though each thrust was deep and swift. But hot and deep as that was, it was only a prelude to what Tommy knew was coming.

I watched, my dick still dripping, and my asshole twitching. My ass flamed red and my body shook. Would Tommy take it? Would I?

Then they were turning the plump Tommy over, onto his back and lifting his thighs, spreading them apart and pushing them back. His shoulders were on the couch, with the exhausted Dean right beside him. His mouth was still full of Grant's cock. Terry and Bobby laughed loudly. Bobby straddled Tommy's crotch and faced Terry. He pointed his dick downward and began to insert it into Tommy's stretched, lubed ass pit. I saw it all, my own asshole quivering.

Then Terry added his own dick from in front. I could see both big bones slowly riding inside Terry's pouting hole. It was amazing.

Suddenly there was a shout. Tommy had spit out Grant's dick. Was he going to protest? Would he beg them to stop?

"*Fuck my sweet ass!*"

Tommy's shriek took us all by surprise. Laughter filled the air; even I emitted a surprised giggle. Tommy wanted them to fuck him! He wanted both dicks up his hungry ass!

"You're out of here! You were told to keep your mouth shut!" Terry said through his own laughter.

And that was it. They shoved Tommy aside, naked and used. He stumbled to his feet and sheepishly grabbed his clothing, heading for the stairs.

"If you ever want to enter another fraternity, you won't tell anyone about this!" Terry warned the departing Tommy.

I was aching with disappointment. I was in; Tommy had caved. But that would mean I wasn't going to get any dick!

Or did it?

The leering seniors were descending upon me. Three of them—three big, juicy dicks. Where would they put them? I opened my mouth and stuck out my tongue, spread my thighs, and raised my butt, silently offering what I had. The images of the past hour flooded through my head and body. My lips tasted dick already, my asshole quivered with sexual longing. Fuck me, I almost cried out. Almost.

My patience was rewarded. Dick—big, fat, and hard—invaded me. My orifices were stuffed. I was porked. I was fucked.

I was in Psi Alpha Sinfonia.

Captured

William Holden

It had been two days since the capture. Two days in which I have had to listen to the star of the football team and president of Alpha Alpha Alpha fraternity call me such names as "little faggot" and "dead cocksucker," just to mention a few.

We were alone most of the time except when the president of Gamma Gamma Gamma came by for a brief visit to see how our prisoner was doing. I was proud that I was given the chance to prove myself worthy of this fraternity. It was one of the most prestigious fraternities on campus, and I was not about to mess this up. Sure, the other members pitched in, helped me arrange the kidnapping, and got him to where he sat today, but I was the one who had made livable spaces out of a couple of rooms in the basement of the house. I was told that he would need to be watched 24-7—no excuses.

So I was left alone with him—this guy who stood at 6 foot 3 and weighed in at 280 pounds. This frat stud whom I was now watching. Me, at 5 foot 7 and a mere 145 pounds. That alone should have been enough to piss him off, but to add to his misery, he was being held by a gay student. That was too much for his ego to accept.

I looked up at the clock in my small room. "Time for dinner," I mumbled to myself. I slid off my bed and walked into the makeshift kitchen. I placed the leftover meatloaf and potatoes in the microwave and pushed the auto-heat button. Tony must have heard the movement in the kitchen. He broke his silence.

"Hey, queer boy!" Tony yelled from his room. "That food better be for me. Or I'll—"

"Or you'll what?" I opened up the door and asked. "Come on, Tony, what will you do?" I loved the power I had over him. It was my time to turn the tables and give back a little of what I and the other gay students around campus had endured over the last year.

He sat in his chair, looking at me with his large brown eyes. His chiseled cheekbones and squared off chin were now overcast with two days of stubble. He looked at me but kept quiet. He was my prisoner and he knew it. His legs were in shackles that only allowed for limited movement. A heavy length of retractable chain connected the shackles to a large eye hook drilled into the floorboards of his room. His wrists were bound in a similar fashion, connected to the eye hook by the same pulley system. He was able to move from the chair to his bed and over to the toilet, but that was as much movement or activity that I allowed him.

"Just give me a few minutes and I'll have your dinner ready."

I shut the door and returned to the kitchen. As I prepared a plate for him I remembered back to the first time I had tried to feed him. The retractable chain didn't allow for much arm movement, so I had to feed him myself. Every time I placed the fork up to his mouth, he would take the food in and then spit it out on my face. That night I had my doubts about this plan—I didn't know if I could actually go through with it. But things did get better. There were times, in fact, when I thought he actually enjoyed being treated like this. One night in particular when I was feeding him, I happened to look down at his crotch and noticed a large bulge in his jeans, as if he was getting off on being hand-fed. Before that I had never thought of Tony in a sexual way. Anger and frustration were the only things that came to mind. But after seeing his swollen crotch, I lay awake that night jerking off over the thought of what was inside his pants.

"Sorry it took so long." I said as I walked back into the room and sat on the edge of his bed, next to where he sat in the chair. "It's leftovers again. Matt hasn't been by to pick up the grocery list."

"I don't have much of a choice now, do I?" Tony barked with a little less bite than normal. "Let's just get this over with. I hate being fed like a baby." He sat still as I brought the first fork of meatloaf to his mouth. He took it quickly, swallowed, and waited for more. We finished with dinner without any hassles or words spoken. As I was getting up to leave, Tony asked me a question.

"Adam, you've had me tied up like this for two days now." He paused, and a brief expression of embarrassment flashed across his face. "I'm really starting to stink. Do you think you could unlock these chains and let me at least take a bath in the tub?" He stopped, then added quickly, "I promise I won't give you any grief." His eyes told a different story.

"Tony." I sat the tray down on the floor and walked back over to him. "I can't do that. We both know you could snap me like a twig with one hand." My eyes moved over his sculpted arms, wondering just how strong he really was. "I can't take that chance. You're just going to have to stay that way until the game is over this weekend."

"That's another three days." Tony replied. "Come on, man, help me out a little here."

"I'm sorry. I have my instructions from the fraternity. Under no circumstance are you to be untied." I turned around and walked out, shutting the door behind me.

"Fuck!" Tony's voice echoed into the next room. "Adam, get your ass back in here and face me like a man!" I could hear him pulling on the chains. "Come on, you pussy, get me out of these things. You're a dead man. You hear me? A dead man!" His voice had started to tremble, whether from anger or frustration I couldn't tell, but there was no way I was letting him loose. I walked back to my room and shut the door to help drown out his voice. I left him there, alone the rest of the night.

By the middle of the next day the heat had raised the temperature in our space by 20 degrees. The air was thick and stagnant. At lunch I had brought in a fan to help circulate the air in Tony's room. He had been quiet all morning. Breakfast was served and eaten in complete silence.

"I'm sorry for the way I acted last night," Tony finally spoke. His voice had changed. His tone was soft, almost apologetic. "I'm just getting a little frustrated. I understand why you are doing this, and actually I'm pretty impressed that you were able to pull it off." He paused and looked up at me. His eyes, unlike yesterday, seemed to be sincere.

"Tony...I thought about the bath situation last night." My voice began to tremble as I thought about what I was getting ready to suggest. "You're not going to like what I'm about to say, but the only way I see being able to let you bathe is if we leave the chains on and you sit in the bathtub and let me wash your body." My face felt flushed as I spoke those last words.

"What!" Tony's voice rose through the air. "Are you out of your mind? There's no way in hell that I'm going to let you bathe me. I'd rather rot in these clothes than be touched..." He paused. "I get it." He voice was much calmer. "This is your way of getting your rocks off, isn't it? Seeing me naked and being able to touch me—that's what this is about. You fags are all the same. You'd give anything to get a chance to get me naked. Well, you can forget it."

"That's not what this is about," I replied angrily. "Just because I'm gay doesn't mean that I want to have sex or get naked with every man. I couldn't give two shits about your body." That was a lie. I couldn't help myself: His body was enough to make anyone look twice. He worked out every day. The tight shirts he wore around campus showed the ripples in his abs. As I stood there I wondered if he had a hairy chest. If he did, was the hair soft and silky, or coarse? Everyone on campus heard stories about his sexual escapades. Was he well-endowed, or did he try to make up for a small dick with his attitude? As I walked to the door I added, "Fine, have it your way. Sit there then for the next few days, smelling yourself sweat." I walked out, leaving him to his own thoughts and me to mine.

The pizza was delivered on time as promised by the company, by this cute Hispanic kid no older than 24. I had answered the door in a pair of boxers and a tank top. His eyes immediately took to my body, checking out all he could through my clothes. His eyes stopped briefly at my chest. I raised one of my hands and ran my fingers through my hair to expose my dark, hairy armpits. He licked his lips as he eyed what I was able to offer him. I was tempted to invite him in for his tip—my growing desire for Tony had gotten the best of me. Wanting to touch Tony's body, to caress his sculpted muscles, I was as sexually frustrated as I had ever been. I knew deep inside that this kid, no matter how horny I was, would not be able to satisfy my increasing desire for Tony. I paid him his money and left him standing on the doorstep as I proceeded to take Tony his dinner. I took a deep breath and tried to hide my needs before entering his room.

I sat the tray down in his lap and started to leave when he spoke.

"Adam, don't leave. I want to talk to you." He grabbed a slice of pizza and tried to bring it to his mouth without any help from me. The pulley system that attached his cuffs to the chain made his movements awkward and slow, but with a little effort he was able to manage that small task.

"Why, so you can verbally abuse me again?" I responded sharply as I turned to face him. "I don't think so. Just eat your dinner, I'll be back later to get the tray."

"Wait, please." His words slurred with the pizza in his mouth. "I can't stay like this any longer. I need a shower."

"We've been over this one before." I was becoming more irritated by the minute. "I'm not unlocking the chains. I've—"

Tony cut me off. "I know," he said abruptly. "I don't like this at all, but if the only way I can get cleaned is to have you bathe me, then I have no choice." He lowered his head and stared at his plate, then looked me directly in my eyes. "After dinner…" He paused as if unsure of his own words. "After dinner, if you could come back in with some soap and clean clothes…" his words failed him. I could tell he was uncomfortable with the idea and just couldn't bring himself to finish the sentence.

"I'll be back in a little bit, then." I left.

The whole idea of bathing him didn't hit me at first, but when it did, it hit me with such force, my heart rate immediately picked up speed. I became nervous with anticipation. I would finally get to see what all of Tony's teammates got to see regularly and with no appreciation. "If only I had a camera," I mumbled to an empty room. "To have a photograph of the star football player, sitting naked in a tub, being bathed by another guy." Hearing those words spoken brought a smile to my face and the start of an erection in my pants.

I came back into the room, with my arms full of bathing items and a clean set of clothes. Tony watched quietly as I placed the items near the tub and brought his clothes over to the bed. I could sense his apprehension about what was about to happen.

"Are you ready?" My voice seemed to fill the entire room. I knelt down in front of him and began unlacing his tennis shoes.

His legs trembled with nerves as I removed his shoes. He jumped slightly as he felt my hand move up his pant leg to remove his sock. He sat still as I removed the second one. His feet were large, with short, stubby toes, one of which appeared crooked, probably from a sports injury. Each toe had a small patch of hair on it. His toenails were perfectly trimmed as if they had been professionally attended to.

Tony's voice cracked as he spoke. "How are you going to get my clothes off without undoing these cuffs and chains?"

His voice came from miles away. My mind had been lost in admiring his feet and looking at the trail of fine dark hair from his legs, which stuck out from underneath his pants. Something in my thoughts brought me back. I looked up at him and realized what he had asked. "With these," I said, in a voice as distant to me as his was. I held up a pair of scissors. "We're going to have to cut the clothes off of you." I noticed the expression on his face change, and then added, "Don't worry, I'm not going to cut you. It's the only way we can do this." I stood up, brought the scissors to the waistband of his shirt, and began to cut.

His shirt was damp from sweat. With each slice of the blades I exposed a little bit more of his body. My hand brushed up against his stomach and I could feel the ripples of his abs, which were covered in a soft blanket of hair. His nerves were getting the best of him; his skin became damp as I continued my cuts. His hair grew thicker as I reached the area in the center of his chest. I could feel his heart racing. His heavy breath brushed across my face as I made my final cut at the neckline.

Tony sat motionless without a word. I spread his shirt open and proceeded to cut out the shoulders and sleeves to remove the shirt. I could begin to see the edges of his dark brown nipples. His tits were erect. I wanted to place my mouth over one and suck on it. I forced myself to concentrate on the cutting instead of his chest. I slowly removed the remains of his shirt and exposed his body to me. The veins in his arms and chest were well-defined as the blood pumped through them. Dark, wet patches of hair stuck out from his armpits.

Without a word I began cutting the edge of his pant legs. His calf and thigh muscles were perfectly sculpted, and covered the same dark hair that I had seen sticking out of his pant legs. I finished the final cut at his waistband on one side and began making the same cuts on the other. Within a matter of seconds his jeans were in half. I went to remove the front half when Tony spoke.

"Wait, please." His voice was that of a small child. He was shaking and almost ashamed. As if the child in him had been caught doing something wrong. "I—" He paused. Looked at me and started again. "I don't think I can do this."

"Tony." I spoke with irritation, mostly from the sexual excitement I was getting from his body. I didn't want this to stop, not yet. "I'm almost done cutting. Why stop now?"

"I don't want…" He stopped again and looked down at his lap. His face became flushed as he looked at me. "I don't want you to think that I'm enjoying this, but I've got a hard-on." His eyes left mine as he spoke those words. "I'm not a fag."

"I never said you were. It's a natural thing. You shouldn't be embarrassed by it. Besides, you mean to tell me that you've never gotten a hard-on while in the shower with your teammates?"

"Well, yeah, but that's different." He turned to face me again. "You're in the shower, washing and touching yourself— sometimes you get turned on by your own touch. It's not because they're touching me."

"Don't worry. I've seen hard dicks before. I'm sure yours is no different." I reached up once again and removed the front half of his pants. He wore a pair of forest-green boxers. The fly didn't have any buttons and stood slightly open from the bulge of his cock. I could see the darkness of his coarse pubic hair below. My hands began to shake for the first time as I began cutting away his boxers. His cock twitched beneath the material each time I brought the scissors together. His thick six-inch cock dangled in front of me as I pulled away its cover. His hairless balls hung heavily off the edge of the chair. The muscles in his cock convulsed, his cock bobbed up and down, and a small drop of pre-come appeared on the head.

"Come on," Tony said anxiously. "Let's get this over with."

I moved away reluctantly to allow Tony to stand up. The chains rattled against one another as he stood. "Hang on, let me get the tub filled," I said, turning around on my knees before standing so Tony would not see the outline of my nine inches pushing against my jeans. As I stood, I could feel the dampness of my own excitement pulling its way through the blond hairs of my crotch.

The sound of the water echoed in my ears as I sat on the edge of the tub. I wanted to look over at Tony standing naked behind me, but I forced myself to watch the water level rise instead. The chains scraped against the concrete floors as Tony moved over next to me. I could feel the heat of his body. His cock swaying between his legs was only inches from my face when he stopped. I swallowed hard to control my urge. I moved out of the way so he could step into the tub and sink his body into the warm water.

"Oh, God, that feels good." He moaned and threw his head back as the water engulfed him. "You have no idea how good this feels." He sat there with his eyes closed as I took the sponge and dipped it in the water.

I mumbled to myself. My voice had seemed to disappear

again. I squeezed the sponge out and let the water run over his head, wetting his hair. I placed a small amount of shampoo in my hand and gently rubbed it in. A soft moan escaped his lips as I massaged his scalp. I looked down and watched as the soap suds fell from my hands and landed on the head of his cock that was sticking out of the water. They slid down his shaft and formed whitecaps in the water, as if surrounding a small deserted island.

"Can you lift your arms up?" I asked as I finished rinsing his hair.

He looked at me questioningly, then raised his arms up as high as the chains would allow. The damp, sweaty odor of his armpits drifted to my nose. I inhaled quietly so he wouldn't notice. My cock responded to his scent and began to throb. The bar of soap lathered quickly in the thick hair. I rubbed the suds up and down his armpits, enjoying the feel of his damp hair against my hand. Reaching down between his legs, I cupped a handful of water to rinse him. I moved my hands down to his chest. My heart was racing. I tried to control my desire but couldn't. As I washed his chest I allowed my fingers to graze over each of his nipples. He didn't try to stop me. Without thinking I rolled one of his nipples between my fingers. He gasped. His body shook, but still he didn't resist.

My hand slid down his chest to his stomach. The touch must have been unexpected. Tony let out another moan. He leaned back against the tub and arched his back. His cock followed his movement and rested against his stomach. As I reached closer to the head of his cock, I paused. My hand trembled. I looked over at him. He was looking directly at me. A small smile of pleasure formed at his mouth.

"Don't stop now." I'm so horny I can't stand it." He reached up and grabbed my arm. "I can't help myself. You're driving me crazy. I've never felt anything like this before." He leaned back up and brought his face up to mine. Our eyes locked on one another. Neither of us could look away. Before I knew what was happening, he brought his lips up to mine. The first touch was electrifying, sending shivers throughout my body. My heart ached as our mouths opened to receive each other's tongue.

The inside of his mouth was warm. His tongue felt like a flame burning inside of me. I don't think I was breathing; all I could feel or hear was the pounding of my heart. Tony pulled me closer to him. He kept pulling our bodies closer together until I was lying in the bathwater with him, my clothes quickly soaking up the water. He tried to put his arms around me, but the chains were in the way. We continued to kiss deeply as if we were both experiencing this act for the first time.

Our cocks pushed against one another: his out and free, mine still confined to the tightness of my pants. I pushed myself back up, then sat on his crotch. I lifted the wet shirt up and over my head. My hairless chest glistened in the soft light of the room. His chest hair stuck to his skin except for the hairs under the water level. They seemed to float carelessly in the water. Tony moved his hand to unfasten my jeans, but again the chains had blocked his reach.

"Fuck!" Tony muttered. "These fucking chains keep getting in the way. Can't you do something about these?"

Without responding I reached into my pocket and brought out the key to his cuffs. Quickly I moved from wrist to wrist and ankle to ankle, unlocking his constraints. We shifted our bodies slightly from side to side as I removed the chains. They rattled as they hit the floor. Suddenly I realized what I had done. I regretted letting him loose; he was going to get out. He sat up quickly. But instead of pushing me aside to escape, he kissed me again, this time more passionately than the first. He dug his fingers into my back as he lowered his mouth to my nipple. He sucked on it

harder and harder as it became erect in his mouth. I pulled him
off me and pushed him back against the tub. His chest and stomach were moving rapidly from his breathing. I stood up over him
and unzipped my pants. They stuck to my body as I tried to pull
them off. My underwear went with them. His eyes got large as he
saw the size of my cock. He looked down at his, then back up at
mine. There was no comparison.

"Let me fuck you?" He gasped as I knelt in front of him. I
think he was afraid I was going to fuck him with my big cock.
"Please, I want it so bad."

"Come here first," I demanded, as I pulled him back up to a
sitting position. I stroked my cock in front of his face, squeezing
the head with each forward movement, to release more precome.

He looked up at me, his eyes glazed and eager. He looked back
down at my nine inches. His lips quivered as they parted. His
tongue came out and touched the tip of my cock. The heat of his
mouth was more intense than before. He parted his mouth further and moved in closer. The head of my dick slowly disappeared into his mouth. I could tell he wasn't sure what to do at
first, but soon he was using his tongue to circle the head.

"Oh, yeah," I moaned. "Your mouth feels so fucking good. Can
you take a little more?"

Without making a sound he slid his mouth farther down my
shaft. I watched with raw desire as the star of the football team
took my meat into his mouth. I didn't have to ask for anything
else. It seemed to come almost instinctively to him now. Slowly he
took another inch into his mouth, each time pausing to get used
to the size. His tongue continued to move over the pulsing veins
as my cock went deeper into his throat. He gagged briefly but
never once stopped me from going deeper.

Tony's nose was buried in my damp pubic hair. He tried to go deeper, but there wasn't any of it left. He took a deep breath through his nose, inhaling my sweat. I pulled my cock out of his mouth and brushed the precome on his cheeks. He panted heavily.

I reached behind me and grabbed his cock. He jumped from my touch. His cock was hot. I could feel the blood running through its swollen veins. I positioned myself over his crotch and slowly lowered myself onto him. I stopped just as the head of his cock touched the entrance to my tight hole.

"Damn it!" His voice rose to a feverish pitch. "Don't stop now! Fuck. You're driving me crazy."

I wiggled my ass to spread his precome around. "You've got a hot little cock, Tony." I smiled at him as I pushed the head of his cock inside. "Oh yeah!" My smile grew as I felt his cock slide deeper into my ass. "Damn, you're so thick!"

"Oh man! Oh shit!" He kept repeating. "Your ass is so tight. Oh yeah, tighten those muscles. Oh fuck!"

"Yeah, there we go. That's it. Let my ass milk your cock." I began riding his cock up and down, deeper and deeper. Before I realized what was happening Tony had his hand around my cock, holding onto it like the reins of a horse. He began stroking it with the same motion and rhythm as I was riding him. The water splashed over our bodies and over the side of the tub.

"Son-of-a-bitch!" Tony spoke each syllable between breaths. "I can feel the come building. My balls are on fire!" He forced himself to a sitting position and buried his tongue into my mouth. We kissed violently, our teeth hitting against one another. I could feel something building inside of Tony's chest. It was faint at first, but each time I forced his cock inside of me, the pressure rose.

He began to moan inside of my mouth. The vibrations of his

voice bounced against my throat. I tried to pull our mouths apart, but he pushed me back to him. The pressure from Tony's chest was making it hard for me to breathe. My heart was beating in my head. I felt dizzy as Tony began to lose all control.

He lifted our bodies up off the floor of the tub with the use of one hand, his other hand still stroking my cock. He fucked me hard, thrusting his hips up and down, slapping my ass with his thighs. His moan became louder and more forceful in my mouth as he reached the point of no return.

My breath was cut off as his voice finally broke, separating our mouths. "Fuck, I'm going to…"

Before he could finish, I felt him unload his hot juice inside of my ass. He continued to fuck me, sending more and more streams of come into me. My ass was sore, there was nothing left in him to give me, but still he continued to fuck my hole.

He panted against my chest and continued to stroke my cock. The force of my orgasm sent us falling back against the tub. Wave and wave of come shot out of my cock, landing on his neck and chest. I collapsed on top of him, mixing my come with each of our sweat-soaked bodies. His arms reached around and held me close.

Saturday came before I knew it. I sat quietly in the bleachers of the football stadium, lost in my own thoughts. The game had been sold-out. Everyone anticipated the star, Tony, to send them to victory once again. I had let him go the morning after his bath. My potential brothers were not happy with my decision. I had failed them and failed my initiation into their fraternity. That afternoon as I was packing up the few things they had let me keep in the house during the capture, Tony came walking by with a few of his friends.

"Hey, I see they finally decided to dump the faggot!" Tony yelled to me. His teammates laughed and patted him on his back. They were so proud of their stud. But that was OK, because I knew deep down inside that I was the best fuck Tony would ever have. He'll be back for more.

The Cigar Race

Terje Anderssen

The sun was *just* over my head. Its heat was so strong, I thought I'd surely burn myself if I reached up for it. I looked to my right, where the Blue River's shallow ripples sparkled in the bright light. It didn't really seem to be flowing, but just resting here among the grassy slopes of prairie. Across the river, which was barely a river and not blue at all, a steep embankment rose about 20 feet above the water. At its edge, two old cottonwoods held on to the sandy cliff with twisted and tangled roots exposed by the river's dark gouge in the hillside. Their shiny leaves tipped and turned in the breeze like dangling discs of isinglass. Another cottonwood sat helplessly horizontal about 20 feet below the others at the edge of the water, having tumbled when the world was eaten out from under it.

I turned my head back in the direction I was facing. Corey was standing right in front of me. His short blond hair; long, thin neck; tan, muscular back and shoulders, biceps, thighs—all of him shone in the sunlight. His body was drizzled with beads of sweat, trickling in crooked rivers through the thin golden fuzz that grew on the tight, muscled slopes of his torso. The salty liquid descended into the hollow of his lower back, then further, down into the furry crevice that divided the pale cheeks of his tightly toned butt.

I wanted to lick the sweat from his body, to slide my tongue into that crevice and drink from his little trickling rivers. I wanted to taste Corey, who was shining golden before me in the blazing sunlight. But that wasn't allowed. And neither was a boner, I reminded myself.

Todd stood in front of Corey, and Brian stood behind me. We all stood, four boys, single file, naked, burning in the hot sun on a short sandy beach at the edge of the Blue River, and we waited. To our left stood four more boys, also naked and burning in a single-file line. Across from us, about 40 feet away, two more lines stood just like us, facing our direction, waiting and sweating in the summer sun. There were 16 of us in all—16 boys, college students, all of us football players, basketball players, gymnasts, swimmers, and runners—standing in sweltering heat on the searing sand. Our bodies pressed so closely together, I could feel the sweat running down Corey's back transfer itself to my furry stomach. And I could feel Brian's thick, heavy cock slap the inside of my thigh when he shifted his weight behind me, and I knew if I got a hard-on now, it would rise between Corey's slick, wet legs and wedge itself in his ass.

But I couldn't let that happen. It was definitely not allowed, I reminded myself. In fact, I was sure it was part of the test—to prove we were men. After today, we were going to be brothers. The sight of our muscular, athletic bodies shining in the sun would not turn me on. The moist, warm skin sliding over my own, the toned muscles twitching and flexing against my own as we stood waiting, the smell of the sweat of all these jocks standing naked—none of that could turn me on. I could not be aroused by the sexuality of this situation. I could not experience the pleasure of what we were doing here. And of course, I could not stop thinking about it.

About 30 men stood around us in a semicircle. Like us, they too were waiting. Like us, they were all athletes. Unlike us, they were clothed, chatting, and laughing, and drinking beer. Unlike us, they were older. And they were in charge.

The Cigar Race

They were watching us. We had to give ourselves freely and completely to the situation. We had to immerse ourselves fully and without question in the tasks presented to us. And they were watching. We had to follow every order they gave us without allowing ourselves to enjoy it. We had to resist the sexuality of this highly sexual situation, and we had to deny the meaning of our actions. We had to prove to them and to ourselves that we too were men, that we were worthy of one another, that we could do anything together—and yet that it would mean nothing to us. If we were men, we could do this. They were watching and waiting to find out.

Todd turned his head and looked back in my direction. Our eyes met, and he smiled the way you smile at someone you are sharing an uncomfortable situation with. I gave him the same smile back. I figured he probably knew what was going through my head more than anyone right now.

"Eyes forward!" The fierce order brought everyone to full attention, though I figured it was meant for Todd. Then again, any order directed at one of us was directed at all of us.

It was Dan who shouted the order, but we had to call him *Master,* because that's who he was. He was a big, handsome guy. His straight brown hair was a couple of inches long on top, but shaved very short in the back and on the sides. His massive shoulders, chest, arms, and legs were evidence that he, like me, was a lineman on the football team. He had a boyish face with round, dimpled cheeks that were usually smiling.

I was the youngest student at the small private college we attended. And despite my 6-foot-4 frame, I had started out the year shy and intimidated by all the older guys, especially the upperclassmen.

When I first decided to pledge Kappa Theta Phi, we were all

instructed to find ourselves a pledge buddy. But I never had to, because he approached me first. I was honored—and elated. I looked up to him. I admired him. And I had a crush on him. He made me feel comfortable and safe.

But today, this event on the banks of the Blue River, the harsh sunlight, his role as Master, all of these things made him a little rougher, a lot meaner, and goddamned formidable. He was no longer the good-natured guy who looked out for me and built me up with confidence and praise. He wasn't my buddy. Not today.

There were two big brown cigars sticking out of his breast pocket. I figured he was just carrying them for effect, because I had never seen him smoke before.

"Close formation!" No one made a move at his command. I don't think we took him seriously. It seemed that we were already in close formation. Our bodies *were* touching, after all.

"Are you all fucking retards?" he shouted. "When I give an order, what do you do?"

"We obey, Master," we all said in unison. We'd had to answer that question more than once in the past week.

"Oh, *fuck,* you shitheads are *hopeless!*" he bellowed. "When I give an order, WHAT DO YOU DO?"

"WE OBEY, MASTER!" we shouted, loudly this time.

"CLOSE FORMATION!" The order was undeniable. "Get in *tight.* I don't want even a molecule of air between your pansy asses!"

We squeezed even closer together. My crotch pressed against Corey's ass and my hairy chest adhered to his shoulder blades, holding us together in a sticky bond of sweat and muscle. Brian, who was at the back of the line, hooked his fingers in my pelvis to pull himself closer to me. Brian was the freshman star of the gymnastics team. His hands were huge, his arms were strong, and his body was tight. I could feel him flexing against my skin in places I didn't even know I had muscles. I felt his pubic hairs tickle my butt as he leaned into me. His hefty cock swung between my legs, and I reflexively tightened my muscles, trapping the tip between my thighs. He gasped slightly and tightened his grip on my waist. His cock swelled suddenly. I relaxed my leg muscles to release it, but it was too late. His meaty prick rose between my thighs and planted itself defiantly at the base of my balls, causing me once again to tighten my muscles and grip his massive hard-on between my legs.

His hot breath fell onto the back of my neck as I heard him whisper, "*Fuck.*"

And there we stood, waiting. None of us knew for what, but we knew something was about to happen, and Dan was enjoying the tension he was building. I might have too, standing there with my hairy bulk pasted to Corey's smooth, slender body. The muscles of his ass twitched nervously against my crotch, as I stood there also straddling Brian's monster of a hard-on that was now wedged tightly between my legs and lifting my balls slightly from behind; all of us stood there dripping with sweat. It was a dream come true and a nightmare all at once. I fought to maintain control of my own dick, which was starting to hang a little lower at this point.

"You BOYS seem to think this is just a game!" Dan shouted as he paced back and forth in front of us.

It *was* a game, I thought, except that we all had to play. We had no choice, really, at this point. And that made it real. I focused my eyes on the glint of tiny golden hairs catching the light on the back of Corey's sun-bronzed neck, which was only inches from my face. I could feel humid musk rising from him like hot breath, and I sucked the aromatic mist deep into my lungs while trying to keep my dick, which was nestled in the crack of Corey's ass, from hanging any heavier.

Brian's pecs pressed his sweaty chest hair against my shoulder blades. I felt them quiver as his dick suddenly throbbed between my legs. I could feel every breath he took as he held his chest and stomach snugly against my backside. They were quick, nervous breaths that struck the back of my neck in short, hot bursts. He had originally hooked his fingers in my pelvis to pull himself closer to me, but now his giant hands were pressed flat against my waist and his long fingers extended downward to the edge of my curly pubic hairs.

He better get control of that thing, I thought to myself.

"DO I NEED TO EXPLAIN THE RULES TO YOU AGAIN?" Dan was shouting in Todd's ear.

"NO, SIR!" Todd shouted loudly, looking straight ahead. Brian's dick throbbed again, pushing against the perineum at the back of my balls, and I heard him suck air. I was beginning to feel nervous for him, and yet my own cock was still threatening to swell.

"WHAT did you just call me?"

"NO, *MASTER!*" Todd corrected himself.

"You just won a drink, you stupid fuck-up!" This had been part of today's ritual from the very beginning: If you did anything wrong, if you fucked up in any way, you had to take a swig of hard liquor. In a way, it made this whole thing a lot more fun. But it was also a trap, because the more you had to drink, the more likely you were to fuck up again. I'd done all right so far. Todd, on the other hand, was hurting—big time.

Each of the guys standing around us was holding a bottle of booze. There was rum, vodka, tequila, gin, a few flavors of schnapps, that licorice-tasting shit, brandy—you name it. Dan motioned to Greg, and a low moan rattled in Todd's throat. Greg was holding the bottle of Red Hot Mama Sauce. It was the worst of all—like drinking 100-proof Tabasco. Todd was going to be puking before too long.

Greg stepped forward. I watched his skeleton move beneath the cotton-white skin of his shirtless torso as he approached our line. The bones of his shoulders protruded with each step of his lanky swagger, and his dark pink nipples popped up and down with the flexing of his pecs as he swung his arms. His muscled stomach narrowed from the base of his ribs to the top of his pelvis, which extended a couple inches above the waistband of his 501s. The top button was undone, and wisps of black hair rose from his fly upward to his navel like smoke from a smoldering fire.

He came to a halt next to Todd and, with a toothy, devilish grin, handed him the bottle. "Drink up, fuck-up!" Dan demanded.

"Yes, Master!" Todd replied, and tipped the bottle back to take a drink. The veins in Todd's neck stood out, and I could imagine the pained grimace that was undoubtedly contorting his face.

Brian's dick was throbbing rhythmically now, swelling and contracting between my legs, pushing against and lifting my balls, then relaxing for an instant before its next spasm. We were sweaty enough that each contraction sent his rigid cock sliding slightly up and down the insides of my thighs. By this time he had figured out that I wasn't going to sell him out to the rest of the guys, and probably even knew that I didn't mind having his big stiff prick pulsating between my legs. And then it dawned on me that the increased motion in his cock was intentional. He was trying to get himself off before he got caught with a hard-on!

With that thought, my own dick, which was not yet hard but definitely feeling much weightier, lurched suddenly against the inside of Corey's leg. He turned his head slightly for a moment, then continued looking forward. I felt precome begin to drizzle out the end of it—and, no doubt, ooze its way down the inside of Corey's thigh. I always liked the way my dick pumped precome when it got aroused, but this really wasn't the time. At least with all this sweat dripping off us, I figured Corey didn't notice.

Dan had turned away from our line and was now yelling in the ear of a guy named Brandon who was in line across from us. I concentrated on keeping my dick from getting hard, but with Brian's big cock sliding up and down between my legs, I realized that I was in trouble.

Brian gripped my waist tighter and reached his right hand further around, burying his fingers in my pubes and just touching the base of my cock. The river was to our right, so no one could see him do this, but he had to squeeze his hand in between my leg and Corey's ass in order to reach in that far. There was no way Corey didn't notice. Corey whispered something in Todd's ear and Todd nodded his head.

Brian leaned his face forward so his lips brushed my right ear and whispered, "Vic, I need to get off, man. Help me out." He pushed his hand down further to get a better feel of my cock and then added, "Maybe you do too. Don't worry about Corey." He moved his index and middle fingers around each side of my dick and squeezed. My cock instantly flared, rising between Corey's sweat-slicked legs and spewing a jet of precome against the back of his balls.

I could have killed Brian. My dick swelled and stiffened, burrowing into the crevice between Corey's thighs, but I still fought to dispel my arousal. I lost the battle when Brian whispered one final word: "*Please…*"

The Cigar Race

Hearing him beg me to help him come, my cock became so tightly swollen, sandwiched between Corey's sweaty legs, there was no way it was going to go soft anytime soon. I was in the same predicament as Brian. I needed to get off too.

In an incredibly smooth motion, Corey rose onto his tiptoes, and Brian quickly used his two fingers to position my dick at the puckered opening of Corey's anus. Corey lowered himself again, and after a moment of exquisite resistance, my swollen prick, slick with sweat and leaking precome everywhere, popped into Corey's tight, warm tunnel. I was just slightly taller than Corey, so as he lowered himself, my fat pecker slid all the way into him and left him slightly suspended so he had to remain just a bit on his toes. I was so hard, I could have held him completely off the ground if I had to. The subtlety of their movement amazed me. None of the other guys noticed a thing.

Except Dan, who turned and walked toward us. He must have sensed the movement or heard Brian's whispering.

Suddenly, everything was different. I had my dick up Corey's ass—and with dozens of guys watching us! I was mortified, yet so turned-on, I had *no choice* but to enjoy it. I *had* to get off—and quick. Corey was going to do everything he could to help me, I realized. He began to rhythmically flex his ass muscles with a power only a champion swimmer like him could have achieved. His tight butt hole pinched the base of my cock as the muscles inside him slid his flesh along the shaft and around the head of my dick. I would be flooding his ass with a torrent of come in no time. Already I was releasing a continuous flow of precome deep inside the warm, comfortable sleeve of his ass. He tipped his head back, burying my nose in his sweaty blond hair, and I breathed him in once again.

Dan stopped a couple of feet from us. We continued to look

straight ahead, but I could see him look us up and down out of the corner of my eye. He pulled one of the fatties from his pocket and placed it in his mouth.

"You boys seem a little restless over here," he said with a sneer. As if in response, Brian's dick throbbed violently between my sweat-slicked thighs. I'm sure Corey could feel my heart pounding between his shoulder blades.

Dan stepped closer to me and leaned forward until his face was just inches from mine. "Hey Vic," he said.

I gulped—audibly. "Corey's got a pretty little ass, don't he? I bet you like standing here with your cock pressed into that pretty little ass of his, don't you?"

"No, Master!" I shouted as my cock began to quake in the tight grip of Corey's asshole.

Dan leaned closer to me, and I could smell the sweet tobacco smell of the cigar in his mouth. "Yeah, right," he whispered in my ear.

He stepped back and turned his attention to Corey, looking him up and down. "Why are you on your toes, boy? You got a problem I should know about?"

"No, Master!" he shouted, and lowered himself even further onto my swollen tool. I felt the head press hard against his prostate. He had now truly filled himself with my cock, stretching himself open to take me in. At the same moment, Brian shifted his position so his cock rose between my ass cheeks. I tightened the muscles of my ass and squeezed his dick as he subtly slid it up and down, massaging my asshole in the process.

"You little peckerheads make me sick!" Dan bellowed, still chewing the cigar. "I think you like standing out here naked together!"

The Cigar Race

"NO, MASTER!" we all shouted. Brian's cock lurched between my legs and Corey's ass squeezed my own, siphoning the precome from my body into his. I thought about how much must have flowed into him by this point, and how any minute now I would be pumping load upon load of come up his ass. I thought of Brian, standing behind me, preparing to coat my own asshole with his hot, sticky semen. I was starting to feel slightly giddy with a combination of arousal and terror.

I looked around at the beautiful, muscular men who were watching us. It turned me on like hell to think that I was fucking Corey up the ass right in front of them; that Brian, our star gymnast, was pushing his huge cock against my own hairy butt; and that Corey—the smooth, blond, boy-next-door Corey—was going to take my load right before their eyes.

Greg, still holding the bottle of Red Hot Mama Sauce, walked in front of us and stopped at the river's edge. He stood with his legs spread and undid the buttons of his fly with one hand, pitching his hips forward and arching his back to take a piss. He tipped his head back and began guzzling a beer, holding the bottle of liquor with his other hand so his cock hung freely and his 501s sagged to expose the crack of his round butt. In that position, he released a torrent of warm, golden piss into the shallow water of the Blue River.

I watched Greg out of the corner of my eyes as he continued to chug the beer and let the piss flow from his body. The breeze caught his piss stream and sent the sparkling gold liquid spattering across the shallow ripples of water.

My knees were getting weak as I began flexing my muscles rhythmically, hoping no one would notice, yet caring less and less if anyone did. A monumental orgasm was approaching. I wanted—needed—to thrust my hips and drive my desperate cock into

Corey's little golden ass. But I couldn't. I could only let my arousal continue to creep with increasing, excruciating patience as my consciousness was pulled downward through my lower abdomen and into my now urgently fragile and very volatile cock.

Hot breath struck my cheek as Dan began shouting in my ear, "Vic, you little pissant! Pay attention!" He grabbed my left nipple, squeezing hard, and I came and came and came with a gasping yelp of pain and ecstasy as my prick finally released me from its torturous control. Load after load of hot sticky come gushed out of me and flooded Corey's beautiful, taut fuck hole.

At the same instant I felt Brian release the first hot jet of come against my asshole. His strong hands held my waist even tighter. Using his own come as lubricant, he pushed his spraying hose inside me, depositing the rest of his spunk up my ass, and I yelped again.

Dan, our Master, was still pinching my nipple between his fingers. Sweat was pouring down my face, and I hoped that it helped hide the fact that tears were streaming from the corners of my eyes as I continued to pump spurts of come into Corey's ass. I looked at Dan, and he was staring into my eyes, the corner of his mouth showing a hint of the dimpled smile that was so familiar to me. Corey's tight asshole was twitching in sync with my own throbbing cock, and I wondered if he was coming too. And I wondered if Dan knew.

Brian was still filling me up with his load as Dan released my nipple and walked away. Our rogue cocks finally began to soften, and I felt Brian's finally slip out of me. My own prick was still lost in the hot embrace of Corey's rectum, bathing in the soupy mix of his ass juice and my come. He relaxed his sphincter, and I felt my prick slowly slither out his spunky-slick chute.

We had done it. And right in front of everyone. I'd fucked

The Cigar Race

Corey up the ass right in front of a group of macho men who surely would have beaten the hell out of us if they knew. My ass was still throbbing from taking Brian's load, which I could feel trickling out of me now, winding its way through the hairs on my ass and inner thigh.

For a moment I was exhilarated by what seemed to be our triumphant act of deception.

But that's when Dan started telling us about the cigar race.

He gripped the cigar in his mouth with his teeth, which caused his face to stretch into a fiendishly toothy smile. "This little exercise is called the Cigar Race," he began, pulling the remaining cigar from his pocket and wiggling it between his fingers. "It's a relay. You pussies know what a relay is, don't you?"

"YES, MASTER!" we shouted.

He walked over to the boys lined up across from us and stuffed a cigar into the mouth of the lead boy in each line.

"When I say the word, you're all going to drop to your hands and knees!" Dan continued, maintaining his drill sergeant persona with burgeoning zeal. "Is that clear?"

"YES, MASTER!" we all shouted again.

"*DROP!*"

We instantly fell to our hands and knees, and I found myself staring directly into the pretty pink pucker of Corey's champion-swimmer ass. The ass that only moments earlier had been stuffed with my spurting dick. The ass that I had so flooded with come that it was now leaking a white trickle down the back of his smooth, hefty balls and dripping onto the searing sand.

I looked ahead of Corey to Todd, and my suspicions were confirmed—Corey had been fucking Todd, because his ass was leaking come too. Somehow, Todd's prick had managed to stay soft throughout the event, probably because he was so trashed.

Dan pointed at the two guys with cigars in their mouths. "You two stay put!" he ordered them. "The rest of you, about-FACE!"

We scrambled on our hands and knees until we were facing the opposite direction. My face was now only inches from Brian's beautifully muscled butt and truly massive cock that hung like a third leg between his dark, hairy thighs. The cock that had just plowed my ass and was now shiny and slick, dripping with come and swinging heavy in the summer sun.

It hadn't yet dawned on me what was about to take place.

"Here's how the race works!" Dan continued. "These two fuckwads over here with cigars in their mouths are going to crawl across the sand and shove their cigars up the ass of the guys across from them!"

A gasp of summer breeze rustled the shiny cottonwood leaves above us and joined the chorus of groans and incredulous laughter that rose from our ranks.

"AT WHICH POINT," Dan raised his voice to shut us up, "these two faggots will pull the cigars from their shit chutes, put them in their mouths, race back across the sand, and shove the cigars in the ass of the guys across from *them!*"

I lowered my head and looked back between my legs to Corey, who was now behind me. Come was still dripping from his dick; a long silver string now descended from its tip and stretched all the way into the sand. Corey looked up through his sun-bleached bangs into my eyes. He licked his lips and smiled.

A bolt of fear shot through me. How would we explain the come that was bubbling out of our assholes? What would our teammates do to us when they stuck the come-soggy cigar into their mouths and realized they were sucking on our jizz?

I thought about making a break for it—dashing across the river, scrambling up the embankment, and disappearing behind the cottonwoods. But I was frozen there on my knees before this group of big, smiling men.

The race was about to begin.

"You get the idea. Are you ready?" Dan gave us no time to think, let alone protest. "Set!"

I looked up to the men standing around us. Some were wearing blue jeans, and a few wore shorts. Most of them were bare-chested, some hairy, some smooth, a spectrum of earthy colors shining sweaty in the sun. A few big guys stood with their arms folded; others had their hands at their hips. They were all watching us. They were all smiling.

"GO!"

Maybe it was the delirium of liquor, or the furnace of summer, but the race seemed to proceed in slow motion. The first two boys scrambled across the short stretch of beach, their feet digging into the sand, their hands clawing at it, spraying the tiny granules several feet into the air.

Todd didn't even flinch when the first boy, squeezing the cigar between his tightly pursed lips, slid it up his ass. Todd reached back and pulled it out, coated wet and shiny with his ass juice and Corey's come, and stuck it into his mouth. He turned tail and headed back across the sand.

When the next guy reached Corey, I thought about the cigar he was sucking on and that he must have no idea it was dipped in Corey's semen. He pushed his face into Corey's butt, and when Corey pulled the cigar out I saw a few big globs of my come fly off it and splatter onto the white sand. Corey was looking up at me as he popped the cigar into his mouth, and I was sure he was savoring my salty fluid as he sped back across the beach.

I glanced up at the men around us. They were laughing at us

and cheering us on. And a few were gripping hard dicks through their denim. Did I really see that?

My turn. It was Chavez who would have the privilege of pushing that cigar into my butt hole. I watched him as he crawled quickly toward me—his muscular, brown shoulders pulling him across the sand; the cigar clenched in his teeth; his bright red lips stretched open; his dark, thick eyebrows arching angrily, giving his face a vicious expression. I felt the cigar slide in until his gruff chin scraped against the back of my balls.

I reached around, pulled the cigar out, and sucked it into my mouth, tasting Brian's sweet cock juice mixed with mine and Corey's. I headed back across the sand and focused my eyes on my target ahead of me. His name was Kirk. He was tall and thin and tan. He was a high jumper, I recalled as I sucked on the gooey, come-slicked cigar in my mouth. He had big balls that hung so low that they hid the rest of his cock from me. His slim waist was bent, his legs were spread, his knees were planted firmly in the sand, and his hairy ass cheeks were spread wide so I could clearly see the pucker of his asshole as it twitched with anticipation. I pushed my face against his little butt, forcing the cigar into him, until my nose was completely buried in his furry ass crack and I felt my lips meet his, which tightened and relaxed to accept the length of the cigar.

I rolled to one side to get out of his way. Kirk dug the cigar out of his hole and shot me a dirty look for having put it in so far as he placed it in his mouth and raced back across the sand where Brian was waiting.

It wasn't until then that I realized that we were winning. The other team was having trouble, due to drunkenness, reluctance, or lack of lube, I figured. When Kirk reached Brian, the race was over.

Of course, we picked the Red Hot Mama Sauce for the losing

team to drink. They all started puking a few minutes later. Brian, Corey, Todd, and I were standing in a circle talking about the race, laughing about all the other guys having tasted each of us and thinking about the fun times we were going to have as fraternity brothers. Dan walked over to us with his old familiar smile back on his face.

"Lookin' good, guys," he said to us, slapping my sticky ass. His finger slid up my ass crack as he did it, and he raised his hand to his lips. He winked at me and then ordered us all to get in the river and "cool off."

"Yes, Master!" we shouted, and jumped in the shallow water. We splashed each other and started wrestling. The water was warm from the heat of the day, but the sun was setting, bathing us in a golden glow. The evening breathed a cooler breeze, and cotton fell like snowflakes from the trees.

Cruel and Unusual

Kyle Stone

Initiation hell week was over. In one way I was disappointed that I had no ordeal to boast about. In another, I was relieved. Now I could relax—and stop putting things on top of the door to warn me when it was opened. I could shed the confining flannel PJs.

I was just drifting off into my favorite dream: watching Brian, my sophomore neighbor across the hall, and a bunch of other naked fraternity boys soap themselves up in the open showers on the second floor. Steam billowed around them. Their muscled naked bodies gleamed, inviting, beckoning my eye to follow the soap as it drifted down Brian's flat stomach to get caught in the thick pubic hair above his lengthening cock. I wanted to touch him so badly I almost stopped breathing, but like in a dream, I couldn't reach out, couldn't do anything but watch and ache.

They were suddenly all around me. I was in the shower too, naked and aroused. I felt their hands on me, on my waist, on my feet. Pulling…jerking…yanking my legs.

"Stop!"

This was no dream.

They were here! Why now?

I tumbled off the bed and thumped heavily on the floor. Shielding my face from their flashlights, I looked up at their tall shifting shadows. Black. All in black, with black hoods on their heads, covering their faces and slashed with scarlet markings. Oh, God, no! The Tribunal!

Cruel and Unusual

I almost lost it and cried out in fear, but one of them bent down and stuffed a bandanna in my mouth, fastening it with duct tape. Another silent figure taped my eyes, my wrists, my ankles. Working like a well-rehearsed team, they rolled me up in a rug and carried me silently down the back stairs and out to the waiting van in the alley behind the fraternity house. All this had taken maybe two minutes. And no one had uttered a sound.

As the van pulled away, I concentrated on breathing in the confines of the rug. Dust and grit got up my nose, and my mouth was dry as the Sahara. I tried to move my jaw to loosen the tape so I could get some air through my mouth, but it didn't work. And I couldn't think of anything else but breathing. My whole world was focused on my nose, pressed up against the inside of a filthy carpet as we sped through the night to some mysterious destination, the idea of which filled me with dread. I was naked, completely at their mercy. This knowledge whispered in my mind, tickled under my skin, made a warm trickle of desire squirm in my bowels.

I had heard of the Tribunal: stories told in whispers, rumors with no known source. It had been active in my uncle's day, but five years ago it had been outlawed, banished from the campus for its cruel and unusual hazing rituals. I used to listen to the stories my two uncles told, forgetful of my presence as they compared notes—what someone had told them, what had happened to old Hap, never about what happened to them. Even then I knew they spoke from personal experience, and it excited me. They talked about beatings and hot wax, being tied up and forced to have sex with a group of anonymous men. The pledge was naked; everyone else was in some sort of long robe. The images even then stirred me, made me feel ashamed of my desire. I didn't know how to process what I felt, didn't know what it meant. Later on I decided these stories were made up, a way of psyching each other out, a weird sort of one-upmanship. Now I was about to find out. Was it a myth? Or had the Tribunal just gone underground?

The road was getting rougher, and I was disoriented, bruised, and totally panicked by the time the van stopped. For a few moments nothing happened. I strained to hear, to get a clue what was going on. Doors slammed. Boots thumped on the ground. Someone coughed. The van door slid open and I was pulled out and dumped on the ground. Someone took one end of the rug and pulled, and the roll slowly unwound, exposing me to their gaze. At once I felt the goose bumps on my bare skin. My teeth were chattering.

Two guys pulled me to my feet and frog-marched me over the rough ground. The earth was very uneven—packed solid, strewn with twigs and leaves, roots of trees. I felt the beginnings of an erection die in the cool air. Then I felt warmth, heard the crackling of a fire. I was released so abruptly I almost lost my balance. For a moment there was complete silence except for the ominous crackle of the bonfire. I tried to stay still, swaying slightly as I found my balance.

A hand ripped the tape from my mouth. Tears leaked out of my eyes as the rest of the tape was removed. Now I could see, but nothing was reassuring. Dark shadows moving about the fire. Candles flaring on a long table, someone squatting over a drum. Coals glowing in a brazier. For a sudden moment I thought of summer camp. Maybe this wouldn't be so bad. Then I saw what looked like a Saint Andrew's cross.

A hand hit my ass. Hard. I cried out.

"What are you?" said a deep voice.

I looked down at the ground. The memorized words of the

old hazing ritual came to me at once: "I am nothing. I am less then nothing."

"What are you?" another voice demanded.

"A worm, sir. Less then a worm."

"What are you?"

I paused. What did they want? I had given the proper response, though this was usually asked when I was fully dressed in shirt and tie like all the newts, and they would then cut my tie in half as a symbol that I was a worm, a lowly worm, and they were…masters. They were masters.

I gulped. "I am your slave?"

Someone hit me again, this time on my thigh. The slap of his hand against my naked skin cracked in the cool night air.

"Step forward, slave. It is time for the inspection." This time it was the short men with the broad shoulders. His voice was familiar, but I couldn't remember the face. I stepped closer to the fire. Now my body was clearly visible; no chance to hide my stiffening penis that shamed me with this obvious sign of sexual excitement. Shamed and surprised me too. Why was I turned-on? It was as if that first slap had awakened my sleeping flesh to the erotic possibilities of this scene. But looking around, I saw only menace and threat.

Then someone stepped up behind me and laid his hands on my ass. No one spoke. I could feel his breath on the back of my neck. A tremor shook my body. His hands moved up to my arms, then back, his fingers sliding into my crack, hands parting my ass. Then he moved closer, his arms encircling me, pressing my nakedness against his clothed, robed body. I forgot the night, the fear, and the cold. His hands warmed me. Everywhere he touched, it was as if he lit a candle under my skin—my nipples, the hollow below my ribs, the trail of dark hair leading down my stomach. My cock began to stiffen, though he hadn't yet touched it directly. I was breathing in quick, shallow pants, pushing back against him, longing for more. My hands were still bound behind my back, and I could feel his hard body under the robes. Everyone else was forgotten, but this tall dark stranger, this anonymous man whose hands teased and aroused and withdrew, owning everywhere he touched.

"You want this, worm?" he whispered in my ear.

"Yes," I breathed.

"Yes, what?"

"Yes, sir."

"You think you're ready?"

"Yes, sir."

He laughed softly, his breath tickling my ear. Suddenly two fingers jabbed under my breastbone. I cried out, shocked, disoriented. He grabbed my left tit and squeezed hard, his fingers twisting, bringing tears to my eyes. I began to shake, the pain confusing me.

"You're not going to forget this night," he went on. "Ever." His lips were so close to my cheek I could feel each puff of breath as he spoke. Then he drew away.

"You think I want you?" he shouted, his voice filling the night. "You think I want a worm—a dirty, naked slave who doesn't know shit?" He pushed me away from him, and I staggered toward the fire and fell, my knees hitting the packed earth hard.

Angry, I tried to get up but one of the men stepped forward and kicked me. This time I fell on my face. I lay still, trying to control my pain and humiliation. I wouldn't fight back again, but I wouldn't show my fear or cry for them either. I'd show them who they were dealing with.

"Prepare him." That voice again. What did he mean? I rolled over on my side and looked up to see a group of them emerge from the shadows. How many were there? For the first time I felt real fear. Who were they? There were too many for them to be from the fraternity house. There had to be more then 20.

Hands reached for me and dragged me over to a large X set up on the other side of the fire. Before I realized what was happening, my hands were untied, then attached roughly to the top pieces of the X. Two men grabbed my feet and attached them to the bottom pieces. I was stretched in the firelight, completely at their mercy. My legs were wide apart, my arms high above my head. My muscles cried out. but I bit back the pain and stared ahead. *They're trying to frighten me,* I said to myself. *It's only a hazing. Or was it? Hazing was officially over.*

Out of the corner of my eyes I saw another man approach with a bowl on a tray. Silver implements gleamed in the firelight.

"Do you know what pain is?" The dark, rich velvet of the leader's voice pulled my eyes toward him. I wish I could see his face, gaze into his eyes. "If you don't know what pain is, you are nothing to me."

I stared at him, feeling the connection between us, feeling his touch even though he was several feet away. What did he want? What was I supposed to say? I wanted him, but did he want me? Or would he walk away?

He turned away and I almost cried out. *Come back! Don't leave me!* What I said was, "Sir, what should I do?"

He whirled around, his long robes flaring out as he moved, the whip I hadn't noticed uncoiling in the air, biting my chest.

I screamed.

He laughed; the whip cracked in the air, making me tremble with fear and anticipation.

"No! Please!" Would it kiss me again? Cut me again? Bite me like a razor blade, flicking my cheek? I was trembling now, stretched out and offered to him, to his whip, to his cruel hands and hot eyes. He hit me again, and this time I bit my lip so hard I tasted blood as the leather thong bit into my thigh, curling against the soft inside skin near, so near, my genitals.

I closed my eyes.

"You can't hide," he said.

I opened them again and glared at him. I stared at his face as he made the whip dance over my hot skin, across my chest, up and down my legs, lighting my whole body on fire.

By now snow could be falling and I wouldn't notice. My whole world was centered on the man with the velvet voice and the cruel touch—the man who had now dropped the whip and was standing so close to me, looking at my body. He reached out and touched one of the small mouths his whip had opened on my chest. His fingers came away with my blood. He touched his tongue to his own fingertips, looking at me all the time, eyes gleaming through the holes in his hood. Then he offered his fingertips to me. I opened my mouth and licked my own blood off his hand.

"Prepare him," he said, turning away.

The man with the tray approached now, and another man came over and stood in front of me. Without a word he knelt down and took my cock in his hand. At once it responded. I turned my head aside, trying to will my cock down, without success. The man chuckled and slapped cream on my balls. And then I felt the touch of cold steel. "Be still" was all he said. I froze, barely daring to breathe as he shaved my genitals. I thought of the gym, of swimming, of the showers at the fraternity house. I would be mortified to be seen naked until this grew out. Casual sex was out too. Damn the Tribunal! I gritted my teeth.

The man was not gentle but at last it was over.

Two men approached me, unshackled me. I took a deep breath, but instead of freeing me all they did was turn me over so my back was exposed. Shackled again, I could not see the whip, but I heard it one second before it bit into my flesh. I opened my mouth against the wood of the cross. As the whipping went on, my tears stained the wood, my smothered cries filled the clearing. *You bastard! You knew I would break!*

Then I felt hands on my ass, the soothing spreading of cream and the touch of steel once again. My ass! They were shaving my ass, my crack, and my hole. Is that what he wanted? Is this only way he wanted me? New? Bare? Nothing hidden?

When they took me down again, I swayed. Someone caught me in his strong arms, held me against his dark robes. That chocolate voice soothed me; his hands moved over my tortured skin. "Hush," he said. "You're ready now. Ready to be mine. It had to be like this."

"Why?" I sobbed, his kindness breaking me down completely, as he had known it would.

"Because I want you for myself. This way, every time you look in the mirror, you will think of me. Every time you feel the caress of your clothing against this complete nakedness I will be with you. You won't ever be able to think of another man, and I know you think of men all the time. But no more. You are ours. As long as you keep your body exposed like this, we are here for you. Now, are you ready?"

I felt his hand on my neck, pressing me down. I sank to my knees. "Turn towards the fire so all can see you," he said.

I did, kneeling on the ground, exposing my shaved genitals to these anonymous men, my cock already hard and gleaming with a new nakedness. I was shaking with tension, desire for the man behind me sending spasms through my body.

"On all fours," he said.

I fell forward on my hands, moving my legs apart for better balance.

"I don't want your cock," the man said, "And I don't want you until my brothers have had you. Do you understand?"

"Yes, sir." My arms were shaking now. I looked up and saw that the men had dropped their robes and they were naked. Someone was beating the drum. They formed a line, and the first man touched my ass, pushed my ass cheeks apart, thrust a greased finger inside me. Then it began. I lost count of the cocks that were thrust up inside me. The drum beat on and on. Blood rushed in my ears. Naked bodies slammed into me, pumping in time with the drum. Faster. Slower. On and on. At one point I fell forward on my face, crying in pain. The one man who was still clothed knelt in front of me and held me as his brothers, the secret members of the Tribunal, fucked my ass.

At last, it was over.

The fire was dying. My master moved away and I lay on the ground gazing after him. The others were back in their robes, standing in a circle around us, holding candles. Someone had put two torches in the ground, and my master stood between them now, holding something in his hand.

"Come here," he said.

I tried to get up but fell back on the ground.

"Crawl," he said. "You are still a worm. Crawl to me."

I pulled myself to my hands and knees and moved toward him, my knees scraped and bruised by the rough terrain.

"Now you belong to the Tribunal," he said, raising his hand.

"To us!" the hoarse cry echoed through the woods.

"As an outward and visible sign of this night, you will always carry our mark. Present your ass to your master."

Beyond thought, I did as I was told. I still wanted him.

Everything in me longed to please him, to hold him inside me as long as I could, for him to fill me with his flesh. I would do anything to please him now.

Two men had moved forward to stand on each side of me. One of them knelt on one knee and grabbed hold of my chest. Hands grabbed my ass and held my cheeks as wide apart as possible. I screamed. Agony flared through me and I almost fainted. A brand. Fire. Steel on my ass, right beside my asshole. I smelt the sickening odor of burned flesh and knew it was my own. I threw up.

One of the men laughed and pulled away. I lay on the ground in my own vomit, shaking with pain.

"It will pass," he said. My master. The man who had done this to me. The man I still wanted.

"Take me," I said though my tears. "Now."

"Give yourself to me," he said.

I struggled up to my knees, lay my forehead on the ground. Abject. Exposed. Throbbing with pain and desire.

"What do you say?"

"Please?"

"Please what?"

"Please, sir."

I felt his hands on my burning flesh, his tongue laving my brand. Then some ointment, soothing the agony, making it bearable. And then I felt his cock, forcing its way past my sore, stretched anus, taking charge of what was rightfully his. His property, I thought suddenly. Through the haze of pain and pleasure, the longing to be one with him, I pushed back against him, forcing him deeper inside. All the way. Always!

His fucking was not like the others. There was nothing brutal about it. There was no drum now, urging him on. He took his time, knowing I was raw and overloaded with pain. Knowing I wanted him more then any other man I had ever met. He lay against me, my face in the dirt, my scarred chest ground against the rough soil as he began to move inside me, taking his time, breathing in my ear. "Mine," he whispered. "Mine. Now you're mine."

"Yes," I said. "Yes, sir."

"Anytime I want you," he said, "you will come."

"Yes," I said, whimpering now as he began to move faster. "Anytime, sir." And he began to buck, driving into my torn, bloody ass, filling me at last with himself, his essence, his desire. Mine, at last.

When I came, I screamed again, but this time with joy.

"Mine," he whispered. "Only mine. You will have no one inside you unless I am present."

"Yes, sir."

"Not even one of us."

"Yes, sir."

"How will you know it is me?"

"I will know, master."

I lay on the ground for a long time, panting and gathering my strength, my eyes closed. For a time I knew he was with me. I felt his hands on me, and his fingers thrust something up my anus. Then he was gone.

When I finally opened my eyes, there was no one left in the clearing. The cross was gone. The fire was almost out. The table and candlesticks had all disappeared. A small pile of clothes was close to me. I staggered down to the stream to wash. I forced myself to sit in the cold water, letting the icy liquid calm the throbbing in my ass where the brand still hummed. At last I dried myself with a T-shirt and put on the track suit they had left for me. The shoes and socks. They were mine, I noticed without surprise. There was no underwear. I couldn't have stood to wear anything tight against my burning skin.

As dawn began to lighten the sky, I made my way down a path where the trucks had chewed up the ground recently, and I found the road. It took a long time to get there because I felt disoriented, almost drugged. I remembered the man pushing something up my anus. Is that why I had slept so long? Numbly I stood by the side of the road, until finally an old pickup appeared.

"Lost?" the guy said, leaning over to open the door.

I nodded. "Are you going into town?"

"Sure thing." He began to drive, humming off-key between his teeth, beating time on the steering wheel with nicotine-stained fingers. I concentrated on the strange sensitivity of my skin, on how the soft track suit caressed my shaved genitals with every tiny move, making me so aware of my own body. I could still feel that dark stranger inside me. I felt hot with pleasure at the thought of him. But how could I find him again?

My local yokel was going right by the college, it turned out, so he dropped me at the fraternity house. As I shook hands, I saw the ring. The fraternity ring! Well, it was almost the same as mine, but with a tiny red stone that winked in the middle of the Greek inscription. I stared at him. The Tribunal had its own ring?

"I'll be in town next week," he said, "in case you need a ride." He winked.

I swallowed. He was one of them. He had been there, had seen me naked and crying, taking it up the ass over and over again like an animal, begging for it on the ground in front of my master. He wasn't my dark man, but he knew him. He knew who he was.

"You're—"

"Hey, man, I'm just the chauffeur," he said. "You want a lift, leave me a message." He handed me a card with a phone number embossed on it. Nothing else.

"I will."

"I know." He winked and was gone.

Brian waved from the porch. I waved back. A few short hours ago I had wanted him so badly I could taste it. Now I didn't care. Every step I took reminded me of what I wanted. Who I wanted. I closed my hand around the card with the Tribunal number on it and slipped it carefully into my zippered pocket.

Alpha Tau Omega—
the Beginning and the End

Paul J. Willis

During the second semester of my freshman year I pledged Alpha Tau Omega fraternity. A couple of guys on my dorm floor asked if I wanted to go with them to an informal rush party.

We were greeted at the front door by a couple of the fraternity's officers. After we signed in, they escorted us to the formal living room, where several active members were talking with potential pledges. I was introduced to the chapter's president, Brother Edwards. He was a junior from a suburb of Chicago, majoring in business administration.

We hit it off immediately. We discovered common interests in tennis and music. The conversation flowed without awkward pauses or the sense that it was forced. I genuinely liked this guy. He told me that he'd rather hang out and talk to me some more, but he needed to meet the other men rushing the house, since he was the president. He told me I'd see him at the end of the golf course. I didn't understand what the hell that meant, but I nodded and said OK.

After making the rounds of introductions and small talk with the other brothers in the room, I was taken on a tour of the house with three other potential pledges. In each bedroom there was a miniature golf hole setup. I was handed a putter and told what par for the hole was. The rule of the course was that you were to chug the beverage of the room if you didn't make par.

I was chugging something in every other room, sometimes several rooms in a row. I had shots of schnapps and tequila. I had several beer bongs. I was getting sloppy, but everyone was in the same condition. The last hole of the course was in the president's room. Brad and his roommate had set up an impossible par 3 complete with water hazard and sand trap. I bogeyed the hole and accepted my Long Island Iced Tea.

I woke up the next morning realizing I wasn't in my dorm room. Everything was fuzzy, but I figured out that I was in Brad's room at the fraternity. The Long Island had been the last straw, and I passed out on his futon.

Someone had removed my jeans and covered me up with a blanket. There wasn't anyone else in the room until the door opened and Brad walked in. He was still wet from his shower with just a towel around his waist.

He acknowledged that I was still alive and that if I wanted to take a shower there was a clean towel in his bottom dresser drawer. He also offered to take me out for breakfast as he stood drying himself off. He took me by surprise when he winked as he saw that I was looking at his rather large cock. He told me to get moving if I wanted that breakfast. I didn't care about the food: I really liked this guy and wanted to get to know him better. After some orange juice and several cups of coffee, I felt almost human again.

I took in every word as he told me more about the history of Alpha Tau Omega. He relayed how much of a positive experience Greek life has been for him. I was sold on the notion of pledging the house. I wanted to join for the experience—and to be around Brad on a regular basis. He already felt like the big brother I was missing in real life.

A week later I received my invitation to join the brotherhood. I gladly accepted and went to the pledge party, where we met our trainer. He went over some basic rules of the house, but this evening was for celebration. We were to meet our big brothers for the first time. I had a feeling that Brad would be my big brother, and I was relieved to have it confirmed. He gave me a fake ID, and we went out with some of the other brothers to a college bar that was promoting stupidity with their 3-dollar "all you can drink" special.

I woke up in Brad's room again. This time I was naked in his bed and he was the one sprawled out on the futon. I had my usual morning hard-on and wanted to track down my clothes while he was still asleep. But I couldn't force myself out of the bed. I was enjoying taking in Brad's scent from his sheets and pillow. My hand went to my dick and I started to jack off, keeping an eye on him to make sure he didn't wake up. I felt strange being aroused by another man's scent but dismissed the thought as nothing other than horniness. I finished the task at hand, found my T-shirt and wiped off, and fell back asleep.

As the semester progressed I spent increasingly more time with Brad—losing interest in dating. I had a few trysts with little sisters of the fraternity, but the experiences were fulfilling a functional need rather than sparking any interest or desire. I just preferred to spend the time with Brad, whether we were studying together at the library, working on a project for the House, or just vegging out on a Sunday watching some sports on TV. He was my big brother and my best friend. I looked to him for advice and companionship. When I was with him, everything felt that much better, regardless of the activity.

During finals week I asked Brad if he wanted to meet up and study together. He took me up on the offer. We met up at the library every night for a good four or five hours. We studied our respective subjects and gave ourselves a reward on the hour by heading outside for a couple of smokes and some conversation. It was pretty late on Thursday night, and the library staff was flashing the lights to signal 15 minutes until locking up. We both had one more exam on Friday afternoon.

Brad mentioned that his roommate had already gone home for the summer. We both felt like we had some more cramming to do, so we went back to his room. There were too many guys finished for the semester to really focus and study: Stereos were cranked and beer was flowing. We gave it our best shot but were distracted by the noise. We set the books aside and took one of our breaks. We each lit a smoke and projected what we would be doing over the summer.

By now it was about 2 A.M. and we were both a little punchy from lack of sleep. On another break we ended up wrestling around until Brad pinned my shoulders to the floor with his knees straddling my chest. The energy shifted from playful to serious as he stared down into my eyes, taunting me by repeating, "What you gonna do now, boy?"

I didn't know what I wanted to do. I could feel my cock getting hard in my jeans.

I felt like I should struggle to try and get loose, but I enjoyed being under his control. I liked the feel of him sitting on my chest with his crotch pushed up close to my face, but he was my big brother—and we weren't gay. Just as I was trying to process what was going on, Brad bent down and kissed my mouth.

It felt natural, like it was the first kiss I ever had. He shifted his body so that he was lying on top of me with his cock pushed up against mine. Our kiss became rougher as we rubbed our hard cocks against each other. I could tell precome was leaking out of my piss slit, as the head periodically got stuck to my underwear. He was reaching for the button on my jeans when some laughter outside the door brought us back to the reality of where we were.

It was too risky to continue our exploration in the House. At any moment someone could barge through the door—drunk off their ass in celebration or speeding on coffee and caffeine pills. Brad had a car, so we decided to get the hell out of there and drive somewhere and talk about what was going on. An awkward silence hung in the Buick as we sped out of town toward the country roads and cornfields of central Illinois.

My cock was still hard and my mind was racing. How could I be attracted to a guy? What would happen if anyone found out? What do two guys even do together? My only exposure to homosexuality was some stuff I had read in a Masters and Johnson sex book I found in my parents' room when in high school. And that had scared the fuck out of me. According to that book, gay guys were often found in the emergency rooms of hospitals with oversize vegetables and lightbulbs shoved up their asses. Homosexuals were perverted and destined to a miserable life.

I didn't want that, but this didn't feel perverted. I loved him, looked up to him. I hadn't ever felt so comfortable with someone. Brad pulled off the side of a country road. We were in the middle of nowhere, about 30 minutes outside of the city and the university. He reached over and grabbed my leg, pulling me toward him. I scooted over and turned to look up at his face. His eyes bore through me with a sharp intensity—a look of desire combined with extreme comfort. His eyes told me that everything would be cool, to let go and experience our need for each other.

He put his hands on both sides of my head and pulled me roughly up to his face. My lips parted, and I felt his tongue enter my mouth. This was an urgent kiss, a hard kiss that took over all senses. I could feel his heartbeat against my chest. The scent of his skin and sweat filled the space. I could hear slight moans escaping my mouth as he explored with his tongue, stopping intermittently to bite my upper lip. He pulled back just long enough to pull my T-shirt up over my head. I did the same and pressed back up against him.

Racing through my mind were thoughts of wanting to touch and taste every part of his body. We were in sync. He lifted his arm, and I moved in to run my tongue through the hair in his pit. He told me to take in the scent that he knew I enjoyed so much. Surprised, I looked up at him. I could tell from his grin that he had seen me the day I had jacked off in his bed. I continued my exploration and sucked his nipple into my mouth. The soft skin of his aureole contrasted with the skin on the rest of his chest. I moved to the other before continuing down to lick around his stomach and poke my tongue in his belly button.

I came up to get another kiss and because the steering wheel was prohibiting any further exploration. He still had a big grin on his face. When eye contact was reestablished, we both started laughing out of a sense of joy. Neither of us had experienced this type of connection—the power of love and the strength of a man. As quickly as the laughter came on, the realization of this joy turned back to a mood of desperate lust. Brad opened his car door and pulled me out behind him. He led me by the hand to the trunk of the car.

He took awhile fumbling with the button and zipper on my Levi's before yanking my pants down to my ankles. He crouched down and took my cock in his mouth. I had never felt anything so incredible as he licked up and down the shaft. He licked the precome out of my piss slit. He kissed it, sucked it, and rubbed it all over his face. He was lost in pleasure experiencing his first cock. I was fighting blowing my load in his mouth. I warned him that I was close, and he sucked harder with purpose.

Alpha Tau Omega

My pelvis kicked into high gear in fucking Brad's face. My legs started buckling as I shot off a huge load in his mouth. It felt like I lost all muscle control. Brad stood up and wrapped his arms around my trembling body. He kissed me hard on the mouth and with his tongue pushed in some come. When he came up for air, he moved his mouth to my ear, biting on the lobe then tonguing inside. He also spoke, saying it was time to open up my hole.

He told me to bend over the trunk of the car. He pulled my ass cheeks apart and rubbed his cock up and down my sweaty crack. He pushed the head of his hard dick up against my hole. I could feel some of his precome slicking it up, but not nearly enough to allow any entry. I knew this was going to hurt, but I needed to feel him inside me, so I pushed back against him. "Not yet, li'l bro" is all he said. He pulled his cock away and bent down behind me.

He started blowing his hot breath on my ass. He stuck out his tongue and ran it around my hole before working it up inside me. I couldn't believe he was doing this and how good it felt. I experienced another jolt of excitement as he alternated smacking my cheeks with his open hand. I was surprised by how much I enjoyed the stinging sensations. I realized that I would let this man do anything with me that he wanted. I needed to be desired, touched, and fucked hard.

He stood up behind me and again rubbed his hard cock all over my ass. He also gently rubbed his hands on my cheeks, telling me how good they looked reddened from his touch, how he liked the warmth they gave off on his crotch. The head of his cock eased into my hole this time when he pushed up against me. The combination of more precome, his spit, and my excitement made for an easy entry. I was tight, but determined.

A whirlwind of thoughts raced through my head as I felt each inch move him farther inside me. At first my attention was focused on making myself relax: I wanted pleasure, not pain. He was a master at knowing when to stop to allow me to get used to his size. He instinctively knew when to proceed, how to move slightly side to side, where to slide over my prostate. He knew how to work my hole for the deepest penetration possible. Once he achieved full penetration, he pushed his body as tightly up against mine as he could and just held himself inside to allow me to fully appreciate the situation and to completely relax into him.

My thoughts were of pure enjoyment. I had never felt so free as I did at that moment—free from guilt and worry, free from loneliness and confusion. He fucked me full with his love and passion for our friendship. He fucked me out of desperation to connect with another man. We worked up to a rhythm where he'd pull all the way out and plunge back in deep with me relaxing and opening my hole. On the outstroke he'd move slowly, with me gripping his cock as hard as I could with my muscles.

The combination of senses was again overwhelming. I could hear his cock pounding in and out of my hole. I could hear our bodies smacking against each other, accentuated by the sweat we were giving off. I could smell that sweat and could still taste the come he had pushed into my mouth. But it was the sense of touch that took over. His hands on my shoulders as he pulled me harder onto his cock. The feel of his cock pushing against the walls of my ass as he worked up to shooting his load.

I felt him shoot off deep inside me, our fuck becoming its most intense. His cock slid through me, much easier coated with his thick come as he continued to pound into my soul. I was overwhelmed by emotion, feelings of pure pleasure, and joy. I felt a great release of guilt and shame. I was a whole person for the first time. I held him inside as long as I could.

The connection with my big brother was the beginning of

self-exploration and becoming a young man. He brought out the realization that I was gay, something that I had tried to deny myself—not wanting to become one of those men that I read about. His love and attitude gave me confidence to be who I was—someone who loved the beauty and strength of men. Our relationship lasted for two years, where we had the backdrop of college as a playground—fraternity parties, hot young men, no real responsibilities.

The relationship with Brad also brought about the end of youthful innocence and ideology. Our two years together ended when I was faced with the harsh reality of being treated as an outcast. A couple of our fraternity brothers took it upon themselves to tell the rest of the brotherhood that Brad and I were fucking each other. I went from having 80 "brothers" to being snubbed and ridiculed.

I wasn't mature enough at the time to handle the hostility that was being directed at me. I associated it all with Brad. Our relationship became complicated and started to deteriorate at that point. I wish I would've had the ability to handle the situation differently, but what I choose to remember now is that time I was bent over the trunk of the car. How Brad's cock took away all the teen years of confusion as he pushed farther up my young hole. How he fucked me into adulthood, feeling passion and lust for a man. I remember a big brother who would feel good to have about now.

Bonfire

Max Reynolds

The screen spread before Drew, wide and white. From his seat in the second row he could see a large seam down the center where it had been repaired. He had made a similar repair himself on campus one night at a screening in the student lounge when an overeager freshman had snapped the screen so hard it had torn almost in half. He remembered that freshman—not his name, but the way his face had colored at Drew's upperclassman displeasure and the way, when he had bent over to pick up the torn piece, his khakis had outlined his ass with the linear perfection of paint-on-glass animation. Drew had turned away then, as he wanted to do now, half-rising from his seat, then sitting again, almost defeated by the screen brightening to color.

Why was he here? It was 3 in the afternoon on a rainy Saturday in early November, and the chill outside had crept into the theater like a malevolent patron. He remembered a movie he had seen in his "Feminism on Film" class—*Variety,* about life at a porno theater in Manhattan. He felt like a cheap stereotype, slunk in his seat in the last remaining men-on-men porn house in town.

All over campus, signs met his gaze on an almost daily basis. When not advertising some queer event, they were lauding coming out dances and gay or lesbian or transgendered or bi-curious get-togethers. He should be at one of those, not in some sleazy theater with come-stained seats that smelled a little too strongly of disinfectant and not enough of popcorn. But Drew had what were commonly called "issues," and one of them was his place on campus. There were no queers in his fraternity, of that he was certain, and there had doubtless been none in that same fraternity when his older brother Scott had been there three years earlier or when his father had been there in the early '80s. Family tradition hadn't gotten him into Penn; that Ivy League benefit had come from hard work and an award-winning documentary in his senior year of high school that had been shown on PBS in his hometown in upstate New York. But the pledge had come with strings and a price: that he knew.

Tall, lean, and just buff enough to have been used as a model at the local art school before he left home for college, Drew was no jock and never would be. He liked swimming, but team sports had failed him as bitterly as he had failed them. His nearly black hair, blue-green eyes, and sleek hairlessness looked good in the water, but it didn't lure the girls like the hulking footballers or the sinewy soccer men. But then Drew hadn't cared; his only girlfriend had been the quirkily intellectual Lisa Loeb–alike, Diana, and she, like he, had been, he now knew, a closet case from that first freshman dance where they had met. She had come out to him right before their senior prom, sweetly teary-eyed and deeply apologetic. She was crazy about Alana, an inaccessible fellow senior she didn't have a prayer of wooing, because Alana, as Drew knew only too well, was nymphomaniacally attached to any dick she could get her hands on, and those had been plenty. He came out to Diana that night but couldn't bring himself to tell her about how Alana had felt him up outside the cafeteria after the last meeting of the Greek club she chaired and he attended.

Diana, good sport and great friend that she was, had dutifully visited Drew on campus at Penn. Her artfully slinky presence had prompted knowing looks and jousting among his fraternity friends. It had also deflected any attention that might have

accrued from what Drew knew to be a hotly dangerous attachment to Jake, the frat's second-in-command and the would-be
lover that had led him to this ridiculous moment at the Bobcat
Sinema.

Bobcat Sinema. Drew nearly laughed out loud. Not quite 21
and already a caricature. What would happen when he was 50? he
wondered, as he discreetly swiveled his head to see who else had
entered the plush little room since the trailers had started.

On-screen the action was beginning. *What was he seeing?*
Right, *Soccer Boys.* Not much imagination in that title, but then
when it came to soccer (and Jake, the Fast Forward as he was
called by the team), Drew's imagination was all that was needed
on the topic of the sport.

The men on the screen were as young, buff, and sinewy as
Jake. And like Jake, their hard-ons strained against their shorts
with the same ferocity as they strained to kick the ball around the
grassy, mud-flaked field. British accents with barely intelligible
slang peppered the room as the men—boys, really—kicked and
scrambled their way into each other, building the tension that
Drew knew would soon be released in the obligatory locker room
scene.

He knew about those scenes. He had gotten into sports in high
school solely to witness them: hard young jocks prancing naked
in front of him, soaping up and wetting down, fondling their own
dicks and balls and rock-hard six-pack abs. And occasionally, as
he had caught one afternoon when he was late for swim practice,
he witnessed exaggerated faux circle jerks meant to dismiss any
notion that the sex was as real as the stiff and spurting cocks
might imply. No moaning like he soon expected and, if he were
honest with himself, hoped for on-screen. Moaning implied con-
sent; he knew this. Moaning implied it wasn't just a whack with a

wet towel or a quick shove into a locker. Moaning implied desire and desire meant queer and queer meant he would be kicked out on his fairy ass from the fraternity his father still talked about and his brother had been president of. Moaning was what he ached to do beneath Jake's slightly less than six-pack abs and taut thighs. Moaning was what barely escaped his lips now, as he found his hands had gone from resting on his thighs to massaging his balls and working up the shaft of his now intensely hard dick.

Why am I here? This time the question came not from inside his own head, where he still hoped to find some way to reconcile his queerness, but from the guy who had lowered himself so quietly into the red seat next to him that he hadn't even noticed.

Drew dropped his hands from his crotch guiltily, as if the nuns had caught him as they had so many other boys at school. "No, don't stop," said the man, taking Drew's hand and putting it back on the bulge in his 501s.

The moaning had begun on-screen, but Drew was staring at the face next to his. Clean-shaven, sandy-haired, 30-ish, taller than his own 5 foot 10, if the legs that stretched out in front of him were any indicator. A brown leather bomber jacket covered a khaki shirt that tapered into jeans much like his own. The legs ended into richly textured cowboy boots. The guy had bucks. What was *he* doing here?

"I'm a film student," Drew quipped as if he'd been caught by one of his frat men. "Research," he added, knowing just how true both statements were. "You?"

Drew's eyes drifted to the guy's package. They were, after all, in a porn house. Wasn't he obligated to look? Stiff as his own cock pulsed the man's dick against the harsh fabric of the jeans. *What had he gotten himself into?*

"I'm Bob." *Had he really just held out his hand as if they had just met for coffee?* "I own this place, and you seem like you might be underage to be here."

Drew didn't know whether to be offended or flattered. The veritable Bobcat himself carding his patrons? Drew knew there would come a time when he'd be happy to be thought younger than he was; he wasn't there yet, however.

"Well over 18 and ready to play ball." The words came so unbidden from him that he felt his color rise the way that fresh-man's had in the student lounge a few weeks back. *What* had *he gotten himself into, indeed.*

"You look like you might play soccer—or swim," nodded Bob, whose gaze had more than drifted—fixated—on Drew's crotch.

"We should watch the film," Drew said, searching for a tone somewhere between demure and offhand. "I hate it when people talk in the movies." The heat had spread up his thighs, through his groin, and into his abdomen. Bob the Cat was no longer just looking. His hand squeezed Drew's thigh so hard it almost hurt; his dick ached, and he instinctively unzipped his pants.

This is how I had wanted it to be at the bonfire last week with Jake, Drew thought as Bob the Cat, owner of the Sinema, became the first man other than himself to touch his cock. Bob the Cat slunk low in the seat and caressed his dick out of his now too-tight Speedos and ran his hand deep under his balls, gripping them strong but not hard, not the way he had grabbed Drew's thigh.

The screen was alive with fucking now. One soccer player was stark naked, another dressed only in a jockstrap. Three others stood, open-shirted but shortsless, massaging their own dicks as the jockstrapped player edged the naked one onto the locker room bench. Beneath the bench—next to a towel, some socks, and a cleated shoe—was a convenient can of lube, and as the jockstrapped player pushed the naked one forward in a sports-manly act of one-upmanship, the naked player let out the moan Drew was holding behind his own clenched teeth.

His own shirt had become unbuttoned to the waist. *How and when had he done that?* wondered Drew as he searched his naked chest and belly for answers. "No hair," murmured the Cat as he ran attractively rough hands over Drew's sleek abdomen and plunged them into his Speedos.

His dick was, as they say in the movies, throbbing. He ached to come but didn't want to—not yet. This was new, this was a little scary, this was so intense and exciting that he was surprised he hadn't come already just from the sheer tension of it all.

He slid down a bit in his seat, spreading his legs wide. *Were there others in the theater? Did it matter?* He'd become part of the screen now. It was one of those real-time split screens, like in that dreadful Mike Figgis movie he had to dissertate on last semester. Three separate sequences played before him. The soccer movie, with Mr. Jockstrap pulling his admirably sized cock out of the white elastic–and–brown leather contraption and slicking it up with lube. The moans from the naked player whose beautiful Latino ass quivered suggestively as Mr. Jockstrap played with his asshole—smearing it with lube and slowly pushing one, then two fingers in, spreading the cheeks wide—had grown just a little more intense, a little more urgent. Mr. Jockstrap whacked at his cock, jerking it off a little and then pushing it against that smooth, dark ass. The head of his dick disappeared into the hole ringed with soft black hair, and the naked player reached desperately for his own cock, but Mr. Jockstrap had that too, fucking and jerking at the same time.

Bob the Cat had seen this movie before, certainly. He was squeezing Drew's balls and stroking his cock with a lightness that was so tantalizing Drew thought he might explode. Not come, just burst into bits all over the small plush room. "Touch me," Drew murmured, his voice suddenly deeper than any 20-year-old's should be. "Put your mouth on me, jerk me off, touch me." His voice held all the urgency his cock felt.

Bob reached into his pocket and pulled out a condom in a mint-green wrapper. Drew took his own dick in his hands and held it as Bob ran the silky pale-green rubber over his steamy cock. Then he put Bob's hand back on the shaft, leaned back, and closed his eyes.

Bonfire Night had been two weeks ago. The game had been a big event for the frathouse. Partying and drinking would be a two-day long ritual, but the game was the intro and Jake had asked that everyone be in attendance. Drew would have gone regardless. He never missed an opportunity to catch Jake in action—skirting the field, his legs nothing but sinew; his thick brown hair sweaty on his forehead; his arms tensed as his feet traversed the field. Jake was a god, there was no denying it. Girls paraded in and out of his room at the house like he was interviewing for jobs. There was no one special girl, Drew knew. Jake claimed practice made perfect—on the field and off—and he was going to get as much practice in as he could before he was forced to settle down back in Michigan at the family law firm.

Drew wasn't sure how he and Jake had ended up at the bonfire together later that night. It had been a blur of a night. The game had been fantastic: fast-paced and tense, a 5-to-4 score with seconds to spare, and Jake, of course, making that final, fabulous goal, the muddied ball a white streak into the net.

They had ended up lying on the grass as the bonfire was lit by underclassmen. Jake was lit himself, two beers chugged in rapid succession and another half gone in his hand. "What a night," he'd exclaimed with all the reverential sadness of a 20-year-old knowing nothing would ever again be this sweet. "What a fabulous, fucking fantastic night, huh Drew?" Jake had fake-slugged Drew then, pushing him down on the grass under the tree and pinning him by the shoulders. Drew had felt himself go hard, harder than he thought he had ever been, and the urge to kiss Jake had been overwhelming. The jet-black eyes had searched his for a second, maybe longer. Had Jake seen the desire streak across his face the way that final goal had streaked into the net?

"Fucking fantastic is right, you asshole!" Drew had arched his body, swung Jake off onto his back, and laughed. It was a cover laugh, he knew it, but perhaps Jake was too drunk to know for sure. The most dangerous moment of his life, the moment when everything might have changed forever, had passed. Or had it?

Jake wanted to wrestle then. "You pussy," he yelled, tossing his beer across the field as sparks flew around them from the bonfire and groups of students cheered and grabbed each other, girls jumping up and down together and guys shoving each other in the way guys do when they want to touch but can't.

They rolled around on the grass for too long. Drew had felt it, when Jake pushed down on him—the hard cock against his thigh. He felt it when Jake continued to rub against him, harder and harder until he knew Jake was going to come, going to come against him, but not on him, not in him, not with him.

"What a fucking night," Jake breathed again as he rolled back onto the grass, leaves crunching under the weight of him. He pulled his shirt out lazily, matter-of-factly, from his pants, covering the stain spreading where seconds before he'd come hard against Drew's thigh. Drew's own dick pulsed in his pants, aching to be touched, aching for Jake to come against it, on it, make it slick with come.

Drew was coming now. He could feel it rising from his balls to his shaft and begin to spurt through the head of his dick. He released the moan he'd held back from Jake, that night and long before that, as he watched the men fuck on-screen. When Bob the Cat had first touched his cock, the first man ever, he realized he was truly queer now. That moan sizzled past his lips, and he grabbed Bob's hair in his hand and felt him suck, suck, suck on his pulsing cock until there was nothing left but the sighs of the men on-screen and the limp, pale-green rubber on his slowly softening dick.

The computer shone blue in the half-light of his room as Drew tried to organize his storyboard for tomorrow's film crit. Images of naked men superimposed themselves over the smooth digital icons he was drafting. Bob the Cat's card lay to the right of the mouse. Discreet as their encounter had been, it read simply BOB CATT FILMS, with number and e-mail address.

Bob *had* taken him for coffee yesterday after the movie ended. They had walked eight blocks to Cosi and had lattes and omelets and talked about film for two hours before Drew took the bus back to campus. Diana had e-mailed him several times. Did he need her to visit next weekend? Otherwise she was going to a women's festival with some classmates.

Did he need her to visit? Nothing had happened to make Drew think Jake even remembered Bonfire Night. Jake had come back to the house and drunk himself into a stupor with two of the other frats and some frat groupies. Drew had picked his way over the bodies on his way out to run the next morning. He and Jake had taken two classes together since then and swum a few laps and had a beer one night at Smoky Joe's. Nothing. Drew was safe because Jake wanted to be safe.

Drew stood, stretched himself out, and walked to the bed, flopping down, his legs wide apart. He closed his eyes and thought of how it felt to come in a man's mouth in a darkened theater, how it felt to have the boy he wanted more than anything rub and rub and rub against his thigh until he could feel the stickiness seeping onto him. His cock hardened at the memories: the flashes of sex between the soccer players; Bob and Jake.

He stood and walked back to the computer. One more semester and he would be out of this school, out of this fraternity, and out of the closet that was tighter and more suffocating than his pants had been yesterday when Bob had made him truly, truly queer.

He squeezed his legs together, his balls touching his thighs in the loose sweatpants, his cock throbbing against his stomach, and he hunched forward and tried to think about his work. It was after midnight and the class was at 8:30. If he were going to show, this was going to be a long night.

The knock on his door rattled his concentration. Jake's voice, slightly slurred, announced his entrance. Jake tipped into the room, his hand around two Sam Adams, one of which he proffered to Drew.

"Can't," Drew waved the beer away, "gotta finish this storyboard for tomorrow's crit." Drew kept his eyes on the screen as Jake ambled to his bed and fluffed the pillows under his head.

"All work and no play, my man," he sneered and pushed at Drew's chair with his outstretched leg.

"Really, man, let me get this done." Drew felt Jake's presence, smelled him—salty and grassy like he had been that night, as if he had just come from the field. He swiveled around in his chair, took the beer, and drank a long draught.

"I don't have the old man's firm to go to, remember, Jakester. I got to work for a living." The joke barely broke the tension between them. Drew felt his breath catch in his throat with the taste of the ale. He could drop to his knees right now and take Jake's thick cock in his hand, his mouth, even up his ass. He was that ready.

Jake leaned over, clinked his bottle against Drew's, and toasted to "the old men."

"Come on, Drew, come over and tell me a story. I screwed up on the field tonight and I'm damned depressed. Play me a little movie for my head in which the goal always hits the net and *I* am *always* the star."

His black eyes sparkled with ale and the half-light and his hair fell low over his broad forehead, and Drew thought, not for the first time, that Jake was indeed a god, a god whose light would fade in the years past school. He would be like Paul Newman in *Cat on a Hot Tin Roof,* replaying the scenes of his youth again and again because they were so acutely perfect and because he would never again be this beautiful; this sexy; this deeply, fabulously, intensely sweet.

Drew stood and walked to the bed. He shoved Jake's leg back with the playfulness of the field. He sat down and turned, looking over the sprawled, beautiful boy who lay before him ready for a story, ready to be taken, perhaps aching to be taken. And then he began to talk about a split-screen montage of a bonfire, a soccer game, and a trip to the movies on a wet, cold November afternoon.

Frathouse Blues

Trebor Healey

They told me it was about brotherhood
but mostly it was a dubious dabbling in drunk-driving
    deliriums
doped up and holed up behind a great cement dam
entombed in the nursery of the straight white male hydro-
    electric powerplant
Daddy turned all the levers
these were the princes of the powerbrokers
drunk, dumb and dosed
in the dungeons of consciousness

And I was running from queer demons
hiding behind walls as thick as these
—they had to be safe
I hid among the big whirring dynamos of electrical boysex
generating the glowing germs of desire
like fireflies I couldn't not see
I ran in place for four years
impressed by turbines and flumes
Drunken I debated delicious dick dichotomy
I convinced myself it was envy for their sex not greed for it
I lost every case
and was sentenced by my penis to hard labor

in a fraternity
I was in a prison made of my own passion
the bars of my cell
were big hard blue-veined cocks
I shook 'em and I wailed
for release

My dreams were kinder to me though
flowering like the blossoms of hard dicks
floating like lotus flowers on a warm white sea of fresh boy cum
flowing from the frightened eyes of these sexy scared boys even
who cried subconsciously for me
—I know they did
they cried for me and they cried for themselves
we cried in brotherhood without ever letting on
for the boy in us all
that was killed when the bell of initiation into this frat
    manhood thing rang
That was the only brotherhood we really ever had
a brotherhood of loss
like our dicks setting down like the sun
when they could have drove deep and found a place to swim
    upstream
upstream where the river still ran wild
and none of 'em ever knew
that I sauntered in a solitary
subversion of semen somnambulance
cuz I was a fag

I'd say it was a heaven
but delicious dick dichotomy determined

Frathouse Blues

it was purgatory
They had these things called 'brotherhoods'
in which they dominated the new pledges
the older boys made us strip and do calisthenics
we were so close
to just letting it go
the room was full of sweat and groaning
so close to realizing my fantasies
and maybe a few others'
We would have done anything the older boys said
to achieve brotherhood

We would have paired up and fucked each other all night
for brotherhood
We would have gotten on our knees for the older guys we so
    wanted approval from
for brotherhood
We would have let them fuck us and welcome us home
We would have sucked each other's 18-year-old stems
for brotherhood
For brotherhood
we would have cummed for distance
instead of vomiting for distance
Ain't it the same thing sublimated?
I mean four years of watching these guys guzzle beer
It always seemed like they were trying to prove to one another
what great cocksuckers
they could have been
how much they could take
Like randy Marlon Brandos on the waterfront:
"I coulda been a cocksucker

You shoulda watched out for me Charlie
—you was my brother."
Brotherhood

And I felt sorry for them
trapped behind that Hoover Dam
that made them strive for fifty-two years
their Daddy's age, stamped on the fuselage of a B-52 bomber
the age of power and privilege
not a place for boys or cocksuckers
Their steelvault hearts I see even today on the streets of this city
10 years later
they could have broken like eggs full of semen
they could have been take-off-that-tie sloppy and sticky
in boy-romping randiness
They didn't have to be fags forever
for brotherhood

Youth wasn't worth shit
to these beautiful adonises
women didn't want it
and their fathers laughed at it
considered it a liability
like a flower was somehow a necessary evil preceding a fruit
They couldn't bear their mother's love
how she thought they were cute
It compromised them into powerless obscurity
So they pretended to prefer the patriarchy's practicality about
    produce
I think that fags and mothers are the only ones who love them
    for what they are

Frathouse Blues

Beautiful little boys unbeknownst
bearing their beautified boners
like bamboo and bougainvillea

Power was all they were provided as a goal
So pansies and petunias be damned
They played their volleyball games
they got their grades and connections for grad school
they harvested their friendships and their fathers
they got their muscles all hard and tight
sleek as machinery
not for the girls
but for the other boys
for power over other boys
for intimidation
for a kind of hierarchy
My dick is bigger than yours kind of thing
I got more horses of power under my hood
A kind of brotherhood
and that's all a big dick was
a pecking pecker order
For brotherhood
as in older brother and younger brother

For true brotherhood
the things I could have shown them
the fields of wildflowers' non-fruit-bearing I could have led
    them through
we were all the same age
generally the same size and strength
A big dick and a smaller one are not that different

in the grand scheme of things now are they?
Not among brothers
in the grand scheme of things
like stars and liberty
equality and fraternity
For brotherhood carries no judgment
Brotherhood does mean love you know
a kind they were afraid of

And yet it was what this living arrangement was supposed
    to be about
Was it a fascination then with something that they couldn't have
that made them talk about it and claim they had it
like how the African-American girls straightened their hair
the sissies lifted weights to look like football stars
And me
I joined a fraternity to be a straight boy
and convince myself everything would be OK
and I will find protection
from losing the love of my family and friends
and all strangers
which I know I must have or I'll die

Were they trying to prove that they could actually be a team?
like all the rulers had told them to be but failed
for competition was the priority always
and if the team didn't serve that
well no one gets rich at a co-op
Their teams are more like alliances I guess
NATO and all that, a common enemy
But real brotherhood—it bankrupted enmity

Frathouse Blues

so brotherhood was relegated to language alone
They were trained to fight, fight, fight
even for brotherhood they were told
Alone, afraid, loading rifles of manproof
Oh, I would say again we had a brotherhood in this way
I was there too protecting my fragile manhood slipping away
they never knew
my sexual subversions
they too walked in a solitary semen somnambulance
their life asleep in their testicles

Was it a fascination with something that they couldn't have?
The whole man-frat thing sure was for me
It was the central theme of my queer childhood
Before I knew what these feelings were
there were feelings of longing to be another little boy
I wanted to be the beautiful blond baseball battin' boy
until my hairless little cock
stood straight up and pointed at him
"That one there; that's who you want to be"
I remember crying very long in my bed one night
when I was only 7
when I accepted that I would give up my family, my room, all
    my toys and all my friends—and Jesus too—
to be that boy
I had three brothers who hated my guts
they would've loved that little blond boy
I couldn't be

No wonder it was sadness I saw
when I first looked upon my male seed in my hand

Trebor Healey

I'd missed my mark
Oh, if my penis had been a boy-seeking missile
or a bird of prey boy-bound

So the frat was a twisted sort of blessing
like a nest I'd stumbled into
and all that longing came back
a dormant seed watered by alcohol in drunken reverie
A nest of beautiful bacchanalian boyness
A cock nest
they were working like bees
honeycombing the college
with hexagonal cum compartments as they masturbated in
    bathroom stalls
and the private cubicles of the library
I wished then my asshole was six-sided
Oh Cinderella lonely queer I'd long
if the cock fits, wear it
I dreamed one might be my prince
but I knew, I knew
we all were princes and we all fit each other perfectly
For brotherhood I longed
The brotherhood they'd each accepted initiation into
And I couldn't just offer up my toys and Jesus and family
    anymore
my hairless little dick
was a loaded 357 magnum now
and my desires felt dangerous

They told me the frat would make me a man
And I thought *Good!*

Frathouse Blues

cuz I'm slippin' into womanhood real fast!'
Oh, when does a boy become a man?
When he signs a contract of brotherhood he plans to break?
When he stops caring about words having meaning?
When he accepts "I'm a Zete" as a tag of brotherhood
simply because it has status and the love be damned
When he decides once and for all to bow down to Daddy
and suck the dick of his dogma instead of the dick of his friend?
—it was happening before my eyes too soon
They were teen-something, twenty-something young guys
When does a boy become a man?
As soon as his cock drops I'd say
droppin' into manhood
every one of 'em
like virile bombs out of the lumbering B-52s that were their
    fathers
cuz they couldn't find brotherhood
no one had shown them a way
And I could have but was afraid

And crossing the river Styx was the first trial most would have
    turned from
Our sticks straining together forcing the pussywillow off the
    bough
and into a fabulous fellated flower full of pollen
For brotherhood I longed
I even lied with them
For Brotherhood
Oh so close
to lie with them is only a conjugation away
like the rules of language

Trebor Healey

the rules of the fathers kept our dicks apart
But still for brotherhood I longed
It's what they promised me you know
I who would never fit in
I knew how to be a brother to them
I was the only one who knew

I was silent
and they told me over and over again
—because I was a lie of what they were and that made them
    trust me—
They kept telling me how well I fit in
And all I could imagine
as I watched their lips pronounce it:
"fit"
How would I fit in each of them
in their assholes, in their mouths
How well all of them could fit and fill me
fit and fill each other
Oh brothers
I dreamed of wild fucking orgies
And I no longer believe they were an impossibility
We all wanted brotherhood
For brotherhood
I think we all could've given ourselves to one epiphany

But my dreams went limp and I left
left with no memory of union
only an infinite repertoire of masturbation material
the steamy showers
and their half-hard boycocks risen from sleep

Frathouse Blues

the tender lines of hair that vertically descended between their
    bellies and their belts
like Chinese writing
I was cheated of the same thing they were
so I'm not bitter
we wanted brotherhood
and none of us got it
and I see it in their eyes today
receded far inward beyond their gray suits
that have formlessly cancelled their male beauty
behind a wall of shapeless fabric
that only speaks for the power of the man
not the boy-joy spring-loaded flowery semen stem
which I hope I do hope
their wives can retrieve something of
as they race into middle age after the spoils
the kingmakers promised

I hug them now when I see them on the businessman's boy
    dead streets
It's a sort of brotherhood I think
that they can still let themselves touch
I hated them for years for refusing to touch me
until I thought of brotherhood and what it could be
And maybe I am the only one of us who knows
I better get to work teachin'

So now I feel a sad lost love for these boys
for what we intended together
even if we failed
we were all scared, brainwashed and running

lost in the deafening deluge of the whirring dynamos of
     electrical boysex
generating the glowing germs of desire
that made us blind and vulnerable to the dogma of B-52s
And how much like 52 they are today
but I know what hangs between their legs is always young
A penis is forever a boy
And when it rises like the sun
it gives the boy in the man away

So these so-called men
are always boys to me
I hug them close
like my dad did me before I grew hair on my dick
I lean forward into their arms
and wish them well
I give them my gift of brotherhood longed for
—Otherwise I'll long forever
and besides I know it's what they want
For brotherhood is how we met
and what we dreamed upon together
10 long years ago
For Brotherhood
I would have mounted them and left them my seed
the gift of spring
like a lucky bag of Indian corn
they could carry through the valley of death
of being a straight white male businessman

And I could have used their lucky bag in those hard years too
Oh, and even if it's only the scrap metal

Frathouse Blues

of a plane that crashed in a field of wildflowers
there is a kind of brotherhood still salvageable in their eyes
I lean forward and hold them
I wish them well as brothers

And at night in my dreams I fall backward into their arms
into the arms of 40 naked athletic boys alive
and scented with sweat
sittin' on the young fine fence of 20 years give or take
I'll give
And bless the boyhood that still breathes in 'em

Contributors

Terje Anderssen spent his formative years splashing in the shallow waters of sandy prairie streams, looking under driftwood, and catching turtles, catfish, and crawdads. A son of America's Great Plains, Terje has worked as a technical writer for most of his professional career. Trading open skies for open minds, he moved to San Francisco in 1997, where he currently works in publishing and can be seen walking to work each morning from his South of Market flat. "The Cigar Race" is his first published work of erotica.

Clark Anthony has Northern roots, but lives and goes to college in the Southern half of the United States. He's such a sweet boy that he blushes when asked whether the events recounted in "Initiation Night" have any basis in his real life. Still, he encourages the curious to get in touch with him at clarkanthony100@hotmail.com and let him know what they think of his story.

M. Christian's work can be seen in the *Best American Erotica, Best Gay Erotica, Best Lesbian Erotica, Best Transgender Erotica, Friction* series, plus over 150 other anthologies, magazines, and Web sites. He's the editor of more than a dozen anthologies, including *Best S/M Erotica, Love Under Foot* (with Greg Wharton), *Bad Boys* (with Paul J. Willis), *The Burning Pen, Guilty Pleasures,* and many others. He's the author of four collections: the Lambda Literary Award–nominated *Dirty Words* (gay erotica), *Speaking Parts* (lesbian erotica), *Body Work* (more gay erotica), and *The Bachelor*

Machine (science fiction erotica). For more information, check out www.mchristian.com.

Todd Gregory is a slutty New Orleans writer who loves to research his writing wherever and whenever he can find someone willing. He has published short stories in *Friction 6*, VelvetMafia.com, and *Latin Boys*. He is currently working on a novel of erotic suspense called *Sunburn*.

Trebor Healey's fiction can be found online at the *Blithe House Quarterly* and *Lodestar Quarterly*. Anthologies where his work appears include *Best Gay Erotica 2003*, *The Bad Boy Book of Erotic Poetry*, *A Day for a Lay*, *Sex Spoken Here*, *Between the Cracks*, *Wilma Loves Betty and Other Hilarious Gay and Lesbian Parodies*, *M2M*, and *Beyond Definition: New Writing from Gay and Lesbian San Francisco*, of which he was coeditor. Trebor also wrote a hit single, "Denny," for Pansy Division. His first novel, *Through It Came Bright Colors* (Haworth Press), was published in August 2003. Visit www.treborhealey.com.

Greg Herren is the author of the novels *Murder in the Rue Dauphine* and *Bourbon Street Blues*, and editor of the anthologies *Shadows of the Night*, *Full Body Contact*, and *Homo for the Holidays*. He has published stories in numerous anthologies, web-sites and magazines, and tries to maintain his sanity while leading an insane life in New Orleans with his partner.

William Holden is a native of Detroit but now lives in Atlanta with his partner of six years. He was working as a corporate accountant for 17 years but has left the corporate scene and is now working towards a master's degree in library and information sciences. His short stories have appeared in anthologies such as *Slow Grind* and *Hard Drive*. This will be William's fifth published story. In his spare time he volunteers for various local gay and lesbian organizations.

The erotic fiction of **Christopher Pierce** has been published in *Three the Hard Way, Saints & Sinners, Sex Buddies, Latin Boys,* and the *Friction* series. He is currently coediting *Men on the Edge* with Michael Huxley for STARBooks Press. Write to him at chris@christopherpierceerotica.com, and visit his Web site at www.ChristopherPierceErotica.com.

Max Reynolds is the pseudonym of an award-winning journalist and author from Philadelphia. His work has appeared in the anthologies *A View to a Thrill* and *Dangerous Liaisons,* and he is currently working on an erotic vampire novel titled *Touches of Evil.*

Michael Rhodes lives on the West Coast, where he works fulltime and writes for pleasure whenever the demands of daily life can be temporarily held at bay. He's new to the erotic writing scene but has several stories awaiting publication. He's also written one unpublished novel and is working on a second. He says that the thing he enjoys most in erotic writing is searching for "new frontiers of violations" wherever he can find them.

Simon Sheppard went to a college so avant-garde it didn't have intercollegiate sports, much less fraternities. There was a Zen monk on staff, though, and Sheppard's philosophy degree has stood him in good stead; his work has appeared in over 80 anthologies, including *Best American Erotica, Best Gay Erotica,* and the *Friction* series. He's also the author of *Kinkorama:*

Contributors

Dispatches from the Front Lines of Perversion and *Hotter Than Hell and Other Stories,* winner of the Erotic Authors Association Award for Best Erotic Anthology by a Single Author of 2001. With M. Christian, he's the coeditor of *Rough Stuff* and *Roughed Up,* and his next short story collection, *In Deep,* will be published by Alyson Books in 2004. He can be found at www.simonsheppard.com.

Steve Soucy was born and raised in upstate New York and holds a master's degree in Professional Writing from the University of Southern California. He lives and works in West Hollywood, Calif., where he writes fiction and screenplays.

Colt Spencer is the pseudonym for a writer who currently resides in Los Angeles, where he is pursuing a career in the entertainment industry and frequently contributes to several gay and lesbian magazines. His erotic fiction has appeared in *First Hand, Guys, Men, Freshmen, In Touch for Men,* and *Playguy* as well as the compilations *Friction 6, Manhandled,* and M. Christian's upcoming bisexual collection *Binary.* His monthly sex column for men, "The Guy Report," appears in *Unzipped,* and he recently completed his first erotic novel, as well as his second adult-film script, *Hard Cops,* for rookie production company Massive Studio. He can be reached at ColtSpencer1@aol.com.

Vancouver, Canada resident **Jay Starre**'s stories have appeared in the gay magazines *Men, Honcho, Torso, America Bear* and *Indulge,* and in numerous anthologies, including Alyson's *Friction* series and Greg Herren's *Full Body Contact.* Regular exercise and plenty of sexual adventures allow him to keep working hard on all the hot stories he writes.

Contributors

Kyle Stone's name first appeared as the author of the scorching S&M/sci-fi erotic adventure novel *The Initiation of PB 500* in 1993 (reissued in 2001). A sequel, *The Citadel,* and three more novels followed. Stone's short stories have appeared in many gay magazines and anthologies. The latest are collected in *MENagerie* (2000).

Troy Storm, who considers himself a fratsex gourmet, has had several hundred gay, straight, and bi erotic short stories published in various magazines and anthologies. Troy's sexy tales appear in *Men For All Seasons* and *Full Body Contact* (Alyson.com) as well as *Buttmen 2* and *Buttmen 3* (WestBeachBooks.com). His book of short stories, revolving around the hot inhabitants of a West Hollywood gym, *Gym Shorts,* is published by Companion Press. Tell 'em Steve Troy sent you.

Davem Verne has lived in Los Angeles, New York, and Boston, working in the theater and film industry before writing poetry and erotic prose. Educated on the East Coast, he has lively memories of his college years that still inspire his work. His short stories have been printed in numerous publications; however, this is the first time his work has been included in an anthology. Mr. Verne hopes many anthologies will follow and dedicates "Tucker the Spy" to the breathless young men of his alma mater.

Paul J. Willis has written reviews and articles for several magazines and newspapers including *Unzipped, ForeWord, Philadelphia Gay News, The Gulf Coast Arts & Entertainment Review,* and New Orleans daily newspaper *The Times-Picayune.* He is the editor of *Sex Buddies: Erotic Stories About Sex Without Strings* (Alyson Books), *View to a Thrill* (STARbooks), and coeditor with Ron

Jackson of the anthology *Kink: Tales of the Sexual Adventurer* (STARbooks). He currently works as the program coordinator for the Tennessee Williams/New Orleans Literary Festival and is the festival organizer for the queer literary event Saints and Sinners. He can be reached at pjwillisnola@aol.com.